GO HOME LAKE

GO HOME LAKE

MEGS BEACH

Second Story Press

Library and Archives Canada Cataloguing in Publication

Beach, Megs, 1963-, author
Go Home Lake / by Megs Beach.

Issued in print and electronic formats.
ISBN 978-1-927583-80-7 (paperback).—
ISBN 978-1-927583-81-4 (epub)

I. Title.

PS8603.E23G65 2015   C813'.6   C2015-903295-4

C2015-903296-2

Edited by Kathryn White
Designed by Melissa Kaita
Cover by Natalie Olsen

Printed and bound in Canada

*Second Story Press gratefully acknowledges the support of the
Ontario Arts Council and the Canada Council for the Arts for our
publishing program. We acknowledge the financial support of the
Government of Canada through the Canada Book Fund.*

ONTARIO ARTS COUNCIL
CONSEIL DES ARTS DE L'ONTARIO
an Ontario government agency
un organisme du gouvernement de l'Ontario

Funded by the Government of Canada
Financé par le gouvernement du Canada

Canada Council   Conseil des Arts
for the Arts   du Canada

Canadä

MIX
Paper from
responsible sources
FSC
www.fsc.org   FSC® C004071

Published by
SECOND STORY PRESS
20 Maud Street, Suite 401
Toronto, ON M5V 2M5
www.secondstorypress.ca

"I truly hate the way you get up early
and bring me breakfast and coffee in bed every single day,"
said No One, ever.
I love living here with you in the Land Of The Good Breakfast.
You make everything possible.

ONE

The Legend of Mad Mag

THERE IS LITTLE LEFT of her that can be held in the hand. A few odd things, dusty and damaged, occupying some gray area between rubbish and memorabilia. A plastic cup, nails from a small horseshoe, a bit of broken plate. Roadside museum quality stuff. Could have been, might have been hers. Or not. There is no hard evidence, nothing clean-cut, no blood or bone. It's all circumstantial.

Nothing remains to directly link her to time or place. She wanders freely within and without, through days and daydreams. Such is the cursed blessing of the serendipitous legend, unhinged from the Now to which she was once tethered, growing larger by degrees as the shadows grow longer over her once bright life.

Memory sometimes binds, sometimes severs.

There remains a single photograph, controversial and undated. The general consensus is that it *is* her. Because even when strained of nostalgia, there is much about it that agrees with fact. There she is, under the big sky that spreads endless and blue over the pristine waters of Go Home Lake. Mad Mag riding the range.

Hold on, Mag.

Tall in the saddle of her brittle rubber horse, its paint chipped and flaking, Mad Mag glares at something beyond the scalloped white border of the image. Her cowboy hat is rakishly tipped to one side. Her reckless spirit is evident in the way she commands the passive steed on its rusted springs, six shooter wedged almost casually in the grosgrain waistband of her intricately smocked dress. She is four. Her arm is in a cast. She broke it falling down the stairs. She will break six more bones in the next five years. The authorities will consider putting her to pasture. The sheriff will look hard and long at the frontier mentality of her tribe. She will hit the ground running, every day, shoot from the hip, and never look back, never ask, never tell. Take what she has coming and hold her ground. Cross her heart and hope to die. Standing. With her boots on. With her clothes on. Soon.

Away on a fast pony laughing…

While she may have believed *her* childhood was the same as any other, universal and generic, Mad Mag, like the humblest of all demigods, failed to recognize she personified the end of her era.

And not a moment too soon.

TWO

Life in the Big City

I DREAM OF THAT HOUSE more than anything else. Every few years I do a drive by. I need to see that the place is still standing, that my memory hasn't failed me, that it really existed and so, one might presume, did my brothers and I.

No more tears. The weeping willow was cut down years ago, but the broad white-brick chimney stands firm. The solid front door made of wood blocks still bars the way. The windows are oblique to the street. No guessing what's inside.

The roof has been replaced three times.

When we left on a Thursday in January, there was snow on the ground and on the roof. The shingles were gray under the snow, which was also gray and bleak and grimy. Six months later, when the house belonged to someone else, and I belonged nowhere and to no one, the sky was a harsh, clear blue, and the roof was black.

I discovered this on the maiden voyage of what was to become a somewhat twisted tradition, to the place in which I was last a child.

Some years later the roof turned a dusty green. Most recent renovations made it gray again. Everything comes and goes. Though sometimes it just goes.

When we first came, in the spring, there was a tall tree in the front yard. Fixed in the center of the lawn, coloring-book-picture style, it had grooved, rough bark and was wide enough to hide a child when required. But only one, the strongest one, who would twist the arms of the weaker and toss them out, sacrificing them to the seeker in Hide and Go Seek. Survival of the fists. Of the fittest.

My mother gave me a brown paper bag of bulbs to plant around the base of the tree in the hope and promise of beautiful things to come. An exercise in futility in the impatient hands of a four-year-old. In an effort to excel, I groomed each bulb by snapping off the untidy green shoot from one end and pulling out the hairy roots from the other. More than two dozen innocent crocuses systematically aborted. I killed them all. My mother waited until I had finished, ensuring she had ample proof that I was both dim-witted and destructive, then she told me. I felt so bad. What went down into the earth would never come up.

But I still cling to hope. Even now, when I've not lived there for nearly forty years. I still look for the crocuses when I pass. The tree I remember coming down, cut to a stump due to disease. This was how the willow came to be planted. And the dogwoods. Weeping and barking all day long.

I am older now, with a house of my own with a silent

shading grapevine and sturdy, thick hedging. I have a car and an income, a submerged sense of rage and a strength of will that could kill if necessary.

I can come and go as I please. Revisit the house whenever I wish. And dream of it whether I wish to or not.

* * *

Split. Level. Oxymoron. Happy. Family.

My bedroom was upstairs next to my parents' bedroom and the full bathroom. The fixtures were the color of the kind of potion my brothers would mix from the condiments in restaurants: a sort of ketchup-non-dairy-creamer-with-a-hint-of-soy-sauce. Neutral, yet caustic. The tiling was a complementary shade of calamine. I wrote my name in iodine with a cotton swab on the inside of the drawer of the vanity. My mother had a fit. I denied it, but I got in trouble anyway.

When we moved in, the floor of the basement rec room was freshly waxed and gleaming. We took off our shoes and went skating in our stocking feet. We bounced off the paneled walls and into each other like unstable atoms. Four children ages four to ten, encouraged to be elsewhere, far from the maddening crowd of boxes. Of course it was "all fun and games until somebody lost an eye." Or their balance. Then broke their nose.

Forward I fell, hard and fast, ruining the game, destroying the peace, and dirtying up the floor. I ruined the upstairs bathmat as well.

"She should have put out her hands to break the fall" was the exasperated conclusion drawn by my brothers. Any idiot would do that. I must have fallen on my nose on purpose. I was always "faking it" it to get attention.

"Oh, Sarah Heartburn!" my mother rolled her eyes and groaned when she heard me begin to wail. When the blood came she grabbed my wrist and marched me up to the bathroom muttering, "For corn's sake! Why on earth didn't you just put out your hands so you wouldn't fall on your face?"

Sadly, in keeping with the theme and theory of my mother's life, the worst was yet to come.

At the peak of bruise formation, as both my eyes blackened and my rosy cheeks turned yellow and green, I was called upon to lead the processional at church for White Gift Sunday.

I wore a white organza dress. A white grosgrain sash. My hair was combed into submission and pulled tight as the wires on a suspension bridge into two glossy braids tied in white satin. I smiled beatifically, oblivious to the pulsating bubble of blood and mucus hanging in my left nostril. My mother was chagrined.

I carried a box, carefully wrapped in white tissue, beautifully tied with a white ribbon, stuffed with tradition, to lay upon the altar. Alms for the poor.

Poor me. I *so* misunderstood. A small child is given a gift and thinks the obvious: *treasures for me*. Living among the knees and crotches of the world, going to bed first, the kiddy cone. Enduring these and so many more indignities should have ensured entitlement. The box was large. There were sparkles embedded in the paper. It may well have felt as empty as it was, but I was brimming with hope.

I had learned my lesson with the bulbs. I would not trim

the performance to dimensions reasonable to a child. I would accept the inexplicable rules of adults, just this once, and part with the gift as requested, silent and beaming, believing the touched expressions of my ecclesiastical audience had something to do with my stellar behavior and nothing to do with my miserable appearance. And my reward would be that very gift, retrieved later, after the performance was over.

What I failed to appreciate was that it was something of a comedy. A farce, in fact.

I returned to my squirmy seat in the hard pew following my part in the service. There I endured my mother's talon poke to my thigh, which meant "Sit still and keep your trap shut." But I had to know what was hidden within the gift so gorgeously wrapped the angels must have had a hand in it.

She poked me again and hissed, "It's a cow."

Naturally I'd favor a pony, but trade was always possible. "How can it fit in the box?" I wanted to know.

"The box is just to *show* we got a cow for the poor people."

Poor people? I was beggared of ponies. This had to be considered a serious privation.

And anyway, what would the poor want of a cow? I knew cows to be large and smelly. A cow needed a barn, a bucket, a bell, and a daisy-chain crown. Sons and daughters of Ham, living in mud huts, subsisting in blissful, noble grace, knowing nothing of Jell-O or white gloves or teaspoons – what on earth would they do with a cow?

Even at my tender age I knew what to do with a pony.

I was devastated. It was a tragedy.

Some interval later I was taken to some unpasteurized green to see the Bovine Presentation to the Impoverished, during which smiling black people (I think my first, outside of *National Geographic*) accepted the unacceptable creature on behalf of the Needy Multitudes. From whence commeth they? I knew not. I cared less.

There are so many, Lord, so many. Moses said so himself. How was a cow to be loaves and fishes to so many?

And me without a pony.

I have an impression of the years that followed, at times unshakably clear, at times watery and ethereal. Days that nostalgia describes in romantic and perfect prose. *Summers of golden sweetness.* Kinder years.

It was a childhood of its time, the textbook dimensions of the baby boom. Four kids, myself and my brothers, Mom and Dad, a dog, a cat, a guinea pig, fish tank, turtles, a house in the suburbs, a cottage on a lake, a station wagon, and (later) a second car. Dad drove to work. Mom stayed home, avoiding invitations to Tupperware parties and lobbying for a dishwasher.

In later years my mother worked as a Pink Lady, volunteering in the local hospital emergency. She had been there so many times with one offspring or another, they knew her by name. It's difficult to say who was doing whom the favor in this arrangement. Perhaps my mother sought to provide the hospital with her assistance as some sort of repayment to them for the various stitches, casts, and medicaments they had doled out to her habitually fractured children. Perhaps the hospital saw fit to occupy my mother with some task other than ferrying gashed heads, petit mal seizures, broken bones, penknife slip-slices, hockey stick abrasions, and other nervous disorders to and from the ward at odd hours. Clearly she had the needed experience to work casualty. Or possibly such work was meant to offer Mother Dearest respite from "the evil four" and allow us to solve our own problems, and hers, by killing one another. Or it might have been wrongly presumed that if our mother was absent, our constant revolt might be put down by a stern and hairy-legged housekeeper like the one who cared for our neighbors the Scharwtz boys, Reinard and Stash. You could see the mud print of Mrs. Dorbrinzki's jackboot on those poor boys' necks at all times.

Whatever the case, Mother seemed suitably distracted. She took the task to heart and told stories at the dinner table of how, with the utmost dignity and dazzling decorum, she wheeled the mangled bodies of car-wreck victims to the morgue (probably humming Elgar's "Pomp and Circumstance" in a minor key all the way).

Much later, I discovered volunteers were forbidden to perform this feat. And years after that, I understood that this particular clinic, something of a boutique hospital, was without a morgue and rarely endured the company of a stiff. It confined its business to boil-lancing and simple fractures, and the odd tonsillectomy or ulcer surgery, just for fun. Patients were routinely shipped off to larger, more diverse facilities long before they were in danger of being pronounced dead.

Apart from that, my mother kept house. Cooked somewhat, though always under protest. Did laundry, as a family of six produces prodigious amounts. My father's suits and shirts went to the cleaners, however, as he considered my mother seriously lacking in pressing and starching talents, and she thought such efforts were beneath her.

She had her hair done twice a week, three times if some function was on the agenda, by Frank at the beauty salon, except for summers when we "cottaged" at Go Home Lake.

June. Centennial year. 1967. Canada's Shining Moment. Three of our nation's obligatory fifteen minutes of fame. Probably more than we deserved at the time.

Ca-na-da

One little two little three Canadians

Infected by Bobby Gimby's virulent ditty we proselytized profusely.

We love thee

We knew all the words and sang them with irritating frequency, less out of a sense of nationalistic pride and more out of the fact that it was the least scratched record in our limited sound library for the Close 'n Play.

Until my father answered our voices raised in glorious song, "I'll wring your neck if you sing it again!" before we'd even got to the multicultural-embracing bilingual French portion.

"When are we going to Expo? Francine is going to Expo." I marched into the modern kitchen in our seven-year-old split-level on Dewmist Crescent and demanded this critical information from my mother.

Francine lived a few doors down the street. She had

an older brother who must have had some sort of calcium deficiency or muscle disorder because grown-ups were forever commenting on how limp his wrists were and on the swishy way he walked. I can't remember what he looked like. I can't even remember his name, but from time to time I'd see Francine in one of her brother's hand-me-down outfits. Not the permanently smelly kangaroo sweaters or mittens with chewed thumbs that I was dealt there at the bottom of the children's wardrobe totem pole. Francine got stripy shirts and blue jeans and running shoes hardly worn. And once a little purple velvety ensemble with a ruffled poet's shirt. I was insanely jealous. Francine was my age, but she was allowed to wear pants. Daddy said it was all right for some girls to wear pants, but I was a girl and should look like one. Not some ragamuffin.

"We're not going to Expo," my mother informed me.

I was genuinely surprised. Everybody was going. Absolutely everybody. All twenty million and their *frères*. For Jacques's sake, it was EXPO 67! "Why not? I want to go. Can't we go? Please? Please?"

My mother was standing at the counter putting the final touches on a cake. It was not a Birthday Cake. Birthday Cake was chocolate cake with boiled frosting. It was Everyday Cake. Everyday Cake was like this: white cake mix, nine-inch square pan. Mix cake as directed. Bake in pan. (This may seem obvious, but my mother loathed cooking of any sort, so a detail like this could be important.) Drink rum and Coke. Leave cake in oven a little too long while reading Irma Bombeck's most recent book. Take cake out of oven and allow to cool. Turn onto plate. Curse crispy corners.

With avocado-green electric carving knife, cut cake in half horizontally, separating top from bottom. Liberally spread the strawberry jam that failed to set, causing several days of marital strife, over bottom half of cake. Replace top. Place one large paper doily on top of cake. Dust with icing sugar. Remove doily. Have a drink to congratulate yourself on a job well done.

"We're not going to Expo," my mother repeated. It was hard to say which she more resented: that it was *we* who were not going, or that it was we who were *not* going. But the results were the same. The ingenuous child that I was, however, I still believed in the power of persistent whining.

"Please. Pleeeeeeease. Pretty please with sugar on top?" I went on evoking various forms of sweets and entreatments for probably close to ten minutes.

Honesty compels me to admit I had less than no clue what Expo was. I knew it was in Montreal, where we were originally from. I knew it was somehow related to Centennial year, and, by association, to that blistering Young Canadians anthem that I so adored. But over and above that, I knew nothing except that Francine was going and had this smarmy self-righteous smirk all over her face. She had Tutti and Her Boyfriend dolls too, as well as the box they came in that looked like an ice-cream parlor. And it wasn't even wrecked. I had out-of-style Barbies with Cleopatra eye makeup and bouffant hairdos with traces of bubble gum from my older second cousin. The dolls were also seriously handicapped, as I had the peculiar habit of gnawing on their feet, favoring the bendable leg style because the metal tibia-fibula rod gave the most molar satisfaction.

But I wasn't jealous. I was a patriotic zealot. I wanted to go to Expo. I would figure it out when I got there. "Pretty, pretty please? With a cherry? Can we go to Expo?"

"No." Mother was getting that edge to her voice. If you badgered her enough at this point, she could almost be counted on to throw up one hand in a gesture of disgust and shout "Oh, I don't care. Just do as you please!" This was what I was aiming for, presuming she would willfully aid and abet what I pleased, meaning she would take me to Expo.

I crossed my arms defiantly, stamping one foot so hard it startled the guinea pig. "Why! I want to go!"

As if that cinched it.

My mother turned on me, avocado carving knife in hand, blades buzzing the same rhythm as her frazzled nerves. I realized then that I should have waited until after the congratulatory cocktail part of the Everyday Cake recipe.

"Quit whining or I'll give you something to whine about! We are not going to any blinkity-blank Expo. We're going to that damned cottage all summer. Now go outside and play."

Oh, yeah. The cottage.

Knowing what was good for me, I ran out the door – the one with the wounded frame where she broke the wooden spoon in two, chasing one of my brothers.

From the perspective of our front door the world narrowed. Physically. Our house formed the beginning of the curve where the road bent to its crescent shape. To the south the front yards were equal to the backyards. To the northeast the lots were more nearly pie shaped – pie that included asphalt drives suitable for two large cars and ending in broad, double garages. Francine's house was three doors to the narrow direction. She had the biggest backyard on the street and invited everyone there to play, one at a time, only long enough to rub one's nose in her superior acreage.

But Francine didn't have a cottage. There was plenty of time before dinner to inform her of this. I marched to her front door and hammered on it hard.

Opening the door about one sixteenth of an inch, Francine partially extruded from it like fleshy putty. She regarded me suspiciously, rocked on one heel, and gnawed on her hair ribbon. "My Mom says I can't play with you," she said, drooling a little over the hair ribbon.

"Well, whoopee-do. I'm going to my cottage the whole summer," I announced triumphantly.

Who's smarmy – I mean sorry – now?

Francine narrowed her eyes. She edged a little more out of the generally closed door. She looked properly skeptical. "What cottage?"

"*My* cottage," I clarified. "We got a boat and a dock and a raft and I can go waterskiing whenever I want. And I got my own rowboat. And my dad's going get me a pony of my very own." A little nuclear blast of envy went off in Francine's central core. I could see the tremors, little shock waves of distress as I pulled way out in the bragging lead. I see your Expo, and I raise you one pony.

Too rich for your blood, sister?

Francine gasped for air and twitched like a fish tossed in the bottom of the boat. I moved in for the kill.

"And I'm going to be a cowboy, a *real* cowboy," I announced, swelling with pride – pride that was doubly felt when Francine burst into jealous tears and ran crying and carrying on into the house. Within seconds, Francine's mother appeared in the doorway. I repeated for her benefit, "I'm going to be cowboy."

"Good for you," Francine's mother responded. She rolled her eyes and looked weary in the extreme. "Run along. Go away, now." And just before she gave the door a good hard shove with her foot, I heard her say, "Stupid brat," not all that quietly.

Of course I always felt that way about Francine. It just surprised me to hear *her mother* say it.

I wandered back down the street to my own house.

It was the optimal neighborhood of its time. Generally the houses were split-level in design. Enormous plate glass "picture" windows were immensely popular, as were patios made from two-foot concrete squares, pink and white or green and white in a checkerboard pattern. It was a given that you would have two cars. In fact, at any particular time we had three or four cars because, apart from the standard-issue station wagon and the smaller second car (a used Datsun until we got the new gold-tone Pinto), my father seemed to have a rotating fleet of MGs. It was probably only two, possibly three. But they seemed to come and go with regularity. We also had, in the back of the garage, a small three-wheeled vehicle called an Isetta. A one-door, front-opening contraption with a motorcycle engine and no explanation.

Trudging along on that late spring afternoon, I was a little bored. My brothers were all at school. Francine was unavailable. There was no one else my age to play with. Around the bend and across the street were Craig and his little sister. Craig ate paste and the ends of pencils and stood over you when you used his markers shouting "Stop pressing so hard!" if you so much as put pen to paper. More interestingly, he could put the entire business end of his toy hammer in his mouth. I tried it out on his sister, thinking it might be a familial thing. She wouldn't play, and I had to make her do it. She acted like a crybaby. (She was about two.) Then their father came out and yelled at me and complained that I was too rough and said I had to go.

"Craig started it!" I protested, because he did, boasting and bragging and giving a demo of his hammer skill, but his dad wouldn't listen.

I surveyed the other houses for potential signs of life. The only other child available to me was Darlene. She was somewhat younger than I. She, too, had an older brother, actually about my age, but there was some carved-in-stone rule about boys never playing with girls. I pushed that envelope once, and he tangled up my skipping rope so badly, I never tried again. Darlene was a possibility if, for once, she wasn't napping, about to nap, or just getting up from a nap.

I knocked on the door. With her hair all whipped up like a candy-floss hurricane, Darlene's mother answered. Her name was Ginny. I knew what gin was and presumed she was fond of it, hence her obvious nickname. No person could ever be properly named after a drink.

"Yes?" she asked in a rushed voice, wiping her hands on her apron. It was a white polyester deal tied with a huge bow in the back. The loops stood out so far that Ginny appeared to have low-flying wings.

"Can I play with Darlene?" I asked, sniffing the air hopefully. Aprons meant kitchen stuff. There could be cookies.

Unfortunately, the only fragrance wafting through the air was Spic and Span.

"Darlene is having a little seep-seep." Ginny told me. No news there.

It annoyed me how much this child slept. I think I had seen her awake maybe two times. "She's always sleeping!" I complained.

Ginny shrugged. "Well, she needs her rest. She has a little cold."

I mulled this over. "Is her nose all runny?" I inquired with what poor Ginny mistook for sympathetic interest.

She sighed and nodded, a clownish sad face twisting her lips. "Yes, poor Darlene has a little button of a runny nose," she squeaked. I think it was supposed to appeal to a child. I just found it a bit creepy.

For a moment, I considered Darlene's unstoppered sinuses. She probably slept so much because she burnt up so much energy manufacturing snot. On those rare occasions when she was awake, there was always a trail of it from one or both of her nostrils streaming down to her mouth, outlined in filth. The only clean spot on her face was the little patch on her upper lip she perpetually licked clean, lapping up snot like it was the nectar of the Gods. She peed her pants a lot too. Toilet training was a very steep learning curve for her.

"Dirtybutter…" I mumbled.

Mrs. Wrangler across the street sometimes made a face and said to my mother, "Here comes Dirtybutter." But when I looked around all I could ever see was Darlene. But it was dawning on me, if you took a good look at the puddle of unappealing bodily fluids that Darlene was, "Dirtybutter" was not a half-bad description.

"What?" said Ginny, her furrowed brow disappearing under her overdone hair.

It never would have occurred to me to *not* tell Ginny that the other mothers on the street referred to her little treasure as "Dirtybutter," but thankfully it didn't specifically occur to me to *tell* her either.

I had more important things to tell her anyway. "My Dad's going to get me a pony and I'm going to be a cowboy," I announced grandly.

"Girl," Ginny corrected helpfully.

"Wha – pardon?"

"Cow*girl*. You're a girl, so you're going to be a cowgirl." Ginny smiled and her eyes crinkled up and vanished. "Bye-bye now," she sang and shut the door on me.

Cowboy. I was going to be a cowboy. I knew what a cowboy was. I fully intended to be one. Ginny just didn't understand. I'd show her. When I was a cowboy, I would show her.

I returned home. My mom had moved on from dessert and was working backwards through the main course. Each day had its own food. Like some proverbial Chinese take-away menu, our meals came in orderly succession, no substitutions. Monday: leftovers; Tuesday: pork chops; Wednesday: chicken; Thursday: steak or ham; Friday: fish was a religious issue for the early years, but it gave way to a casserole or another form of chicken in later years; Saturday: spaghetti, or, in Stanley Cup season, pizza from Millano's; and finally, every Sunday without fail (sing with me if you know the tune): roast beef, brussels sprouts, mashed potatoes, and gravy.

In my many years of marriage, I have never cooked a roast beef. My children couldn't pick one out of a butcher's shop window if their lives depended on it. And we've lived this long. As a child, I would not have believed this to be possible.

Every meal had dessert, frequently two, because dessert was a vital food group. This was in the days before it was pointed out to us in a national fitness campaign that the average fifty-year-old Swede was more fit than the average thirty-year-old Canadian. Not that we gave up desserts as a result. We did all buy jogging suits and Adidas running shoes, which made us look more like the Swede. Then we had our Everyday Cake, and ate it too.

I sat at the kitchen table and fed Petunia, the guinea pig, bread crusts left over from lunch. She snuffled a little, clearly enjoying this little gourmet interlude. Reaching through the door in her wire cage, I tried cautiously to pick her up. I was very careful to avoid her hindquarters, careful not to startle her. I would not be the one responsible for maiming her. Because, as everyone knows, if you pick up a guinea pig by the tail its eyes fall out.

"Can I have an after-school snack?" I asked my mother.

"No," I was told, omitting comment on the fact that I neither went to school nor was school completed for the day.

"I'm hungry," I complained, coveting Petunia's bread crusts for an instant before realizing they wouldn't taste any better than when I had rejected them at lunch.

"Well, we're having dinner early. And you're going to bed early," my mother continued, "because we'll be getting

up at the crack of dawn tomorrow to go to the cottage."
Unbelievably, she did not sound thrilled about it.

"Hooray!" I cheered. "We're going to the cottage. Can I
go swimming when we get there?"

"It will be too cold. Don't be silly."

I jumped to my feet the way I might launch myself from
the dock. "I can just put my feet in off the raft." I kicked
blithely at the imaginary water.

"They'll turn blue and drop off." My mother looked
peeved as I commenced my lake crossing though the kitchen,
using a stylized sort of butterfly front crawl that most resembled the explosion of a windmill.

"Then can I get a pony?" I spun from vertical to horizon-
tal and into a dizzy canter.

"Simmer down."

Not having heard "yes" immediately, reflex triggered me
into full beg mode. My lip quivered. Tears sprung to my eyes.
I slapped my hands to my face and massaged it into a suitably
desperate expression. "But Daddy said. He did say it. He said
he'd buy me a pony."

"He would," my mother said ruefully. "And guess who
will have to clean up after it?"

"I'll take care of it. All by myself. I'll do everything." I
meant this, of course, from the bottom of my heart, not ever
having stopped to consider that horses, even small ones, were
living, breathing, eating, *defecating* creatures. *Cleaning up
after* meant ensuring one's toys and shoes were put away. I
would be the pony's only amusement. So the possibility of
pony toys strewn about the place was a nonstarter. And I was
personally out of the "hang up your coat" loop due to height

restrictions. The pony might have a blue blanket sort of dressing gown to wear prior to show jumping. But surely there would be someone taller than me to help out with that.

Besides, I knew all I really needed to know.

Any cowboy worth his beans had an equally worthy partner in his beloved horse. This benevolent bond was silent and sacred. Your horse could be counted on to carry you in times of trouble, through swift-moving rivers, over snow-capped mountains, forever and a day under the big sky and into the sunset. In return for this undying devotion, your horse asked for nothing and expected less, secure in the knowledge you'd treat him to a wormy apple from time to time. After first picking out the worms to fish with, of course. Most importantly, your horse knew you were kin. He knew you'd be there, with your saddle and a bridal and spurs and a gun. A gun that you'd put to that horse's head and pull the trigger without hesitation if he was foolish enough to screw you over by fracturing a leg.

Such was the Way of the West.

My mother pointed to the door and abruptly shouted. "Go set the table. Your brothers will be home from school soon. Supper time is early today. I want you guys fed, washed, and ready for bed before your father comes home."

Big sigh, "All right…." She may as well have slapped a ball and chain on my leg and sent me out to split rocks with a short-handled pick.

THREE

Wagon Train

A GRAND OLD DAME I once met told me of how she went out West in a covered wagon. The real deal. Up before dawn to whip up some Johnny Cake and lard, break camp, gather herd, flock, and kin, amble along behind the windy end of some ruminant, repeating the process in reverse at dusk. Circle the wagons to contain the cattle, swine, horses, and exhaustion. Look into your beloved's eyes again long enough to wonder what devil possessed him to bring you along on such a journey, free of comfort and easy access to water. Without apparent reason or end, through a bleak, incommodious wilderness, in which the presence of insects in your hair and underwear was a simple fact to be accepted.

Well, the expedition didn't kill this good lady, obviously, as she lived to tell the tale, so it must have made her stronger.

She became resolute in her appreciation of running water and soap and toilets and screened windows. She remained disdainful of blackflies and fleas and peeing in wide-open spaces all her life. Loo roll was the best thing ever invented, she thought.

Can't really argue with that.

As a child I had imagined the cottage as mysterious and potentially lethal as the wild, angry wilderness of Edwardian children's tales and Rudyard Kipling's India – and just as desirable and exciting. As my father careened around the dirt-road corners, ever downwards toward the lake's shore, I would have been equally unsurprised if we'd hit a moose or a feral child raised by wolves, bearing down on a terrified gopher.

So, reasonably, I viewed the family migration from suburb here to cottage there as not dissimilar to Madame Homesteader's prairie schooner cruise, except perhaps in duration.

She and her party endured wicked weather, animals, and insects.

Same for us.

They feared rustlers and violence from the properly peeved First Nations whose land they trespassed and rivers they piddled in. They feared hunger and thirst and sickness.

We feared hippies and hitchhikers, panhandling for supper or space in the car, for we believed them to be of some virulent untouchable caste. I feared the violence of my brothers, inevitable in a closed, groaning space tactile with second-hand cigarette smoke. Both my parents smoked.

We also feared hunger and thirst, though this was a habitual state for three growing boys and myself in competition.

And in Dad's New Car there was no eating allowed due to spills and spews. One of my brothers was frequently carsick. And, unlike the covered wagons of old, the design of the Ford LTD *luxury* model station wagon was not conducive to puking over the side onto the dusty trail.

But apart from that tiny flaw, it has to be said that the Ford was immeasurably more comfortable than the pioneers' original conveyance. Roughly the size of the Space Station Mir, no cushy detail was spared. This beast of a car had everything: two tons of chrome rounding the bumpers, simulated wood panels (blue, naturally, like the rest of the heap), electric antenna, fine Corinthian leather upholstery, 8-track tape deck, loads of tapes, an after-market rearview mirror device that spanned the entire front of the car and included a view of the full breadth of our fair country of Canada, the second largest (geographically speaking) nation on the planet.

The best part, at least on such occasions as these, was the LTD's built-in roof racks, designed to most resemble the O.K. Corral with tail fins. You could have packed an aircraft carrier up there.

But we needed the space. The perspiration and planning that must have gone into the packing for an old- or new-fashioned wagon ride must have been significant. Packed up were all the basic foods and medicines and, in our modern case, loo rolls that might be wanted in the coming months. Sugar in sacks and ketchup in industrial-size tins; as many packs of hotdogs and pounds of hamburger as could be fit into the freezer; Sunlight soap and Spic and Span by the giant boxful; sterilized milk; and an entire brickwork's worth of pale margarine in wax paper, pockmarked by the accompanying capsule of butter-yellow color, for those who could face the economical fake but not the white, white reality.

Naturally, we took some clothes and towels and a couple of bags of marshmallows for roasting and a storehouse of canned goods. Coffee, stale and strong enough for any cowboy, but reserved only for my mother's precious percolator, the CorningWare cornflower blue twin of the one we had at home. The flannel sheets that came home to the city filthy at Thanksgiving returned to roost and eventually fester on our cottage beds. Once we took a toy boat, which my mother named *Bugtussel*, and once a new mailbox to erect at the top of the road.

But in true detail, only God and Mom knew what we took. Both of them wisely stood back while my father packed it all. He did not entertain commentary on technique or tie-down methods. He attacked this biannual task (because, of course, so much had to be loaded up for the return trip at the end of the summer) with a drive and devotion we rarely saw in him.

Whatever the inventory, it was all hoisted and balanced on the roof of the station wagon. Then the whole conglomeration of suitcases, boxes, baskets, and garbage bags was tarped and roped in like an ornery bull escaped from the herd.

As my father set the mildewed golden canvas tarp in flight, I watched in delight as it floated into place like the proverbial western sunset. It sunk slowly over the hills and valleys of the vast range of goods atop the car, grommets glinting, father cursing like a mule skinner.

I could not suppress a romantic sigh.

This was too perfect. Life was unfolding exactly as it

should. Come sunup, this soon-to-be cowboy would be making her way west in a covered wagon.

Actually northeast was more like it, geographically, but *west* filled out the headline better.

★ ★ ★

It was a less idyllic moment the next morning when we were roused from sleep, not at the crack of dawn, but long before it. Bleary, too sleepy to be hungry yet, we dressed, staggered out to the car and piled in. It was still early in the season. Mornings were cold and damp. The summer clothes we had donned in eternal hope were woefully inadequate to keep us warm. A battle thus ensued to avoid the most-rear seats, the pop-up ones in the back of beyond, remote and distant from the last heating vent. All objections were quickly laid to rest when Dad promised to knock some sense into us by knocking our heads together. The clinical theory behind this Three Stooges therapy was not clear to me, but it was a treatment I desired not to endure. My middle brother, Kieffer, was inclined to try out all of Larry, Moe, and Curly's antics on me. Over time, the humor was completely lost. Silently, though not agreeably, I took the seat I was assigned.

We probably waited until after we were past the end of Dewmist Crescent to ask for the first of many, many times "How much longer?" Probably. But maybe not.

I am not sure what we had to complain about in terms of distance. Traffic volume was much less of an issue in those days, and I suspect the entire trip, start to finish, was less than three hours. And that Ford flew! In spite of how it was weighed down with goods and creatures (only the inhabitants of the fish tank stayed behind), we barreled down the highway.

Dad always drove. Mom did not like highway driving – hers or anyone else's. She sat, rigid and white-knuckled in the passenger seat, becoming one with the blue Naugahyde, pressing simultaneously with all her might on the headrest behind her and the imaginary break she willed to appear beneath her foot. She tended to emit this low, eerie sort of noise. Had it not continued from the point at which we left the driveway to the point at which we arrived, I might have been distressed by such a strangled, desperate sound. But as it was, she made it continuously on every long car trip, so I came to believe it was normal, almost comforting, and very likely useful in warding off deer that might wander onto the road.

The trip always felt endless.

At some point, some well-meaning soul gave my brothers and me a Car Bingo game. Literacy was required. So I was the first and biggest loser there. Patience and concentrated observation skills were an asset, so none of the boys were truly suited. But most significantly, the game was designed for an American cross-country trip. It featured license plates from fifty states in rows. As you spotted the various plates, you marked them off, and once you found enough to connect an entire line, BINGO, you were the winner! Even the hearty highway-loving folk who embarked on huge national excursions must have been challenged by this. How often can one see an Oregon plate on a Texas highway? Way up here, careening across highway 401, the great Quebec-Ontario corridor, the most exotic plate to be seen was that of a wayward Nova Scotian returning home, or a camper from New York State blazing a trail across that which he called "The North Country." To play the game with the intention of winning, we would still be out there to this day, crisscrossing the United States.

There was another game, more loosely structured, which had to do with spotting horses. Being the first person to shout out "Horse!" was in itself a reward. Conversely, wrongly identifying a pasture of cows as their equine associates, was a humiliating defeat in the extreme, and usually brought along with it a hail of insults and a couple of good, solid punches to the arm if anyone could reach you. Then came my father's refrain about knocking our heads together, and he'd flail his arm behind him and take a whack at whomever he could reach. The pitch of Mom's peculiar gurgle-wheeze would elevate to the point where it became a silent dog whistle. The cats would commence howling in their cages; someone would cry. Usually me. But if it wasn't me, I'd join in quickly enough and lead the chorus in no time.

And then suddenly, we were there.

Not *there* at the cottage. But *there* at the Gulf Station, Gas Bar and Restaurant. This title was boldly emblazoned in huge type, the height of which exceeded the actual height of the building on which it was displayed. This was the official pit stop of the journey. Sort of like the mountain pass where the homesteaders were forced to winter, many of them starving to death, going quite mad, and resorting to cannibalism. Except the food was actually quite good at the Gulf.

(It took me until the mid-70s to sort out why there was

no driving range or mini-putt included in the deal, as in *golf*. Had there been no oil crisis to force me into a deeper appreciation of homonyms, I'm sure I would be just as confused today.)

It was not a grandiose establishment by any means. There was a counter with six or eight stools, a table and chairs, maybe a booth in the window for those who wished to dine alfresco with a full view of the gas pumps. An array of "gift and novelty" items were on display to amuse and tempt the weary traveler. There was pinball for the sports-minded, a clean washroom to relieve my mother, who by this time was wont to declare "My back teeth are floating," and a magazine rack for the literati of the crowd, replete with Dad's favorites: *Penthouse* and *Playboy*.

We'd all pile out of the car, legs stiff, still cold, starved, and miserable. And still the skinny lady behind the counter in her starched nurse-like uniform and peach-colored hair stood smiling in beatific welcome. Doris. God love her.

She wore a little lace crown.

She smoked like a chimney.

Doris must have had a good memory to remember us among the innumerable average suburban hordes that funneled through her establishment on the way to cottage country every year. She remembered that we had good appetites, that my brothers were inclined to mix mischievous potions of any and all available sauces and salt, and that we were a very "boisterous group."

While Mr. Doris and Dad shot the breeze a bit, told a few dirty jokes, and gassed up the station wagon, Mom marched us off to the bathroom and then attempted to affix us to the counter stools and establish what we wanted for breakfast. Spinning like exceptionally devout dervishes, the four of us whirled madly, laughing like hyenas on speed.

At length, either Mom or Dad would convince us we were courting danger if we kept the spinning up one second longer. But by then the orders were in, so being grounded didn't matter. The synthesis of breakfast on the wide-open plane of the restaurant grill was something of a floor show. Doris buttered toast, flipped eggs, sausage, and bacon with the showmanship of Liberace. Liberace with a cigarette with a perilously long ash on the bobbing end. With a few sequins and a candelabra she could have taken the act on the road. Could have fetched a regular spot on the CBC.

After we inhaled our meals, my brothers and I wandered about in the otherwise empty shop and admired the goods on display, while Mom and Dad consumed about nine cups of coffee so slowly it was a wonder it didn't evaporate more quickly.

The boys were drawn to the pinball machine. It was immaterial that they hadn't the change to operate it. They made up their own scenarios and sound effects, won every time without tilting, and fought over free games, even though they were all free.

Unable to shake the yoke of a typical girl, I lusted after the display of "Native" gifts and dolls. Those lovely Caucasian pseudo-Barbies with bad dye jobs, California tanned skin, and off-the-shoulder doeskin outfits. They all had bright blue eyes. There were also on display little moccasins that never came in my size and never could, as my feet were "the size of gun boats," my mother said. There were tomahawks with neon-dyed chicken feathers suspended decoratively from leatherette thongs that dangled off the handle. Also garishly beaded, carved, faux leather wallets, whip stitched together with shiny brown plastic. It was all so beautiful, the perfect way for the aspiring cowboy to properly accessorize.

Also for my perusal was a tall circling rack of embroidered patches, spotlighting popular characters and slogans of the day: "Keep on Truckin'," "Save Water, Shower with a Friend," the big lips and tongue of the Rolling Stones, and a series of bizarre cartoons featuring two infants in utero – one girl (you could tell from the bow in her hair) and one boy – both with amazingly large eyes. They exchanged something of a timely, witty repartee, all of which is lost to me now.

Peanuts characters were also in vogue, especially Snoopy and Woodstock. And right where I could reach it, I discovered a patch that featured Lucy, posturing in fury, waving her fist defiantly, a boldly lettered word bubble ballooning from her mouth. I could relate to Lucy: my genius was also frustratingly unrecognized; I, too, was always trussed into a short dress with puffed sleeves and Mary Jane shoes. I latched on to this find and ran to my parents, begging all the way. "Can I have this. Please? Can I Can I Can I?" I yodeled in rapid fire. "Please buy it for me, please please please?"

Much to my stunned delight, Mom and Dad did not respond with the usual thin translations of "NO" such as, "not today," "don't be silly," or "we'll see." Astoundingly, they not only laughed themselves to pieces over the patch, but they promptly purchased it as well.

But not for me.

For my mother.

I should have known it was too good to be true.

The details that so eluded me and so delighted my parents were these: Lucy's dress humped over a pregnant belly that, if scaled up to real-life proportions would have put her in about her fourteenth month of gestation to quints. And the words she spoke with such wrath were "GOD DAMN YOU, CHARLIE BROWN!"

Even after it was explained to me, I didn't get it. Glancing around at the reassuring sight of our "boisterous group," my parents chug-a-lugging coffee, my brothers up to their usual tricks with cafe chemistry in a juice glass, it was quite beyond my comprehension. Why would anyone not want to have babies, and lots of them too?

Stuffed back into the station wagon, this time in the very back (our seating plan rearranged in the futile interest of peace), I looked out the window for a long time. It was still some miles before the turnoff to The Bumpy Road, an avenue so named for its gravel and washboard construction style, but it was not so very long before the road sign that announced the thriving municipality of Bird's Creek, population 267.

We never missed the opportunity, not once, no matter how rough things got.

"Bird's Creek!" Dad would shout out when the sign came into view. Primed and ready, we responded immediately on cue:

"So *oil* them!"

Then my father did his impression of a crow call.

Those *were* the days. But what were they? I am still figuring it out....

After Bird's Creek, which Mom explained "You can tell it's a big city because it has houses on both sides of the street," the cottage was only a series of landmarks away: the riding stables, the train stop that had not seen a train in over thirty years, then the LeBlanc's house, teeming with redheaded children.

My mother said that "Mrs." LeBlanc was the local "Lady of the Evening."

Putting on a party dress, shiny shoes, and perfume and going out for the evening for a living? Other than being a full-time princess, *Lady of the Evening* had to be the best job for any girl ever! Must have been like what Cinderella did before she married the prince. Some fairy godmother had to be part of the bargain, or poor Mrs. LeBlanc could never have made a go of it. She looked hopelessly worn and dowdy in her daylight clothes. Her red hair was never done. With all those kids, she must have spent a fortune on baby-sitters. I thought that once grown up, I could do a better job of being a Lady of the Evening than she.

I announced my plans out loud and was immediately drowned out with roars of "Good Lord, don't be stupid," "No way *anybody* pays *you* for that, *ever*," "What a moron," and such. My mother just rolled her eyes and said she would explain later.

"She goes with men for money," my father chimed in with a sideways grin.

What Mrs. LeBlanc did when she "goes with men" still

wasn't clear to me. But that twisty smile on my father's face in the rearview mirror probably meant it wasn't nice. That was enough for me.

Dad told me more anyway. "No two of her ruddy hoards has the same sire," he said. Mother poked him in the arm and hissed. That was the end of that talk on Career Choices.

I threw all thoughts of Mrs. LeBlanc, her redheaded children, and how she brought home the bacon out of my head, out the window, and onto the dirt road in hopes the next car coming would run them over. But the image of the many LeBlancs returned vividly in grade 13 biology class. She could not have obtained her consistently carrot-topped offspring practicing the *oldest profession*, as she'd been accused of. She was a true redhead, same as every kid I ever recall around her. She would have had to have carefully limited her bodily rentals to clients who'd gone for genetic testing, or to those who could demonstrate themselves as true redheads also – crown to hairy toes and in between.

Just past the LeBlanc's was a bright white, or maybe blue church on a sunny elevation, making it look especially pious, and finally, a farmhouse in which lived a remarkably dense dog named, imaginatively enough, Rover.

If Rover had another brain it would be lonely.

But he had tenacity and a singular passion: he loved to chase cars.

Teeth gnashing, barking insanely, frothing, running full tilt, with a total reckless disregard for his own safety, he kept pace with anything on wheels for as long as he possibly could before his short legs finally gave out – whereupon he dropped as suddenly as he had sprinted. Sprawled comically in the middle of the old dirt road he continued his barrage of snarls, ruffs, and howls.

Prone, he was significantly less menacing.

I was still afraid of him. He was loud and he was angry. Given my family, one might have thought I'd be used to that. When someone impatiently interrupted my fearful sobs by asking, "What the heck would he do with a car if he caught it, anyway?" I was little comforted.

Miraculously, in all those years, after all those cars – for ours was not the exception but the Rover Rule – that stupid dog was never injured in his idiotic pursuit. God must have loved that dog. No one else did.

Getting past Rover was like a medieval trial by ordeal. In order to obtain your heavenly reward, you had to escape The Beast. But once you managed this task, it was barely a moment until you reached the almost invisible roadway that descended into the lush and utopian surroundings of Go Home Lake.

There it was for real. The Cottage.

Relief was palpable. To emerge from the confines of the car, to stretch and spread out and breathe in. Smell that fresh air. Listen, what do you hear? The lake on the shore, the breeze through the trees, birds, frogs, chipmunks, the call of the wild…

"Mom! I'm hungry!"

"You ate only an hour ago."

"But I'm hungry." Fresh air will do that to you. "And I'm thirsty."

"Hello, Thirsty," came Dad's pat answer, "I'm Friday. Come back Saturday and have a Sundae…."

"Ha, ha, ha. So funny I forgot to laugh."

And if you didn't forget to laugh, you soon would when some weighty parcel was tossed into your arms like a medicine ball and your lungs collapsed from the strain. All needs and desires were put on indefinite hold while the station wagon was unloaded.

Finally, after endlessly lifting that barge and toting that bale (Ramses could expect no greater effort from the beleaguered slaves of Egypt), laying bare the LTD, and stuffing the little cottage, it was time.

We suited up.

Running on down to the lake, we made a beeline for the water.

Of course, it was late May or mid-June at best.

Now, there are a few details of nature that should be considered when embarking on any aquatic endeavor in regions north of the tropics at that time of year. For instance, it's cold.

Not chilly.

Cold. Cold like Scott of the Antarctic. Like Penguin's little feet. Like Shackleton rowing to Elephant Island. Like the bottom of the North Atlantic where the Titanic mourned in frozen silence.

The air was also cold. A light wind was worth a warm coat. Once in our bathing suits you were well-advised to wrap up in a towel, the bigger the better. And definitely button up that embarrassing terry cloth garment called a beach jacket that Mom made you wear. None of us cared that we most resembled a troop of goofy cabana boys from a teen beach movie. We layered on any attire, no matter how humiliating, that helped keep our teeth from chattering. The fashion police were never to find us as we sat along the old log at the top of the beach while Dad raked the "seaweed" off the sand.

Mom would drag down a couple of lawn chairs. The folding ones with the metal frames and woven plastic webbing that tended to spontaneously refold with you in them. And blankets for herself and Dad. And something "warming" to drink. And a big spray can of insect repellent.

Because if the cold wasn't enough, there were always the blackflies: hideous carnivorous insects that weren't satisfied to merely sting or suck blood. They swarmed in and chomped off chunks of flesh, leaving behind a gaping wound as well as the customary swollen, itchy, painful bump. Later in the season their ranks diminished, giving way to the mosquitoes and deerflies. But early in the year the nasty blackflies reigned supreme. Another good reason to cover up. And a compelling reason to plunge directly into the water when the "all clear" was finally given.

And every year the first swim was just as painful and the reason was just as shocking to my brothers and me: the water was cold.

No, really.

Had the lake been large enough, surely there would have been icebergs.

Had we thought about it, we would have understood that it was only a short time ago that the full expanse of Go Home Lake was sufficiently frozen over to constitute a miniature ice cap. But that was ancient history for a child anxious to get into the water, easily forgotten in the face of desire. Damn the torpedoes, cold, and the blackflies. All I wanted to do was immerse myself in the lake water, among the turtles and sunfish, the minnows and crayfish. Wash the dust from the dusty trail off me. Cowboy's delight. A scrub in the water hole, once a year, whether you needed it or not.

It wasn't long before our lips turned blue. This was one of the two universally accepted indicators that you had to get out of the water. Blue lips and thunderstorms.

Climbing out, mummified in soggy towels liberally laced with sand, we shook uncontrollably and hopped about on feet we could no longer feel in an effort to warm up. It didn't work, but that never stopped us. For the rest of the summer we repeated the ceremony as many as half a dozen times daily, in and out of the lake. After that first rush into the water, the towels were never dry again until Labor Day.

FOUR

Home on the Range

IT WAS A DIFFERENT time and place. You could drink the water and live to tell. Though whom you would tell and how you might get word to them was another story entirely. Sometimes I wonder if, back then, those rural routes were still serviced by the Pony Express. There was no telephone. Cellular phones were not even a gleam in Ma Bell's eye. If a *coureur de bois* had come stumbling out of the woods with a load of beaver pelts, asking directions to the nearest Hudson's Bay outlet, it would have seemed quite natural.

For a child, the cottage was heaven on earth.

We didn't even miss the television.

There was nowhere to be but exactly where we were, so that one day flowed into the next, only vaguely divided by time to rest, time to eat, and time to set fire to things. Weekends stand out because that's when Dad came up to the cottage, as do my brothers' birthdays, Victoria Day, and Dominion Day.

Firecrackers were quite legal then. It's amazing we still have all digits accounted for and functioning. (Our current occasional shakes from alcohol notwithstanding.)

Mornings were, of course, cold, even in the heat of July, when it finally came. Between sandy flannel sheets we awoke in tree-shaded darkness, the cottage perpetually in the shadow of the forest above it. We would literally be shaken into consciousness when the whole structure shuddered on its stilts with Mom's first insensible steps across the linoleum. She staggered out of a dead sleep groping myopically toward the wood stove, spitting thinly veiled curses in frustration, vainly attempting to intimidate the fire into igniting.

"She-I-T! Darn, darn, darn!"

Once roused, fed, and dressed, we were unceremoniously ejected. There were several acres of outdoors so, unless there was a monsoon, we were to make good use of them, vacating the cottage and "getting out from under" Mother Dear's feet.

You couldn't possibly go swimming until a full hour after eating, any idiot knew that. To do so was to guarantee a quick trip to the bottom of the lake, never to return. Unless at a haunting on bonfire night.

The order of the day's beginning was to negotiate how to occupy the time until the okay was given to swim. The same suggestions were routinely tabled and usually shot down:

"Want to go to the swamp?"

"Naw...."

"The cave?"

"Naw...."

"Pick berries?"

"Aren't any yet."

"Want to build a fort?"

"Naw...."

"Go to the island?"

Silence. But no detractors. So by default it was decided. We would go to the island.

Naturally, preparation and planning were deemed key, and a lot of our pent-up energy went into them, an amusing point, when you consider that the island was all of thirty feet, if that much, offshore. In hip waders we could have walked faster than the boat could ever go.

To call it The Island was probably overstating things. It was more of a stubborn hump of rock that had strongly resisted the last ice age, then rested from its efforts. A single, small, fairly flat surface facing the sky. There, left to the assaults of weather and waste on its igneous complexion, it developed layers of lichens and moss, eventually some grasses and two or three shrubs, then finally a spindly tree. Not bad for a parcel of highly threatened "land" measuring no more than five by six feet. Less when the water was high.

Early in the season, long before the other cottagers settled in, the water was, in fact, very high. The island was certainly waterlogged. The lake was all but deserted. We had our run of the place.

Because he was the oldest, all of eleven, Buck was somewhat in charge. "Go get the life jackets from the porch," Buck started up with either James or Kieffer. There was little hope of anyone actually getting down to business. It was a sort of call and answer game.

"Make me," was the automatic reply.

To which the proper response was, "I don't make monkeys."

Then followed some very strange (to a small child) invitation to chew, suck, eat, or otherwise apply the structures of the oral cavity to the genitals, as indicated by the spreading of the legs and pointing.

"You wish" or "You'd love it" (choose one only).

Then, "Homo."

Once on the track, there was no derailing this train, so I just hung out and hoped they'd run out of steam soon.

"It takes one to know one!"

"Me? You're the one that mo's your pillow and calls it 'Brucie.'"

Note: until I had the misfortune to ask an adult, I had thought *mo* had something to do with cutting one's grass, as in "to mow the lawn." It was an irritated adult who clarified: It was short for *molest*. When I pressed the point, asking for a full definition, the response was "Nobody likes a tattletale," a short look, and exasperated huff.

But I already knew *that*. Loose lips were likely to be punched. Cowboys were loyal. The strong *silent* type was the best. Stand by your man. Or your horse. Or the ranch. Whatever.

And I didn't need The Code of the West to tell me that. I had learned too often and too much the hard way that, at least as far as my brothers were concerned, that my observations on their behavior were not to be shared, unless I really wanted a good beating.

I felt a little sick to my stomach. I didn't know who I

"told on." But no matter how awful I felt, I knew I'd feel worse when the offended brother(s) got a hold of me later.

"No way. You're the homo."

"Homo homo homo."

As far as I knew, "homo" was just a short form of "homogenized." It was just a kind of milk. How was milk insulting? I couldn't tell you. But "homo" was an accusation that had to be defended against. The best retort was to say, "Go shove a flaming hot ramrod up your rosy red rectum."

Such alliteration always sent me into fits of giggles. And I made a point of not spoiling the fun by asking what a rectum was.

If the boys were in the mood, some knocking about of each other might happen, but not always.

When that bit of mirth more or less ran its course, Buck would work on me. "You go get the life jackets."

Being the youngest, I was the most malleable. Which is not to say I was actually cooperative.

"Why?" I had to know.

"Just do it," he told me.

Still smarting from his last convincing wallop, I did. Besides, there was no way we were going to be allowed to go out on the water without life jackets.

Kieffer and James went off to find the oars. They took them over to the old log on the beach. Balancing on either end they tried to knock one another off and into the sand. Buck told them to be careful or they'd break the oars, and then we'd all be in trouble.

In light of the fact that we were embarking on an *overseas* journey, Buck sent me to the kitchen to fill the canteen with water. I went to the bathroom because I could reach the taps there. He asked Mom for some food for the trip. "Can we have some sandwiches to take to the island?"

Mom looked up from digging the ashes out of the woodstove. "I don't see a piano tied to your right arm."

I took a quick glance around the corner to be sure. Nope. No piano. What a silly thing for Mom to say.

"There's nobody sitting on your chest," she went on. "A giant isn't chasing you down the street."

There were no streets around the cottage. Just the bumpy road. I didn't get it.

But by the roll of his eyes I knew Buck did. He sighed and shuffled into the kitchen. I fiddled with the top on the canteen. I got it off first try, and it only took me three tries to get it on straight. I jammed it under the faucet in the tiny sink and let the water run before it spurted out the top. It sloshed a little as I yanked the canteen out, but way more than half the water stayed in. Pretty slick work on my part.

"You're over seven years of age. You're in perfectly good health," Mom continued through the cloud of ash she was creating, waving the metal scoop for emphasis. "What did your last slave die of?"

Buck got some peanut butter and jam from the cupboard and some bread from the box. "Slave was insolent. So I shot 'im," he muttered under his breath.

Laying out an uneven number of slices of bread, Buck slapped together a few PB&J's and a foldie. Lacking our mother's talent for the magic self-sealing-corners-under wax-paper wrap, Buck pulled off a long sheet and made a sort of jellyroll Christmas-cracker sandwich stack. Twisting the ends, he stuffed the arrangement into a slightly too small knapsack.

"It's squashed," I said sadly, regarding the poor little sandwiches folded so tightly they were more like peanut butter origami than a picnic.

"It's all going to the same place," Buck said. He took the canteen from me and gave it a shake.

"Didn't I tell you to fill it?" he asked, unscrewing the lid and peering inside.

"I tried, but the lid got stuck and it spilled." In fact I couldn't quite manage to maneuver the canteen opening around the faucet without tipping much of the water out, and it was really too heavy for me when full. But there was no saying "I can't." Little *girls* said "I can't." Cowboys just ambled on and got the job done.

Buck refilled the canteen and screwed the lid on tight. "Try to not be so useless and bring the knapsack," he told me and started for the door. I held the pack in front of me as carefully as I could, hoping to reduce the squash factor. Glancing back at me, Buck pushed through the screen door and let it swing back. On me. And our lunch.

"Ohhhh," I whined.

Buck shrugged. "It's all going to be crap coming out of your bum anyway," he said with a grin.

"Don't say bum," I said, feeling creepy just saying it myself. "That's a bad word."

Eventually we got all we needed for the voyage. The oars were pried out of the crack in the old log where James and Kieffer had wedged them, but not before the lunch pack was drop-kicked through them as if they were goalposts. Kieffer and Buck successfully attached the electric trolling motor to the minuscule boat then spent a little time using it to tear up the lake bottom at the shallow end of the dock, just to see the fish scatter. Then we loaded up the boat.

In our fluorescent-orange, keyhole-style life preservers, we looked like four cervical injury patients on a day pass from the Home for the Chronically Stunned. You couldn't turn your head in one of those things if your life depended on it. Every little ripple you crossed on the water jerked your head suddenly, causing momentary panic that the force exerted on the life vest might be too sharp and sudden, thereby popping your head completely off.

But the lake was calm as we puttered across the distance from the end of our dock to the island. It must have been a Monday or a Tuesday, because the motor ran well. It was powered off a car battery, which had a seriously limited life span. Dad did such mysterious things as charging it up when he came up on weekends.

We stuck close to the shoreline, moving slowly beyond the Barker's cottage, past the Deiter's cottage, where sometimes a girl named Karen stayed, and farther out into the bay to avoid capsizing on the rocky point of the Canadian Shield that jutted into the water near the opening to the swamp. That's where the Lanza's cottage was.

Had the water been rock-free and perfectly flat, I still would have kept well clear of that point because I didn't like the Lanzas. They were a bunch of wild teen boys with invisible parents. Their cottage was set on a wide rock plate that was frequently used to stake out living frogs and shot-filled birds, downed but not quite killed by the Lanza boys.

Darren, the youngest, was the creepiest kid I had ever met. Small for his age with his tiny eyes set too far apart, he had an evil way of looking at you. A sort of evil-clown smile never left his face. He never smiled *at* anyone, only to himself, probably about whatever rotten idea he was hatching. He had cigarette burns on his hands and fingers. He laughed until he cried when I reacted with little-girl horror at the sight of his penis poking through his swim trunks. I thought there was something wrong with him. (I had yet to understand some of those favored phrases of my brothers: "hard on" and "woody.") He smoked as much as he could steal. He stole anything he could, whether he wanted it or not. It was like a reflex. He was ten.

Soon we arrived at the island and circled it a few times. What were we looking for? An airstrip put in by the native inhabitants during the winter? A hippo hiding among the saturated moss mounds? As a land mass, it wasn't exactly sure of itself. Depending on the season, the island would shrink and grow. There was barely anything that wasn't very wet.

A minor scuffle took place while it was decided where to tie up and how to disembark. Potential dangers were many. The rocks were slippery; there was nowhere to pull the boat up on shore. Actually there was precious little shore. We all got soakers while trying to claim enough island space on which to stand. None of us was particularly disturbed by the prospect of falling into the lake fully clothed. It had been proven, time and time again, that we were unsinkable. We'd all fallen in at one time or another, probably recently. But if the motor got dumped, the battery was submerged, or Kieffer lost his glasses, we were really going to get it. To commit such an act was to be feared. The dreaded cottage confinement that would invariably follow was strictly enforced. Those who failed to observe water safety rules, and that meant returning to shore with the same number of bodies, conveyances, and accompanying hardware that you left with were treated most harshly. It would be preferable to lose a limb than to lose the rope or bailing bucket.

Somehow we all managed to get on the island, but there was certainly no room for us to sit down and have a picnic.

Back into the boat we went, retracing our journey. This time I was on the opposite side of the boat and didn't have to look at the Lanza's place.

Somewhere mid-voyage someone came up with the brilliant notion of a shipboard meal. We broke open our lunch, or rather, we extruded it from the now wet knapsack.

It was not the least bit appetizing – remarkable because we would eat almost anything.

Gamely I nibbled on the driest corner of the least damp sandwich I could find. Kieffer and James broke theirs up, formed them into little sticky balls, and pelted them at one another. Buck, keenly noticing that the rain of white bread and peanut butter attracted all manner of underwater creatures, proceeded to feed his sandwich to the fish.

This was fun for a while, but short-lived, owing to the finite nature of the lunch.

We returned, feeling for all the world like conquering heroes, hard, worn, and exhausted after years away on a crusade. It was surprising we didn't all have long beards and toenails. The entire event took just over thirty-seven minutes. I had expected it to be long after midnight. Surely we had crossed the international dateline a couple of times before coming back to this time zone.

I believe it was Kieffer who said it best. Speaking for us all he declared "Mom, I'm hungry."

We needed fuel. There were a hundred adventures yet to go – today alone.

If it was a cold day and not too damp, the swamp was a splendid destination. Ornate with grasses and cattails, lily pads and algae, the swamp was a rich and busy place. Fat bullfrogs lounged extravagantly about the edges of the bog, dipping occasionally in the opaque green water, then draping themselves about the sides again. They tasted flies as if they were at some exclusive frog gourmet resort. Snapping turtles, lumbering and inept, the size of serving bowls, threatened us in Sam Peckinpah slow motion, opening their pointy jaws and clapping them shut with a cold look in their eyes.

"Don't get too close," Buck solemnly advised me. "They'll bite your fingers right off."

I cautiously jammed my hands in my pockets, just in case, then sought confirmation. "Really?" I asked Kieffer. Four years my senior, he seemed so much older and wiser than I.

"Oh, for sure," Kieffer agreed. "I knew a kid that it happened to. The turtle snapped off his whole hand. Took it off at the wrist and ate it in one big gulp."

"Really…" I stepped back from the water's edge. The turtles floating among the rotting vegetation near the surface appeared to be advancing. And getting larger.

"Yeah," Kieffer went on, his unblinking eyes staring straight at me, "And the worst thing was that the kid could still feel his hand as the turtle chewed and chewed and swallowed it down into his slimy, acid turtle guts."

James snickered behind me. But Kieffer kept his cool. With a stick he reached out and nudged a sleeping turtle. It suddenly shifted and dropped deep in the water out of sight. I wanted to go home. For all I could tell that bloodthirsty turtle was about to resurface in the middle of the road under my feet and bite off the whole lower half of my body.

I looked at my brothers sideways and said doubtfully, "No way," but they could tell it was all posturing.

"Yes way," they all insisted.

But a cowboy feared nothing. This was good training. Throwing back my head, hands on hips, I bravely proclaimed, "Whoopee-do!"

Naturally, I had the last word. There was simply no response to "whoopee-do."

Back at the cottage we ate pink-and-white ice-cream wafers. None of us could stand them, but it was either that or go hungry. God only knew how long until supper. Maybe as much as three quarters of an hour. On the verge of starvation, we gnawed on those hateful ice-cream wafers and tried to keep our strength up.

The blackflies came and went. Voluptuous bullfrog tadpoles and the little skinny leopard frog ones sprouted legs and experimented with the life of the landlubber. We dug in for the season. The supplies of ice cream, milk, and fresh bread rapidly declined. We replenished on weekend trips to town when Dad, and hence the car, were there. Even so, there were times we had to rip into the emergency rations of sterilized milk in the little triangular packages with the little purple cows all over. It tasted kind of funny, but nothing that a heaping helping of strawberry Quik couldn't cure.

Summer progressed. The surrounding cottages slowly filled up. It was not as much the wilderness that it was at the beginning, but it still retained its wild side.

I broke my index finger falling off the stairs. James helped. He felt I was moving too slowly and propelled me to the bottom of the flight with his foot. I landed "tail over teakettle" on a jutting rock and let out such a shriek, Mother actually came to the door. She made a disgusted face when I held up my hand, finger bent wrong-ways around. But it meant some much desired Mom and Me Time when she dragged me by the arm up the back path to Auntie Lil's cottage, waving my misshapen hand before us like a particularly dirty sock. Auntie Lil, Mom's *cousin*, not really an aunt, owned one of the two cottages close to ours.

"For corn's sake, can you help me deal with this?" she asked Auntie Lil.

"Ohmygooooooodness!" Auntie Lil scurried for her keys and off we went to the hospital in hopes of finding an actual doctor on duty.

There was a man in a white coat with white hair and glasses. Might have been Colonel Sanders, for all we knew. He smiled with a twinkle and jammed my finger back rightways. That hurt too, but not as much as the first time. He gave me a lollipop, a green one. But there was no fancy cast like when I broke my arm.

"Can you paint flowers on this one like on my broken arm?" I looked sadly at the Popsicle-stick-and-adhesive-tape cast on my finger.

"Don't be foolish," Mother sniffed. "It's too small, and I only did that so you'd stop hitting your brothers with it. I had to take you in and have it replastered twice, you know."

"Sorry, Mom," I said. I was too. I missed that cast now. It had been useful in fending off the boys. I was sorry it had to come off.

"Now maybe you'll stop picking your nose all the time," Mother suggested cheerfully about my finger binding, "or you're going to wind up with big, huge nostrils."

"I never pick my nose!" I whined, knowing full well I did. And I bit my fingernails. And my toenails, for that matter. And I chewed my hair. Lord only knew what was going to become of me as a result of all those nasty habits. I'd be a snub-toed, blunt-fingered, head-caved-in, wide-nostriled, fuzz-headed freak.

Auntie Lil's brother Don (again, Mother's cousin) owned another cottage near ours. He very rarely visited. He was an actor by trade and in the midst of a divorce. The combination of the two kept him in the city most of the time, often leaving his cottage empty, although it was occasionally rented out.

But one time Don brought a girlfriend with him, who had extraordinarily long black hair. She was excruciatingly thin. She claimed to be a witch. They both wore caftans with African motifs and smiled in a sleepy, vacant way. They stumbled and giggled a lot. But it *was* the sixties.

Don caught a bat in a jar one day. Like Moses descending

from the mountain, complete with flowing robe and hair, Don came down to the beach proudly bearing his canned rodent as if it were the original clay tablets of God.

Fascinated by this wondrous find, we all crowded around him, gawking at the poor thing as it fluttered and flapped nervously in its glass prison.

Mom called down to us emphatically, "You've got to let him play ball, kids. It's *his* bat!" All the grown-ups laughed, fit to be tied. They were so weird.

Auntie Lil, her husband, Marlow, and their youngest daughter, Suzanne, spent the lion's share of the summer at the lake. Their other children were grown and living away from home, but they were known to visit now and then.

We all worshiped Suzanne. She was the quintessential teenager at the quintessential time to be a teenager. And she did it so well. She wore with panache little boots and hip-huggers, complexly engineered bathing suits with big plastic rings holding the top and bottom portions together, or bikinis that defied all natural laws and remained firmly attached regardless of the conditions.

Suzanne knew all the groovy music, looked good in white lipstick, which is *really* saying a lot. She ironed her hair each morning – with a clothes iron – on the ironing board. She kept us up to date at all times with the latest in trend-setting words.

"Isn't that *marvy*?"

Suzanne was marvy.

When I think about it now, I probably only wanted to be a cowboy because being Suzanne was already taken.

We were all pleased when Suzanne arrived for the season

because it invariably meant that many of the more memo-rable events of the summer were about to take place.

Once, it was body painting. With brushes that tickled and cold watercolor paints that itched when they dried, Suzanne painted us all one night with hearts and flowers and peace signs, and the word *LUV* written out in sausage-style letters.

I wanted more than a flower on my face, but I was reluc-tant to expose the skin required for a greater masterpiece. Suzanne assured me kindly, "It doesn't matter. You can take your top off. You're only little."

But I was big enough to know boys and girls were dif-ferent and that ladies did not go without tops. Except in my father's collection of magazines.

"Yeah, sure, stick 'em out. That's what you got 'em for," or words to that effect from the penis – *peanut* – gallery. Brotherly support in the form of gloating. Thanks. *They* were painted all over. They had funny cartoon faces that changed expression when they rolled their bellies or shifted their shoulder blades. I was pea green with envy.

So off came the top to pre-pubescent hoots and catcalls. I felt horribly exposed, and I knew I was doing something terribly bad, but I couldn't tell what. I just didn't want to be shortchanged again just because I was weaker, younger, inept at climbing trees, and unable to throw a football.

Another night, in the grand style of *Twilight Zone* and *Tales From the Crypt*, Suzanne helped us set up a house of horrors, which was not even slightly horrible, but it was a great deal of fun, with its eight-year-old vampires and beard-less youth wolfmen.

Under her dilettante tutelage we attempted to contact the dead (not that we knew any) with a Ouija board.

We also tried hypnosis and levitation.

Surrounding a supine body on the floor, we were instructed to concentrate hard and repeat the words Suzanne chanted in a low voice:

"She sleeps."

"She sleeps."

"She's sick."

"She's sick."

"She's dead."

"She's dead."

"She floats."

"She floats."

It was mind over matter. At this moment, had we been successful, the subject was supposed to rise up into the air. Moved by the strength of our mental powers, we would be able to lift the body of the entranced human with just two fingers each.

Suzanne swore she and her friend Jennifer had achieved the higher state required.

We never quite made it. It was generally agreed that it was my fault for giggling, or just failing to concentrate hard enough.

But I still believed. It had to be possible.

FIVE

Hard Knock Life

THE BARKERS – consisting of Mrs. Barker, Timmy, and some elderly relation, who was pale to the point of being transparent (as a result of never putting foot outside the door), were also full-summer cottagers. Naturally, Mr. Barker came on weekends. And, like Auntie Lil's tribe, there were older siblings who appeared on the scene now and then.

I had a monster crush on one of Timmy's older brothers. Damned if I can remember his name. He could play guitar, at least well enough to convince a young child such as myself. One wonderful afternoon he organized a barbecue and sing-in. The sum total of youth and children at our end of the lake was assembled on the overturned cedar-strip boat at the foot of the Barker's property, maybe about twenty of us, to sing folk songs. "If I Had a Hammer," "Blowin' in the Wind,"

"Ain't Gonna Study War No More." We belted them out, badly, and we had a *marvy* time.

And as the sun slowly set over Go Home Lake, I complained I was cold. Timmy's brother got me a sweatshirt that used to be his but was too small for the galumphing Timmy. I put it on, feeling like the chosen one, very superior because Timmy was the dimensions of a big, hairless bear. I too, was a little on the heavy side. A thick little kid with a big head and a big frame, I was often called Piggy. But in that sweatshirt I felt the love. The love of a beautiful, gentle, young man for a little girl (accent on *little*). I figured he had to love me more than anyone because he believed I was cold. The normal response to my complaining about anything was either "Stop complaining or I'll give you something to complain about," or "You're just faking it to get attention."

The sweatshirt consumed me. It hung past my knees. When Timmy's brother rolled the sleeves up so I could find my hands, he had to take so many turns in the fabric it looked like I was wearing water wings around my wrists. The sweatshirt was blue with a picture of a ship's steering wheel with the words Cape Cod in the middle.

I cherished it until I was thirteen when it finally disintegrated.

I did so love Timmy's brother.

Timmy was another matter.

Not so secretly, Mom referred to Timmy as "the error of aging parents."

He was probably four years older than me, which put him at the right age to be in with my brothers. They would have nothing to do with him, however, unless, of course, it was to torment him relentlessly. I should have felt sorry for him, but it was nice to be out of the teasing spotlight from time to time. And Timmy was a pretty tormentable kind of kid.

He was tall, very fair, doughy, and inclined to cry. And when he cried he turned a definitively female shade of pink. He batted his eyes. He moaned with his lips ruffled and flapping. Then he turned and skip-ran to his mother or indoor relation, holding his sit-upon cheeks to keep them from jiggling and increasing his audience's hysteria.

If that weren't enough he had a far more impressive collection of Barbie dolls than I did. Okay, they were Ken dolls. Nevertheless they were dolls, and they weren't GI Joes.

Even when I didn't get the embarrassing weight placed on this fact, I knew it was grave and beyond forgiveness.

For the first few seasons Mrs. Barker tirelessly lobbied Mom to ensure that the boys cease and desist their agitation and that all we children play nicely together.

"I can't make them play with him," Mom insisted. And it was true, she couldn't. Even under constant and careful supervision, some way could always be found by my brothers to torture Timmy. It was simply irresistible.

Just to make matters worse, every summer Mr. and Mrs. Barker went off to Europe on vacation, abandoning Timmy to the housebound, antique relation, with no one to canvass on his behalf.

But sometimes Mom would feel sorry for Timmy, possibly even a little guilty for looking the other way while Timmy howled in anguish, well aware her little darlings were at the root of it. And then opportunity to recoup a little might present itself in the form of my being unceremoniously ejected from some guy thing that my brothers were into. (This wouldn't happen when I was a cowboy.) Mom would drag me out of the fray for my own protection and shove me in the direction of the Barkers.

"Why don't you go play with Timmy." It wasn't a question; it was an order. I would have rather played with roadkill.

Though I confess there were times I was *that* desperate for a playmate that even Timmy didn't seem all bad.

The water was neutral territory. Timmy and I could go swimming together. There was some agreement there. Besides, Timmy had every inflatable water toy known to mankind and no stinky brothers around to share them with. It was a great opportunity to lord it over Timmy and his toys. Why miss out on that?

I was already in my swimsuit most of the time. Except for the cold early mornings and sundowns, I spent most of my cottage life in a wet bathing suit. In those days the average girl's swim costume was of some unconscionable design, thickly knit so that it never totally dried. Any elastic material was confined to the leg holes, so that the fabric expanded and the seat sagged when worn, effectively trapping about three cubic yards of sand and gravel in the butt end daily.

It was disgusting. But I was little. I didn't care.

Timmy usually promenaded about in some Little Lord Eaton's Haberdashery getup – something overly coordinated, buttoned up, starched, and ironed.

"I know!" I declared in my best television commercial voice. "Let's go swimming!"

I had learned early to dramatically feign enthusiasm for all sorts of dull diversions and fourth-place finishes. Young advertising thespians were excellent teachers, consistently bursting with joy, as they did, over everything from novel recipes for lima beans and processed cheese to useless toys that functioned only through the magic of TV. ("I know! Let's have steamed spinach Popsicles after we recreate an Andy Warhol in pin lights!")

"I'm not dressed for swimming," Timmy sighed.

Well anyone could see that. And I had a great idea what to do about it. "I know! You can *put on* your swim suit!" This time I added a palms-up pose and wide eyes.

"It's not really hot out today." Timmy extended his bread-dough arm and waved it about like the blond fuzz that covered it was some thermo sensing material. "I only really like swimming when it's really, really hot out."

What "hot"? It was hot. My lips were not blue and I could still feel my feet. I refreshed my happy face and tried again. "I know – let's just try it!" Then I quoted directly from, I think, an ad for an upset stomach remedy: "Try it! You'll like it." I tried to keep my own upset stomach settled. Timmy was so dumb! He was starting to make me mad.

Timmy hung his head to one side and let his pink lips slack open. He looked to the sky and blinked a lot. "What if it rains?"

That was just infuriating. If he didn't smarten up soon, I was going to have to smack him. He knew it wasn't going to rain. And even if it did, you could still stay in the water so long as there were no thunder storms. Those were the RULES. "Timmy stop being – " I held my hands in fists and stepped close to Timmy's fat, annoying face. I didn't want anyone, not even God – who, according to Sunday school heard everything – to hear me. "Just stop being a…" I said a tiny prayer to myself that since God was fairly old, he was probably also fairly deaf, like grandpa. "Stop being a *bum!*"

There. I said it.

Timmy heard it. He recoiled in horror. "You said a bad word," he accused, as if that feeling of having swallowed a hot, wet, woolly mitten didn't confirm it. "I'm telling!" he said. But he didn't move. For sure we were both thinking the same thing: Who would he tell?

Mr. and Mrs. Barker had gone continental a week ago and were no doubt, that very moment, cursing the serious shortage of perked coffee and modern plumbing in some charming Italian village.

He could tell the washed-up relation, but to *do* anything about it, said relation would actually have to leave the cottage to chase me. That would never happen. All that might happen was that Timmy would be dragged in and sighed at every time he played with his Ken dolls.

There was no possibility of Timmy being able to repeat the word to my mother, who would almost certainly tell him to mind his own bee's wax and stop being a tattletale.

So there was a use to profanity after all.

I was giddy with power. Ha! I gave him a squinty sort of angry look. "You had just better *shut up.*"

Two bad words! I was getting good at this. But of course I would have to be when I was a real cowboy. "Timmy," I said almost sprouting chaps as I strode in circles around him, "you better just quit faking it. Everybody knows you're just *faking it* to get attention."

What he was faking and how it might benefit him was

immaterial. And given past experiences, the last thing Timmy could want around here was attention, because it was always nasty. But even so, the accusation worked its charm.

Relieved of any notion of personal choice, Timmy accepted defeat, grabbed his jiggly behind, and scurried off to get his swimsuit.

I followed along.

Timmy's bedroom was at the back of his cottage. It was a separate room with an actual door that closed with a push-button privacy lock. The first time I saw it I was almost sick with jealousy. Unlike my room, which was not so much a room as an especially wide hallway that connected the original old cabin to the addition where my brothers slept, Timmy's had defined boundaries, wallpaper, and matching bedding. I had unequal right-of-way to a bed in a corner, water-damaged chipboard on the walls and ceiling, and an old desk with two drawers and a broken leg. The whole of the free world could access anything I might like to claim as my own. Timmy had his very own side table and a lamp with a fringed shade, a white ceiling dome light, and a wall sconce over his bed for reading. He had a copy of *Heidi* and *Black Beauty* on his bedside table. I had a bare bulb suspended from the ceiling that I couldn't reach the switch for and several comic books with pages missing that I couldn't actually read. But, sure as shootin' I would certainly be able to read 'em and weep, cowboy style, when I had a snazzy wall sconce like Timmy's.

Next to his clean, white chest of drawers with gold trim, Timmy had a green-floral-chintz-covered slipper chair. I con-sidered taking a seat there, just for the sheer pleasure of it, but being that I sported something like a stone of wet cement in my drawers, I decided I'd only get in trouble when I ruined it. I remained standing at attention as Timmy stripped to the pink.

Timmy said, "Don't look."

I wasn't looking.

And believe me I had less than no desire to. Seeing Timmy wearing only his pallid birthday suit was like seeing a lurid *bonhomme de neige* naked. But Timmy was about twice my height and lacked the essential creativity required for him to figure out to turn his back to me, so I couldn't help but look.

Maybe I said "Ewyeew."

Probably I made a face.

Timmy had strange and minute genitalia. I had three brothers, so I had a passing knowledge of what these things were supposed to look like, and they weren't supposed to look like what Timmy had.

The proportions were all wrong. Of course children don't have an idea of large or small. They attach no meaning to it – that's an adult's hang-up. The *other*, what the opposite sex had and how it functioned, was a curious sort of thing and worth a glance when you got the opportunity. But Timmy's was hardly large enough to *be* looked at. His Lilliputian penis, shadowed under the looming rings of his milky white tummy, was like an infant's. It appeared to retreat shyly within a vertical fold that looked more like what I had. His balls, if he had any, were hidden between his Rubenesque thighs. It just looked wrong.

"Don't look!" Timmy reprimanded when he saw me looking.

"I'm not!" I snapped back, and then I looked some more. I got a funny feeling in the pit of my stomach. That nightmarish feeling like in a dream, when I wanted to run or scream, but nothing happened. Or like when Grand-Pappa died, but my housecoat still smelled of his pipe from when he read me stories last. I felt terribly sorry but didn't know why. All this for having seen almost nothing at all.

Timmy dressed hastily in his swim trunks. We went off to play in the water. I didn't even hog his blow-up dolphin, though I would have been justified on the grounds that I was The Guest.

We played the usual games: underwater talking, King of the Castle on the air mattress, belly flop contests. Timmy always won belly flops. I just let him win everything. Anything to make the day be over. Anything to not be in it. I just acted the happy playmate. I recited every happy line of every whitewashed, happy story I had ever seen on television.

All of these games pleased Timmy to no end. That very day I swallowed that infantile pill and behaved less like the snarky quick-witted kid I thought myself to be, the kid I'd have to be to survive as a cowboy. Now all those smarty pants sayings stuck in my throat. I just kept my inanely grinning mug above water, babbling and gesturing like, well, just like Timmy. I mirrored his every daft move just to stay afloat while my thoughts were rapidly swimming in circles.

Some serpentine understanding was worming its way through my dense head. Apples to oranges. Apples were made by God, as were boys and girls, men and women, from strong will and a rib, I learned in Sunday school. Timmy was singular, without an orange or an apple or a rib to hold up to him. He was a mistake – my mother was right – made too late in the lives of trifling parents who had lost their recipe for children.

A popular family joke of the day referred to The Three Stooges:

"Why did the mom and dad name their twins Curly and Larry?"

"I dunno, why?"

"Because they didn't want no mo."

I never got the joke, though it was repeated to me several times, louder with each telling. I guessed that "mo'" was not a slur of "more" but the name of the premiere Stooge, Moe. And how could Curly and Larry be twins? They didn't look at all alike. Moe looked older than them. So did the parents not want him because the twins were cuter as new babies? Were they tired of always trimming Moe's soup-bowl haircut? Is that why those grown brothers fought like boys all the time?

It dawned on me that somehow Timmy's being so hate-worthy was preordained. He was faulted by his own malformations. This was big. It was biblical. It was knowledge. Timmy's parents abandoned him for Europe because they had looked and seen all of Timmy, in all his awfulness. They knew. And they didn't want no mo'.

As we played, I occasionally watched Timmy, his delicate rubber features contorted in cartoon laughter, his wet hair transparent, his large bloated trunk billowing over his swim shorts, buoyant like so much Styrofoam. I felt something sickly and unrecognizable.

It would be years before I could describe it. It was pity.

When lunchtime came, we went off to our separate kitchen tables, probably for the first time without me in a rage or Timmy in tears. Just before I left he grabbed my arm and hissed intensely, "Don't tell."

I ran off without saying anything.

I never told.

But then, I never told about anything. No one ever believed me about anything, and besides, a cowboy was a solemn and solitary soul.

By the middle of the summer the lake was warm and the weather was hot. But I hardly noticed. Each day folded into another without seams or rends. The sun and rain rolled over the intermittent night. Other cottagers came and went – sometimes people we knew well and disliked for good reason. They were mean and hated us because we owned the only natural sand beach on the lake. That's what Mom said. Others – mostly renters – we didn't know, but we learned to hate them pretty fast. Maybe they were dried up and old, or stingy with their marshmallows. Maybe they didn't have kids, or maybe they had kids who whined all the time, who couldn't take a joke, who bruised easily or couldn't hold their breath underwater for a normal length of time, no matter how we helped hold them at the bottom of the lake (only ever in the shallow part, of course). None of these useless kids had a penknife or a BB gun. Half the time they wore life jackets in swimming. Their parents wouldn't let them have firecrackers, even on Victoria Day or Dominion Day. One of them cut his hand open on a rock. How stupid do you have to be to cut yourself on a rock? His mom told our mom it was because Kieffer and James pushed him down in the old mine. But what did she expect when the kid walked so slow?

Soon enough the water was dark and the air was cold again. Without knowing it, I felt the change. The inevitable was coming: school, socks, hard-soled shoes, washed hair, going to bed early, and getting up earlier. The seven-supper rotation from Roast Beef Sunday to Roast Beef Sunday. *Auntie Em, Auntie Em* – the twister reversed its frenetic pattern and everything that was not eaten, burnt in a bonfire, or carted to the dump was bunched and stuffed and bundled for the return to the city.

Kieffer had a raccoon's tail that he'd found in the woods. What became of the rest of the raccoon was anybody's guess. I think he believed he'd find it conveniently cleaned and shaped into a hat next summer in the same woods. He placed the tail (with a certain amount of raccoon flesh and bone still in it) on an inside window ledge for winter storage with an eye to reuniting the related pelts Daniel Boone style. But my father instructed Buck to take the "bloody thing" and hurl it as far into the trees as possible.

Seeing what the fate of such character-enhancing head gear could be, I stole away with my cowboy hat, filled it with mothballs, and put it under my bed. I got hit for "playing" with the mothballs, and hit again for denying I knew where they got to, but the security in knowing my cowboy hat, and thus my future, were safe was worth the sting.

In leaving, we had to drive past the remains of an old storefront. All of ten-feet square, at that time most of it was still standing. Suzanne said she recalled buying penny candy there, so it couldn't have been too long ago that there was a real operation going on. Other than the odd black ball or licorice whip to some kid, or a ball of twine or a hurricane lamp to a local, it could not have offered much. By our time, the shutters were nailed over the broken windows and sun-bleached boarding. For a long while a faded For Sale sign was pinned haplessly to the front. It flapped rhythmically in the least bit of breeze and whistled like a giant reed if the wind was slightly stronger.

Attached to this grand establishment like a modern-day garage was a singular horse stall, also in an advanced state of disrepair.

But that summer, as we were driving away from the cottage for the last time, I saw an old dust-colored horse closed in the stall.

"Hey, look at the horse!" I shouted.

"Shut up, or – "

"I'm not playing that game," my brothers said.

Mom said, "Sit down and be quiet. It's a long drive."

I wanted Dad to stop the car. I wanted to make sure that someone was going to take care of the horse, take it away for the winter. This was a summer place. Nothing could survive here past Thanksgiving. Panic swelled inexplicably. I had horrible visions of the poor animal slowly starving and dying a long and painful death. Suddenly I knew and feared death, knew my own was as possible and as likely as that horse's. After all, a cowboy was only as good as his trusty horse. Another year had come and gone and I didn't have one, even though Dad had promised. He *promised*. All my aspirations, my dreams of cowboyhood, were imprisoned, locked in that stall, expiring with that horse, and no one even cared.

In subsequent years I hated to pass that tumble-down store and stall. Though I could see with my own eyes that the horse was not there, I always feared it would be, dead and decaying, its dried skin and stringy muscles looped in putrid bunting over the skeleton, its head still draped over the door of the stall.

That never happened, but the fear played over and over again in my imagination, so that every time we rounded the bend in the road to the site of that old store, I believed that the dead horse was there. I averted my eyes, looked steadily away, for to look would undoubtedly yield the same wretched feeling as when I saw Timmy Barker naked.

SIX

Wintering In

AUTUMN ALWAYS FELT more like its common name: fall. Though "plummet" might have been a better word for it. After the acquisition of the Vestments of Great Hope – new shoes and a first day of school outfit – it was not so much *all downhill from there* but *all downhill at breakneck speed and over a cliff and into cold, rocky water* from there.

I might have fared better if I was one of the pretty, popular girls. I didn't buy Mother's "pretty is as pretty does." Pretty was more like nasty to those who, by the sin of some evil genetic punch up, were not pretty at all.

But I didn't do much to help myself.

I was good at skipping and could manage a decent double Dutch. I had my own skipping rope. Secretly I referred to it as my lasso and, under cloak of darkness in the garage, I practiced spinning a loop over my head so I could capture a stray calf while standing on the saddle of my swiftly running pony. Whoa, bend those knees as the pony jumps the creek!

I never really managed to get the rope moving in that perfect circle. I suspect now the weight of the wooden handle (painted green with pink-and-white spots and bells on the end) of the skipping rope put it all off balance. To cut them off would have required absconding with The Good Scissors, and I valued my life too much to risk that.

Winter was bright and white and sparkly clean. Children in our neighborhood chased each other about and "washed" each other's faces in snow. Being that I insisted on insinuating myself into the games of my brothers and their all male friends, and that I was the smallest and therefore slowest moving, I was regularly scrubbed with heaping handfuls of snow and ice held in half-frozen mittens.

I had the cleanest face in town. I hated it. But giving up such fun was the same as giving in.

And there was no giving in for a cowboy.

For the good of our health, sleet or hail, blizzard or whiteout, we were sent out for a minimum of two hours a day to get some Fresh Air.

This probably served to advance the cause of the tobacco industry in our demographic. Two-thirds of us took up smoking by age thirteen, mostly because we wanted to look cool. We wanted to feel the heat and thaw out our frozen lungs a bit from all that Fresh Air.

During these therapeutic sessions, our parents never joined us. Adult health was not reliant on the Fresh Air factor. Mother remained inside smoking and drinking and studying such conflicting works of the time as *The Women's Room* and *The Total Woman*, the former a story of women's liberation, the latter a how-to guide on wifely cleaving and submission. No telling which one helped her get our father onside with her next little scheme. He was dead set against her going out and getting a job, so she convinced him that she was just entertaining herself with a mere *pastime*; why, you couldn't even really call it *work* at all. And it might make her a little pocket money.

She would breed dogs.

Big dogs. No little yappy crackies need apply.

She started with a best-in-show-worthy male with superior breeding potential. She would have a dog capital in stature, a dog that strode, not trotted, one that set off her recently acquired pantsuit, whose leash matched her shoes. One might think Golden Lab or even Afghan hound. Pure bred. Pure elegance.

But no.

Out of the canine blue, Mother settled on having a Saint Bernard.

These Swiss mountain dogs were probably best known for their daring-do in the Alps. Dispatched to uncover avalanche victims or rescue downed skiers, Saint Bernards typically arrived just before hypothermia set in and offered the little brandy-filled cask they carried under their chins. Perhaps Mother thought they were born that way, genetically endowed mini-barrel outer gland, flowing with medicinal drink.

Of course the puppy did not arrive so equipped. Less appealing liquids streamed from ostensibly limitless reservoirs and glands *within* his body. Drool spilled unstoppable from his bunting-like jowls. He left a slobbery trail everywhere he went like a giant, dog-breathed snail. Mother never revealed any hint of disappointment.

To his credit that dog (whose official show name was Prince Primo but was commonly known as Jethro) was about as happy as a creature could be in this life or any other. Happiness extruded and poured out of him. He peed, pooped, and puked and, naturally, drooled for joy, so when there wasn't sufficient dew or dampness to support his almost palpable cloud of wet-dog smell, he created his own humidity and stench. And he was happy, happy, *happy* about it.

We learned to close the door pretty fast after Jethro came. If ever we failed, the dog's instincts bowled us over. Provoked by the smallest crack of daylight, that dog was across the floor, down the stairs, out the door, and just a spot on the horizon before you could blink. He barked madly, hopped about, taunting the party of manic, shouting children (some or all of my brothers and I), and only gave up when he was tired and wanted a break. That took an awfully long time because this game of chase was the greatest fun he could imagine.

So suddenly, out of nowhere it seemed to me, a puppy appeared in the house.

It was no pony.

I tried to see the bright side of a dog. According to a child's social hierarchy, having a puppy should have meant an elevation in neighborhood stature – street credibility by vicarious cuteness. It was way better than having a baby sibling. Those were a dime a dozen in the baby-boom years. Our generation was jaded against scene-stealing toddlers who hid behind the chesterfield to grunt and fill their diapers.

I learned speedily that large dogs came as large puppies that became bigger so fast it was hardly worth spreading the Good Puppy Word back then. Today's tech-savvy kid could flash the message electronically to a wide and thrilled audience who would be clamoring to visit in an instant. By the time I was able to convince my peers I actually had a real puppy in the house, that it wasn't just another phantom pony, the dog was a good fifty pounds and inclined to knock over the most solid of children and slather them in drool.

The dog was not the big drawing card I hoped for.

Where once I was simply *the girl with the mean brothers*, I was now *the girl with the mean brothers and the huge, scary dog*.

It was no fair. My brothers were probably not *that* much meaner than anybody else's, and the dog was not *that* scary. He was just a bit stupid and totally overwhelming. But there was no getting around his size: extra-grand-gross. The best I might hope for was that other kids would keep their distance based on the dog's startling girth alone. This would keep them from being struck by how foul, smelly, and ceaselessly drooling the beast was.

I wanted to love the dog. But I hated it. It was just another unruly male animal that barked at me and thought it was a game to shove me to the ground and run off.

Once, enraged that I could not get the still immature creature to stop its relentless barking, I dragged it into the walkway between our house and the neighbor's and beat it with the end of the leather leash until it cowered and shook. It took a horribly long time and left me exhausted, but briefly satisfied. My relief was short-lived, however, because I chose to commit this crime in full view of the neighbor's kitchen window. I was too short and too engaged in fury to notice that he was watching me the whole time. Not that he called a halt to the attack. But he did report it to my mother who declared me a mis-er-a-ble chi-ld (each syllable a slap) and elevated the dog to the status of Most Favored Youngster in the house.

I willed the summer to come quickly. This would be The One. Daddy would get me a pony like he said. A few days in the fresh air would blow the mothball stink out of my hat. I could put it in the ice house next to the cottage. No one ever went in there. It was pretty much wrecked. There were a lot of holes in the walls and some in the roof. Rain and snow had done their damage over the years. By the time I came to it in late spring each year, the ice house was ice- and water-free. It was pretty much empty except for some old broken wood furniture. But that was fine. The wind could blow through, and my cowboy hat would be clean in no time. Maybe I could claim a pair of James's old jeans. I needed a badge of some sort. Something for a deputy. A deputy was a kind of cowboy policeman. I spent a long time thinking it over and convinced myself there was a real gold star pin in the glass case next to the black balls at Fitzgerald's General Store. I could probably buy a saddle there, too. And a kerchief to tie around my neck. I could get apples and sugar cubes for my pony at the IGA in town.

But all this would cost money.

Wherever I walked, I kept looking down in hopes of finding loose change. Once I found a dime.

"Trade you," Buck offered, holding out *two* coins. Two for one. That had to be a good deal. I agreed. "And here's a tip," he told me, putting one, two pennies in my hand. "Don't take any wooden nickels."

I showed the shiny copper results of my high finances to Kieffer who slapped his forehead and said, "What a maroon! What a miragey!" in his best Bugs Bunny accent. Then he slapped my forehead. It hurt a bit. "Buck took your dime and gave you two cents. What a dunderhead." That hurt a little more.

But they looked so nice, and each one was bigger than the little one I exchanged. "Are they wooden nickels?" I asked, just a little uneasy. They didn't look like wood.

"No, brainless, you traded a dime, worth ten cents, for two one cents."

"Wha...pardon?"

"Ten cents," Kieffer started to shout. "He's got ten cents, ten whole cents." He waved both open hands full of wagging fingers in my face. "And you got two cents," which was a peace sign. It was not *V* for victory.

"Oh."

There was nothing in my immediate suburban world that could be had for two cents only. We weren't allowed bubble gum, so the grocery store crank machine was out of the question.

Seeing my defeat, Kieffer said, "Well if you don't want it, I'll take it."

I gave my two cents to him. It didn't make me any richer, but it got rid of any evidence that I was a dunderhead.

* * *

But there was a will and a way to work the Cottage-Cowboy dream. Every craft in kindergarten was geared toward The Cottage. I made kites from construction paper and targets for shooting practice. I made a butterfly net with an old nylon stocking and some pipe cleaners. And I made many ashtrays from asbestos clay and painted them with poster paint. It may have been flammable.

Smoke if you got 'em. But watch out for those exploding cigars.

It was all for My Cottage, Our Cottage. Our Lake. The Boat. The Island. The Mine and the Cave. The Swamp. The Marshmallows. The Every Night Sing-Along led by Timmy's brother who just loved me so much. I did not allow myself to wonder what presents he would have for me this year. It's not nice to ask. I would just say thank you when he brought them out at the Campfires. The Fish Fries –

But I had to stop stressing that one because the thought of eating a fish that had been caught, cleaned, wrapped in foil, and tossed in the fire to cook before your very eyes was too much for most of my peers. Even before I got to the part where my father popped out the fish eyeball with his pocket-knife and ate it – eyeballs or black-eyed peas, any kid knows it's not nice to eat off your knife.

Just a few weeks left in school. Still ample opportunity to lure my friends and classmates into my cottage dreamtime, to regale them with my near-cowboy stories and explain how the naturalization would take place. Explain it *scientifically*. Convince them.

It would be a long time before I recognized who really needed the convincing.

"It's because I live in the country so much," I informed the gathering crowd, or, at least the Nixon girls, Nancy and Nina, who had moved in next door. Lucky I had time to spell it out for them. They were almost never around. They were always being dragged off to ballet or baton twirling or some other sparkly pink costume thing. "I actually need a pony to get around."

They stared at me intensely. The older one, Nancy, looked at me sideways. "But you guys got a car." She pointed to the faux blue wood-paneled tank in the driveway.

"Yeah, but my dad needs that to go to work. He's an executive," I added for the good measure of class.

"Yeah?" Nancy stood up straight next to Nina. "So's our dad. He's an executive too."

The focus of this little talk was getting off track. If I didn't take care, I was going to have to mix it up with the Nixon girls over some "my dad is bigger than your dad" thing. And then I'd be in trouble because their dad *was* bigger than my dad, and we'd have to drag them out and measure them up and then they'd have to fight. My mom was already mad as a hatter at my dad for fighting with Uncle Pete all over the front lawn a while back, so I really wanted to steer the subject back where it was supposed to be. On me. The true, rural, western me.

"The thing is," I explained patiently, "I am going to be a Real Country Girl. My mom's a nurse, and she told me that I only had to spend one more summer at the cottage and I would be a Real Country Girl."

Country Girl was an interim step. Like caterpillar, cocoon, butterfly, but it went, regular kid, country girl/boy, cowboy. Anybody knew that. Except the Nixon girls. They were looking a bit dubious. At least Nancy was. Nina was looking at the hunk of booger she had just scraped out of her nose.

"Really? Is your mom a nurse?" Nancy asked. Her uncertainty was enough for me to ignore the question.

No, no. I know. My mother was not a nurse, but before she was married she was briefly a medical secretary in a hospital. It was pretty much the exact same thing. At least close enough to support my claim. For sure she was qualified to assess human development on this intense micro level.

"And when I am a Real Country Girl," I continued with authority, "I can ride a pony to school and everything."

"To Millbrook School?" Nina asked, so amazed at the prospect she dropped her booger. "Can you take me doubles?" She would be in kindergarten next year at the same school, so I guess she figured it was all right to ride on my scholarly, pastoral coattails. And my pony.

"Nope," I said with shrug. "I just can't. You won't be a Country Girl and you won't know how to ride a horse. Besides, Elmer the Safety Elephant says nobody should ride doubles."

Riding doubles was the practice of one person driving a bike in the conventional way with a second one perched on the handle bars. This was much easier when you had those big looping handle bars that looked like upside down J's. Nina was small, a lot smaller than me, but I sure didn't see her riding between the ears of my pony.

Nina accepted the words of Our Savior Elmer with awed respect. Nancy, who was a bit more haughty and in grade two, rolled her eyes so hard, I thought she'd get dizzy and fall over. "You're not allowed to ride a pony to school. It's against the rules."

But I had an answer for her. "Is not."

"Is too," she insisted.

I *tsk-tisked* her and shook my head. "Not."

"TOO!"

"NOT NOT NOT!"

Was that the best she could do?

"IS TOO. It IS TOO. IT IS TOO."

"It is *not* times infinity," I said matter-of-factly. You couldn't fight infinity. Nancy tried, still chanting, "Is too, is too, is too," until Nina started to cry, and their mother came out to see what the fuss was.

"Penny won't let me ride her pony," I could hear Nina wailing as she was dragged inside.

"Penny doesn't have a pony, and I told you never to talk to her anyway," was all her mother had to say.

Forget her. She was only jealous. I was going to get a pony. A real live pony. Daddy said so.

SEVEN

Back to the Land

AS USUAL, WE LEFT for the cottage at break of dawn a day or two before school was out. We swooped down on the long-suffering, chain-smoking Doris at the Gulf Restaurant and Gas Bar. Also, as usual, we made short work of the place in that charming cyclone-like way we had.

What a sight we must have been, in our Trudeau trotters and matching "Fuddle duddle" T-shirts, responding enthusiastically to the unspoken direction "enter screaming."

Trudeau mania had afflicted us. We had a near fatal case.

Pierre Elliott Trudeau – P.E.T. for short. Some Canadian synthesis of a free lovin' hippie and the ultimate New Renaissance Man. He had something for everyone. For the grown-ups, he played politics; for the paranoid, he executed the War Measures Act during the FLQ crisis; for the young and the young at heart, he squired hip chicks such as Leona Boyd and Barbra Streisand; for the children, he was the only Canadian prime minister to closely resemble a Dr. Seuss character, namely the Grinch.

He was young, smart, and unmarried.

He was marvy. He wore safari suits and sandals. We wore safari suits and sandals. And we called the sandals Trudeau trotters. And it was good.

Once, not thinking much of the comments of an opposition member in the House of Commons, our illustrious prime minister (following in the great tradition of Sir John A. MacDonald, who was said to have vomited all over his desk in lieu of remarks on a particular bill) declared to the members and public gallery, "Fuddle duddle!"

Or, that is what he is *quoted as declaring* by the very proper Hansard, the official transcript of the House of Commons. The recorders of Hansard politely demurred from inscribing what Prime Minister Trudeau actually *did* say. Whatever it was, all we know for certain is that it was so shocking, the other ministers repeated it after him.

So in Hansard it reads today something to the effect of, "Some honorable members: Fuddle duddle."

This is how it was explained to me as I put on my Fuddle duddle T-shirt with its Grinchy image of P.E.T., his smile most serene and knowing, his right middle finger pointing heavenward like some icon in training.

June, 1968. The Summer of Love.

I loved ponies and horses.

Clip-clop, clip-clop. I trotted around lost in my happy cowboy world in that battered, white, felt cowboy hat. I reentered the real world from time to time, usually under duress. I stayed only long enough for a peanut butter sandwich and a cup of Freshie or sterilized milk. Once in a while I came upon some discarded article that I adopted or adapted as a prop for my cowboy life. In the kitchen I found a tin plate and a plastic cup, which was blue with a white rim, so I believed it was also tin. Perfect for future cowboy meals by the campfire. I picked up a torn length of jute from the road and formed it into a circle and wore it as my lasso, though it wasn't really large enough to make a good-sized loop, let alone down a wild pinto. But if nothing else, I was stubborn. I could make, at least myself, believe the farthest-fetched things.

I found a holster, but no gun, under some other old toys at the bottom of a box of discards. Didn't matter. Sometimes it was better to stand and deliver a mean look than to shoot. But only sometimes. I didn't stand too tall, and my mean look usually only caused adults to feed me some horrible mixture of sand, stagnant water, and chalk called Milk of Magnesia. So I was overjoyed when I found the gun under a chair. I whooped it up like a Native bearing down on a raging buffalo. Big mistake. Just as I was about to case my weapon, James saw it and grabbed it away. "Hey! My cap gun!"

"Give that back," I demanded.

"It's mine." James jammed it in his pocket. Right away I knew I was on the wrong end of things. He had pockets.

Anything you could get your hands on could be yours if you could fit it in a pocket. Cowboys had plenty of them because they wore proper cowboy jeans. Possession was almost everything. Or so I was constantly told. That was the first law of the jungle. A jungle that did not easily include girls who wore dresses, skirts, or, at the most casual, elastic-waist pull-on slacks without pockets. Should pockets be mistakenly included in any garment I might wear, my mother sewed them shut lest I put anything in them and spoil the line of my outfit or, worse yet, put my hands in my pockets and slouch.

"I found it!" I protested. I wasn't going to give up without a fight. James wasn't going to take my gun and a piece of my cowboy soul. "Mom! James took my gun!" I shrieked.

She was disinclined to mediate her children's arguments. The theory was that, without interference, we would learn to reasonably mediate ourselves like proper gentlemen and lady. Like cream, we would rise above our childish inclinations to simply snatch what we wanted and beat all opposers over the head with it.

But she was right here in the room knitting as the whole thing went down. That made her my key witness, really. I tried to properly build my case.

"I found it. You saw me. I found it under the chair. Finders Keepers, right?" Wasn't that the second law of the jungle?

Apparently not. Not this jungle. "Penny, it's your brother's toy. Leave him, and *it*, alone." My mother drawled. And sighed. She found it rather a drag to be right all the time.

But this was wrong. This was totally unfair. "If James is so in love with his gun, why was it under the chair? He couldn't care less." I shouted. I knew I was going down fast. I wasn't about to go down quiet.

"Well, if you weren't carrying on like a banshee, maybe he would share it with you."

Self-control was not a behavior well modeled for me. My best effort saw me turning my back on Mom so I could give James my mean look. It didn't work at all. James giggled. My voice shook even as I held it steady between clenched teeth. My hand was the same as I reached out for James to give me the gun. "Please, James, may I use your gun?"

"No way," he said, grinning. "You yelled."

"But Mom!" I wailed.

"But nothing," she said and went back to her knitting.

"Butts are in cigarettes!" chimed in James.

I could not suppress a primal scream as I ran out of the cottage.

A little later on, when James found some caps, he and Kieffer pulled the holster off me and took that too. Then they gave me a "pistol whipping" with the cap gun just like they saw in some secret agent movie. That really hurt. If I had ever considered it in the past, I was sure then that espionage was not for me.

I took up whittling instead. That was totally cowboy.

My first attempts were made with the paring knife from the cottage kitchen. I showed some skill in being able to cut down a green branch with a dandy point for a marshmallow. Better yet, unlike my brothers, I could be trusted not to open any arteries in the process. Best of all, it kept me busy and out of everyone else's hair.

Astonishingly enough, a slightly dull pocketknife was purchased for my express use. I loved it. I loved it as much as the cowboy hat I yet managed to keep for my own western uses. And the pony I knew was coming to me.

Last time I asked him about a pony, Daddy said "We'll see," which I was sure meant he was in the throes of careful consideration and planning. It had to mean "Soon." Really soon.

Knowing it was pretty much pony days any time now, I literally and joyfully whittled my days away, creating not only a mountain of wood chips, but also a huge collection of quality weenie-roasting sticks and several very fine pickle spears.

I indulged in other cowboy-esque activities as well. I practiced my lasso skills with a skipping rope, attempted to light fires by rubbing two sticks together, and captured garter snakes in my bare hands. I didn't eat them, though. Mom still made hotdogs and hamburgers, and it wouldn't be fittin' to refuse the kindness or cookin' of a lady.

I once tied up Timmy to a tree and left him there because he was the bad guy in the game.

I *was* going to come back.

I got in big trouble anyway, but not for long because nobody else could stand Timmy. His parents had gone away to Europe again, and the old custodial relation had little patience for children underfoot and a blessedly short memory. I was back tormenting him in short order. As soon as I so much as cast a shadow in anyone's way, it was suggested, "Why don't you go play with Timmy?" and I was pushed out the door before I could begin to list the zillions of reasons.

Timmy showed me a "rusher" he had created to help speed his parents' return home. It was constructed out of paper tracings of Timmy's hands that were cut out and strung on a piece of red wool, the fingers all pointing down and numbered in reverse sequence, each representing a day his parents were away. Just before bed every night, he tore off one finger. When all of the digits were similarly amputated, it would be the day of his parents' return.

I was impressed by his devotion.

On a whim I decided to take up missing my father as a full-time occupation. "When's Daddy coming?" I moaned regularly.

"On Friday," was always the answer. Except once when it was embellished by, "And he's bringing a surprise for you kids."

A surprise? Could it be? Dare I say it? I didn't dare, but I thought it. I believed it. Because I could believe in all things cowboy. And because he promised.

I was convinced he was bringing me a pony.

What went through my child's mind is beyond me. Did I think he was just going to pick one up at Beckers with a jug of milk and a loaf of bread?

"Jug of homo and some hotdog buns, please."

"Will that be all, sir?"

"Uhhhmm..." he would pause thoughtfully. "No. Give me a Fudgsicle and a pony, too."

"White or brown?"

"White."

And if I could believe that, which I could, it was just a short leap to believe he could fit it in the LTD. Probably it would ride in the back, but possibly it might sit up in the passenger seat beside him, chatting away like Mr. Ed.

I was nothing short of devastated when it turned out that the surprise was Bruce Humphries, a cohort of my brothers. Just for the record, I note here, Bruce was not a pony.

I was about as lonely as a lonesome cowboy could get. Perhaps even more so without a trusty, four-hoofed companion. The dog might have been man's best friend, but it wasn't mine. I didn't even have the teeny shoulder of Petunia the guinea pig to cry on. She had passed away the previous winter. I went out into the big wide country world to search for a friend.

What I found was a bucket of frogs.

In a pressboard container with a tight lid, two dozen or so leopard frogs waited in cramped ignorance to meet their doom as fish food. Impaled on a hook, they would make fine bait for the great male-bonding fishing expedition being planned for the next morning.

I did not know this. I swear I didn't know. When I pried the lid off that bucket, I wasn't even thinking about the contents, I was only fidgeting and picking in that careless, derelict way of sulking children. Of course, when the frogs began to leap out, I was ecstatic! There were frogs everywhere, hopping about like green laughter, chirping and burping with excitement. It was fantastic.

Until I heard my father call my name.

"Pennyyyyyyyyyyyy!" his voice increasing in pitch and volume as he drew to the end of it. I knew it. I was in Big Trouble. So big, he set aside his general rule of never hitting a girl (except Mom, of course. That was different).

The ice house was too far away. I'd never make it there fast enough to reasonably deny springing the frogs. I knew I'd be caught eventually. Caught in the ice house, I'd get a double dose for being where I shouldn't be. My only other choice was to make a real break for it, hit the road, and never come back. I had spent some time working out just such a plan after the whole cap-gun thing left my head sore, inside and out. While I had most of the details worked out – travel by night, sleep by day, move south and west, carry your pack on your head when crossing rivers to keep your bread and shoes dry – there were a few things I hadn't got around to yet, like getting together a pack of Lolas and Pop-Tarts and hiding it by the side of the road so I could pick it up on my way out.

There was no getting around this one. I sighed.

I walked up the steps and into the cottage where Dad waited for me. My brothers and Bruce Humphries formed a mock honor guard and sang in soft falsetto, "You're going to get it. You're going to get it."

I considered myself lucky I didn't get the belt. Luckier still that Mom was in no way a fan of fishing. Fish, according to her, should be left alone to swim about or cleaned and cooked by "him what caught 'em." Not that things tended to play out that way. She unhappily cleaned many fish without ever catching one.

Had Mom been the offended party, it would have been her wicked right arm and the wooden spoon coming down on my behind. As it was she talked Dad down a bit as I inadvertently spared her some of the gutting and cleaning she would have had to do for the frog-baited bountiful catch. *What would Jesus do?* Mom might have asked Dad, suggesting turning the other cheek and not paddling mine. He must have taken it somewhat to heart. I only got a fraction of the forty-nine lashes Jesus got. *He* must have been happy, though. This little child was certainly suffering enough to come unto Him.

But I took it like a man, because that was the Way of the West.

I also stopped missing my father.

EIGHT

A Stranger 'Round These Parts

THERE WAS A SECOND surprise visitor that summer: Mahow. He was neither pony nor child. He was just one more way-bigger-than-me male in my already over-masculin-ized world. By gender alone he would necessarily have the upper hand. His confounded "guest" status would make him virtually untouchable.

Long before he arrived I wanted him gone.

I was filled with silent, steaming resentment when I was told he would have *my* bed and *my* room at the cottage. But it never crossed my mind to complain. Not out loud. Any vocal protest was sure to have the opposite effect.

We were told to share and treat him extra special. Which meant he could have just about anything he wanted. No doubt he'd get James's cap gun and even my beloved cowboy hat if he took a liking to them. That any extra dessert would end up as seconds for Mahow was a foregone conclusion. I knew one little cowboy who was going to be put on long-term disability when the stranger, Mahow, came to Go Home Lake.

The single saving grace that might nullify the unpleasantness of Mahow's visit, as far as I was concerned, was that he was an adult. He could probably be counted on to pretty much ignore me, rather than join the mob when my brothers took a notion to pummel me for whatever reason.

I was rarely privy to the reason, even when they tried their hardest to pound it through my thick head. And they put plenty of muscle into the task.

In an osmotic sort of way, I understood quite early that there was a top-down hostility flow at work in our family. Mom and Dad fought like miffed weasels. Now and again, sometimes more than words and spit flew. Lighters, ashtrays, palms, and fists hit hard and fast, like un-forecast tornadoes. Both of them got mad at the boys. James or Buck were the preferred go-to guys in the series. They tended to be a little more energetic and a lot more volatile. But Kieffer was not Teflon all over and endured more than his fifteen minutes of fame as The Most Rotten Child in the House. And as always, there I was on the grimy bottom, blamed by default, whether I had done the crime or not.

Of course, now and then I did. A shot to the backside (parents) or a punch in the arm (brothers) were common responses. Those time-limited and familiar discomforts might be far less horrible to endure than the pain and frustration of not getting, or doing, what I thought I wanted at the time. Sometimes it was just worth it to damn the torpedoes.

Or sometimes I could claim "not guilty by reason of immature insanity" – like what happened with the whole frog freedom thing.

Yes, I was punished. Fact of the matter was it was wrong to think like a child. I knew that. Only I couldn't help it. Because I was one.

* * *

Mahow was an auxiliary of my father's. Like an apprentice executive. He was sponsored by my father's company, a large multinational cigarette manufacturer.

Mahow was a young man from some African country once rustled and ravaged by the English, a place where Great Britain still had enough paternalistic sway that they could force former colonists to play nice with each other. A place where someone improperly believed that plain, often frozen, generally bland and pasty Canadian white-collar, middle-class Christian men could give something more than a cow to those from the depths and darkness of Africa (which most Canadians were yet to learn was neither dark nor deep). You know, the "poor" black people, people who enjoyed health and happiness in complex and sophisticated societies for hundreds and hundreds of years. People who knew the riches of their world and each other long before John Cabot left smelly, infested old Europe, sailed up the St. Lawrence to Quebec, sat on the terrace at the Chateau Frontenac, and drank tea made from pine bark to cure himself of scurvy and nostalgia.

There was *something* about Mahow.

He was, in the politically correct vernacular of the time, *colored*.

We weren't. We were white. Any printing technician or laundress could tell you: white was not a color.

Mom gathered us all together and insisted we "sit down and listen." This was not usually a good sign. Most frequently it meant we were going to have The Riot Act read to us. A riot, I knew, was the same thing as a rumble. There was a rumble in *West Side Story*, but I was never allowed to see it because they said bad words and somebody got stabbed. An act was part of a play. But Mom never read from any play about a rumble, she only ever gave speeches about how we were never going to get to do – fill in the blank – unless we shaped up and pulled ourselves up by our bootstraps.

Straps were like belts, and getting the belt or the strap was painful. Any cowboy I could think of had a fine set of boots, but I couldn't picture any of them belted or strapped in any way. Maybe they were like braces, which were what I called suspenders. They held your pants or "britches" up. Timmy was once hung in his britches by his braces on a hook on a wall. That sure pulled him up. But we got the strap for that.

Though we weren't inclined to actually listen, this time we were willing to give it a try. Because this reading was served up with refreshments.

The fact that Mahow was colored was something so astonishing it had to be imparted with a proper sit-down tea with brown sugar toast and apple slices, lest any one of us should go into shock or something. It was a medical fact that those dumb-ass ice-cream wafers would never do the trick if your blood sugar started to plummet. Thank goodness we always had Pop-Tarts on hand should anyone need sudden intensive care.

"You must show him the utmost respect," Mom explained.

Glassy-eyed, we heaped more spoonfuls of sugar into our already syrupy cups. No one asked for clarification. We didn't care. *Yeah, sure, respect. We got it.* Kieffer challenged James to a Crunch Contest, a sporting event in which combatants attempted to take toast chomps at ever increasing decibels.

"As much respect as you would show any man," she continued. I had a slight idea of what she meant by respect. It had something to do with not telling a fat, smelly person they were fat and smelly, because they could still play piano just fine. Or not laughing when Gramps farted really loud during dinner because he was too old to hear himself.

"Show him the respect you show your father." As Mom carried on, the whole thing made even less sense.

Buck found this a pretty silly notion. He bugged his eyes out a bit and lolled his head like it was going to fall off. Then, just before I burst out laughing, he pinched my leg under the table: He was out of Mom's line of sight while I was front and center. Even I knew she would not appreciate the joke, and the last thing anyone wanted was a swift end to this revival of the Rights and Freedoms of Man and the clearing of the tea table. "For he *is* exactly the same as *every other* man."

This was in direct conflict with the *everybody's different* thing that was going to make being a cowboy possible. This sales pitch was not working for me. But the tea was, and so was the white toast, liberally spread with margarine and brown sugar.

"You must consider only his character, his great character, when you treat him the same as anyone else."

"Well, that would be kind of a step down, dontcha think?" Buck mumbled, rolling his eyes again.

I couldn't be bothered thinking at all. But thanks anyway, Martin Luther Mom.

In the end, the grand address had its desired effect. Because we treated Mahow better than Mom could have asked for. We treated him with awe and wonder. We treated him like a curious being from a place far, far away. Because he was. That made him simply amazing, totally interesting. It made him better than us.

For one thing, he was never described as having a last name.

And *colored* didn't do him justice. He was exceptionally dark-skinned.

We had very limited experience with those who were not the same pale pinky peach as us. We enjoyed a fictional acquaintance with the likes of Tonto, Nanook, and Friday. Perhaps, then, one might reasonably conclude that it's normal for a man of color to have but one name.

God knows we were liberal. There was just no opportunity for practical application in the suburbs from whence we came.

On some level, Mahow's visit must have been a social coup for Mom, who could now rightfully take her place among the ranks of those who blithely claimed, "Some of my best friends are black."

Until Mahow's visit, we'd had liberal *thoughts*. That was the best we could do.

Now, to Mom's defense, the past several years had seen a brutal parade of racially motivated beatings, riots, murders – too many evils. Her heart was in the right place, even if her sense of the dramatic took her straight over the edge. And it was the Canadian way to believe that such events only took place in the deep American South. Sadly, as a nation, we were just more covert about any sort of prejudice. More than once in our short history we beat back or turned away legions of refugees of all stripes and solids from every shore that wasn't ice-locked. Without a second thought we sent them sailing up the D'Nile River without a paddle or a prayer.

But these times they were a-changin'. Mom wanted to be sure we would not grow up to be ignorant white supremacist slobs.

Naturally, she didn't want us to become slobs of any description. But as we later learned from George Orwell, some pigs are more equal than others. It simply had to be that some slobs were more repugnant than others.

By the time poor Mahow arrived, we were so pumped up with cautions and courtesies we were afraid to open our mouths for fear of offending his colored self.

Suzanne told me that even the darkest of colored people were white on their soles and palms. Could it be? She showed me a magazine picture of Bill Cosby, but it was black-and-white, so it was pretty hard to tell.

Mahow arrived with my father (but without a pony) at the regular Friday-night time slot.

I had never seen a stranger-looking human being in all my experience. And it wasn't the hue of his skin. It was the way he was dressed. He wore a black dress suit, a white shirt, and a tie. He carried a small, solidly built suitcase, and his oxford shoes were black and unscuffed. What a freak! He looked like he was going to church or a birthday party or something. Bermuda shorts and a short-sleeved shirt and Hush Puppies – that's what my father was wearing. *That's* what a normal person was supposed to wear to the cottage.

When he was a kid, Mahow was probably one of those weirdos that went to Catholic School. They were always running around in shirts and ties. They were so strange they had to have their own school. What was that all about? What bizarre things did they do in there while we were doing regular stuff in the public school?

"Buck, Kieffer, James, Penny," my father pointed to each one of us as he said our names, "this is Mahow."

The boys shook hands. I wanted to offer my hand, show off my strong cowboy grip (and maybe test the credibility of Suzanne's claim), but under the weighty glare of my mother, I dropped into a quick, straight-backed curtsy. (The bent-back curtsy was in case of royalty, like if maybe the queen happened down The Bumpy Road to the cottage and wanted to jealously review the only natural sand beach on Go Home Lake.)

It was probably a good thing I was too short and too busy trying to catch a glimpse of his hands to see Mahow's face. It must have been completely muddled. There he stood at quiet attention, in what he believed was proper attire to be presented to his host's fine wife and family, confronted by a band of four dirty little savages, dressed for, at best, a dog fight, in worn clothes and bare feet. The Trudeau Trotters were reserved for rare visits to town.

His reverie was interrupted when Buck was instructed to take Mahow's suitcase, and Mom led him to "his" room.

My room.

We all followed in and then were promptly ejected. "Get out, or I'll knock your heads together," Dad said, pointing to the door. We shuffled around a bit, giving the illusion of movement. James was closest, and Dad gave him a good smack to the back of the head. That convinced us. Out the door and down the steps we went.

Mom thought Mahow was marvy. You could tell by the way she put on lipstick and smiled all sparkly. She set the table for dinner, folding the paper napkins into little triangles and fanning them out between the tines of a fork at each place. So fancy. She even set the table for breakfast! And brought drinks around on a tray. Rum and Coke for the grown-ups. Freshie for us.

Mahow remained an enigma.

Even his pajamas were ironed. He did have a pair of shorts and a short-sleeved shirt in the form of a sharply pressed leisure suit. No speck of dirt or biting insect dared land on his flawless form. He had a ramrod straight spine. In the four days he was with us, I think he sat down only for meals, lay down only to sleep. The rest of his time he politely posed, upright and elegant, like a formal-wear model in the Eaton's Catalog.

We tried to entertain him. We showed him frogs and turtles and presented him with a recently shed snakeskin Kieffer found. Dad tried to take Mahow fishing, and we kids relentlessly entreated him to come for a swim. He would watch us closely in the water, or sometimes just stare at the water itself, but would not go farther in than his knees. Every now and then he would bend down and touch the water, running his open hand through it, gauging temperature and texture, like it was something strange and foreign.

Sitting waist-deep in the shallow water along the beach, I marveled at Mahow's amazingly dry swim trunks. "How come you don't come for a swim, Mahow?"

He smiled and opened his hands (yes, Suzanne was right, his palms *were* pale). "I don't know how," he said. "When I was a little boy, I never learned."

He must be joking! There was no such thing as a grown man who did not know how to swim.

I fell back in the water laughing and splashing Mahow. Suddenly his back curved out and his hands flew out in front of him, like he was trying to keep a solid footing. Like the water drops might throw him over.

Buck came up behind me and stuffed my head under the water to shut me up. "Way to go, moron." He pushed me under again when I popped up and gasped. "It's not funny," Buck said. "He really can't swim. Really."

Mahow told Buck to leave me alone. I beefed up the gasping sound in hopes of getting Mom's attention, but it didn't work. But out of "respect" for Mahow, Buck hit me in the face instead.

"No…. Your sister," Mahow said, sad and quiet to Buck. But I ducked under the water and swam away fast. No point sticking around to see if Mahow could talk Buck into letting me off easy. There was probably no way.

I swam underwater as long as I could and floated far away by myself. I was sure Mahow hated me. I had no respect. I was mean to a guest. I made a colored man upset. I was probably a white supremacist slob, whatever that was.

* * *

One day someone provided my brothers and me with a package of balloons to play with. Soon discontent with the conventional air-filled variety, the boys were seized with the notion of water balloons. Bombs. Guerrilla attacks. Snipers in the trees.

When the call to arms came, I was too busy trying to rub a balloon on my damp, slightly greasy hair and stick it to my dress to take notice. Lowest in rank and last in line, I was relegated to a couple of puny balloons, one with a rip and one an already aborted attempt at a water bomb, barely a quarter filled before it was tied off.

"Think fast!" A water balloon came sailing past my head and landed on a sandy bit of ground. It didn't splatter. But I nearly did when James flew past calling, "Not fast enough!" and scooped it up, knocking me flat in the process.

"I'm not playing," I shouted, collecting myself and my two crappy balloons. "I want to play catch." It was an idea that didn't instantly catch on. "Who wants to play catch with balloons?" The answer was silence, followed by a direct hit to my backside and a rush of cold. My clothes were soaked from my crotch all the way down. Balloon bomb water, greenish-yellow because it had been pumped in from the lake.

The boys burst out laughing. "Penny wet her pants!"

I looked horrible. My wet skirt clung to my legs, wrapped tight around my butt, and tucked between my cheeks. For a second I wondered if I actually did pee myself.

"I did not!" I was pretty sure I hadn't. It had been, well, ages since I'd had an accident. And that was because I was trapped in my snowsuit. And it wasn't even my snowsuit. It was James's old one. And it was brown. And you had to close the zipper with a pin. And I didn't know how to open the pin.

But this was worse. Way worse. I felt my face go hot and guilty red.

"I see England, I see France, I see Penny's underpants!" chimed James and Kieffer from behind me.

Humiliation in the extreme. You were *never* allowed to let anyone, *especially* a boy, see your underwear. Not even a brother. Doctors even had to close their eyes if they brought you in an ambulance. Plain and simple. That was *not nice*.

And cottage costume was typically well worn. Usually too small, too short, thin, and grubby. Now properly saturated, it was transparent.

"Yeah well, you think that's bad?" challenged Buck, who was facing me, screwing up his face and pointing somewhere south of my belly button. "I can see Penny's twat. Penny's dirty twat!"

Well, if I wasn't acquainted with that term before, I knew it then. A body part so disgusting by nature, my mother used a phlegm-filled noise to refer to it: the place where "tinkle" came from on girls was called an "a-hem." The boys were allowed to be more nonchalant about those playing pieces of "pocket pool" kept behind their flys. They had a "woo-ee" that felt tickley when admiring pictures of *niiiiiiiiiiice* girls in my father's magazines. Male parts were funny, if not down-right useful. They could be used for responding to the call of nature when far from modern plumbing. My mother called them picnic gadgets.

Embarrassment thundered through me with a sickly, burning ache. My face was blushing brilliantly. I felt as if my threadbare undies and everything that was supposed to be discreetly contained in them were flaming, neon, and blinking on and off. And not nice. Not nice at all.

"Penny's got a dirty twat!" the boys' voices chimed out, each syllable piqued and poisoned. "Dirty twat" over and over with unbridled hilarity. "Dirty twat! Dirty twat!" I could feel and hear and smell and taste each repetition. It shot through every cell and every pore. It ran through my hair and scalded my skin inside and out. Senses overloaded, I was locked in place, choked by inertia. I wanted to scream in fury. But anger burned like acid on my tongue and embittered me completely, and all I could breathe was the acrid smell: "dirty twat dirty twat dirty twat filthy stinking pissy dirty twat."

They waved their hands to beat away the stench. They held their noses, and the berating persisted, atonal, through their sinuses until finally, the "pissy dirt twat" collided with gasping laughter. In the heartless and brief pause a fresh barrage of balloon bombfire was pummeled my way.

The shock of it moved my feet and I followed them, stumbling and spastic. As I ran, I clutched my wet clothes uselessly against me.

✷ ✷ ✷

In Sunday school I'd learned that Eve and Adam were cast out from the good graces of God's garden because, at Eve's insistence, ill-advised by the serpent, they ate from the *Tree of Knowledge.*

"*Then* what did they know?" I had asked, anticipating nothing less than a gruesome answer, only hoping it was not so despicable as to be unspeakable. I wanted to hear.

"They knew that they were naked," was the unsatisfactory reply.

When they were giving out smarts you thought they said farts so you said, "I don't want any."

Could it be that Adam and Eve were hard of hearing? If not, they had to be pretty dumb not to know they were wearing nothing but their birthday suits under those lovely leafy arrangements.

But in that instant I felt the smack of cold comprehension of my own flesh, head to toe and back to front. It was at once shocking and revolting. I *was* naked. And it was not good.

At least there remained no Eden for me to be cast from.

I made my way as fast as I could toward the cottage.

But I stopped short. Refugees were unaccepted in that territory, civilian or military. Accusations of maltreatment at the hands of invading balloon armies would be met with unsympathetic and familiar reminders.

"You shouldn't be playing boys' games like that," or, "If you wouldn't torment your brothers, they wouldn't lose their tempers."

I might wail *it's not my fault,* but I knew better. I put my unmentionables on display. It didn't matter that I hadn't meant to. *The road to hell is paved with good intentions.*

It was probably best to beat a hasty retreat from the cold

hardness of the grown-up folk. Such city slickers were sure to find my appearance as objectionable as my brothers did. I left familiar territory and slipped uneasily into the badlands. Carefully checking around me for witnesses, I walked backwards into the shadows, then into the uncharted wild.

I stepped gingerly into the slatted brightness of the ice house. Belying its name, the interior was inert with heat. The yellow light smelled of dust and dryness. It felt like something less. Something less than nothing. Twice the normal air was needed to fill the lungs, but there was less than half the oxygen.

Or maybe breath was strangled by fear.

Again and again I had been threatened never to cross the threshold of the ice house, lest the beams and joists rain down on my head and squash it flat.

I glanced up, then quickly threw my eyes down. Not to protect myself from the falling sky but from the brightness of it. Had the ceiling actually tumbled down, it most likely would have been around me, not on top of me. The gaps between the dried-out struts were such that one could have easily dropped our large dog through them.

I scanned the place for Jethro. I listened closely for his padding trot. All was safely silent.

There was very little left in the structure. The rough shelving that once lined the walls had long since splintered and collapsed to the floor. The floor was dirt, packed hard by time and rain and snow. There were still the desiccated remains of dry, ancient straw. I found I was ankle deep in a sort of hairy powder that once formed an insulating layer around the blocks of ice, dragged in from the lake in winter, many ages ago.

Cruel-looking calipers used to clamp those untouchable blocks stood awkwardly on bowed legs in the corner.

Other than that, the building contained a short-legged chair, a half-dozen iron hooks on the rafters, and an old, block table.

I took my wet outer clothes off, laid them on the table, and pushed it into the largest and most intense patch of sun. I stood in a separate shaft of heat and light, very still, very silent, in my underpants and waited for them to dry. They did. Though I was unaware of the amount of time it took, if any at all. I was aware of almost nothing. I was captivated by the bands of solid brilliance that filled the ice house.

Once dried out and looking decent again, I left the ice house by the back window. That way I could move, unseen, into the trees behind and make my way down to the road. I could skirt around the beach where the boys were still shouting, though no longer at me, and remain out of sight and off their radar.

The balloon I had wanted to play catch with had followed me as far as the road when I made my wailing retreat. Calmly, it bobbled along the ferns now, waiting patiently, unaware of all the commotion that had just gone on around it. There was something about its hapless fragility that cut me hard and deep. If I abandoned it, it was destined to amble its way into the cottage roses and surely be destroyed. Feeling profoundly sorry for it, almost as much as I did for myself, I felt exactly as I thought *it* did: like an utterly disposable object of infinitesimal significance. Acid tears welled up in me. They came in torrents. I was gobsmacked by emotion. These weren't the angry high-volume, high-velocity tears that hit when I ran away from the boys' insults and accusations. These were hard-drawn and suffocating. They caused me to crumple and fall, limp, on the side of the road.

Mahow happened upon me as I sobbed in superfluous self-pity, all balled up under a tree. He did not run to fetch my mother, who would have surely called me "Sarah Heartburn" and told me to "get up and stop acting like a fool." He did not ignore me, rather than risk getting snot or dusty tears all over his neatly pressed outfit. He leaned down close, patted my heaving shoulder, and asked kindly, "What are you crying for?"

I don't remember if he had an accent. I just remember Mahow had an extraordinarily quiet voice. All around me everyone was always yelling. My brothers yelled at me, I yelled back. They yelled at each other. Mom yelled at us. Dad came up on the weekends and yelled loudest of all. Then we stopped yelling for a little while because Mom and Dad were yelling at each other so much, it was simply too exhausting to try to be heard above the din. Now here was Mahow, speaking so quietly I could hardly hear him, and his voice filled my ears.

Between sniffs and hiccups I explained the thinnest version of my predicament, avoiding the sin and shame of my horrible display, how I wanted to play balloon catch, but the boys didn't, and I couldn't now because there wasn't enough air in the balloon. It's a wonder he could make out even half of what I was saying between the blubbering. But Mahow listened. He offered to help and again, patted my shoulder in a comforting way.

I knew it was no use. The same geography that kept Mahow from learning to swim also kept him ignorant of balloon facts. He just couldn't know; once a balloon was knotted it was irreversible. But I wasn't going to tell him after he'd been so nice to me.

Undaunted by the impossible, Mahow sat down beside me and proceeded to make a valiant attempt at the challenge. I watched through a haze of tears. And wonder of wonders, he actually pulled it off! He untied my balloon! He was magic! He was amazing!

So overjoyed by Mahow's awesome achievement, I almost completely forgot the horrors of the recent past. Mahow stretched out the balloon between his long fingers, then blew it up into a big gorgeous orb. He grinned widely and bounced it off my upturned, astonished face, and I chuckled delightedly.

We batted the balloon back and forth, high and low. We made a fine game of trying to keep it in the air as long as we could. But better than the knot reversal, better than playing the game as I wanted to play it, it was a fabulous and fantastic thing to have the willing and undivided attention of a grown-up. This was bliss.

"You are happy now?" Mahow asked rhetorically, as I fell to the ground, weak with laughter. The real thing. I was delirious.

And also still curious.

"Mahow?" I asked with caution. "How come you can't swim?"

He shrugged. The question did not seem to disturb him at all. He almost seemed to believe it was unremarkable – either for me to ask, or for him not to swim.

"When I was a little child, there was no lake like this," he told me.

"Was the lake too deep? Did it smell like dead fish?" Lake Ontario, bordering Toronto, was like that. We never went near it for those reasons.

Mahow smiled. "No. There was no lake at all," he explained. "There was a river. But you could not swim in it. There were crocodiles."

I gasped. That was horrid. Mahow laughed. To him, I was funny.

Added to my personal list of reasons not to hang out at the swamp was now crocodiles.

But while he was here, we did take Mahow on a trek to the cave.

The cave was said to be an abandoned feldspar and quartz mine. Feldspar, I was told, was used in the manufacture of cookware. This formed a rather interesting picture in my mind involving pioneer ladies in hoop skirts, chipping pots and pans out of blocks of peach-colored rock and then using the pots to make pancakes. I figured Laura Secord carried one under her arm as decoy on her way to warn Fitzgibbon of the advancing American troops. Might have been handy if she'd been attacked (though it couldn't have done much good against the blackflies). She must have made her first chocolates and bonbons in a feldspar cauldron. Thus Canadian confectionery history was born, probably right in this very mine!

There were also loads of quartz. Quartz looked enough like cut diamonds to be desirable for the gorgeous crystals it formed – especially the pink variety. There was black quartz as well, darkened from radiation exposure when the planet was just a baby.

The site must have been closed many years before we laid eyes on it. There were no signs of any roads or structures or anything man-made in the vicinity. When extraterrestrial intervention became a popular theory in the 1970s, used to explain any number of ancient monumental achievements, I thought a lot about the cave and figured it was a prime example of what an alien with a little spare time on his hands could do to confuse and enrage us dull humans.

But everyone said it was an abandoned mine, so for the time being, I went along with that explanation.

Any way you looked at it, it was pretty awesome. It was beautiful, but I was very afraid of the place.

Carved deep into an enormous rock shield, it was a colossal, pinkish-orange half sphere, like a giant cantaloupe turned on its side. The floor was littered with huge chunks of broken rock. Walking into it was treacherous, and standing there, surrounded by the jaggedly cut ceiling and walls, was foreboding.

"One time a kid was standing *there*, just where you're standing," Kieffer proceeded to tell me, "and a bear walked by. At first the kid clammed up, but then saw the bear was coming closer. And CLOSER. That kid was so scared he screamed. And the scream echoed. And the echo caused an avalanche. And he was buried alive." His voice dropped and he said the last words slowly. "Right. Under. Your. Feet."

As I listened to Kieffer, completely drawn into his story, James sneaked up behind me and kicked at my foot. I thought for sure it was that kid buried under the rubble. I nearly jumped out of my skin.

Of course I shrieked something fierce.

"Shhh!!" Kieffer and James warned me, laughing loudly. "You're going to cause an avalanche."

"Really?" I turned to Mahow, obviously an expert on Canadian geology. He shook his head, but said nothing, reassuring me only slightly.

He was a kind man, Mahow. In summers that followed I asked after him, hoping he might return for a longer visit. It was hard for me to fathom that his home was on the other side of the world. To comprehend that there even was another side to the world was difficult. To believe that the world might be different, might even be better beyond my limited territory, was impossible.

NINE

When the Going Gets Rough, the Tough Get Stuck

MAHOW LEFT WITH DAD at the end of the week. Apart from the water balloon brouhaha and getting pushed under the water for questioning Mahow's inability to swim and maybe the "scream-cident" in the cave, time was unusually mellow while Mahow was there.

But by the time Dad came back for the next weekend, the push was on to make up for any recent lack of hard noise. Mom and Dad did more yelling than usual. That was quite the feat; they did a lot of yelling to begin with. The more obsessed and absorbed they became with how one was willfully destroying the other by minute and nefarious means, the less they observed the fact that they had children who should be regularly dealt with.

So we were obliged to deal with ourselves. Success and failure were difficult to differentiate.

At first the weather was good, and there was reason to stay outside all day. Kieffer took to his favorite tree and literally hung out for hours. Buck went off with a small pick hammer to search for quartz crystals in the mine. I vacillated between a swing that hung off a tree near Auntie Lil's cottage and holing up in the pump house, listening to the engine turn over every time somebody flushed. James just sort of blended in to the commotion. Sometimes he'd throw rocks at the fish, capture frogs, and ignite them with firecrackers, or see what he could hit with his BB gun. If he was out of BBs, it didn't matter. He would just whack anything in his path stupid enough to remain still with the butt or barrel end. Occasionally, he might hike on over to the Lanza's to see if anyone was around to join him in these light-hearted games of destruction.

Then the weather turned. It was duller, sedate with gray. It stayed cold long into the morning. The distant but regular grumble of thunder kept us out of the water for fear of electrocution, for modern meteorology taught us that where there is smoke, there is a forest fire, and where there was thunder, lightning was sure to appear out of nowhere. Sheet lightning was our greatest fear, because it would surely strike the super conductor of Go Home Lake and steam or stir fry all who were foolish enough to be in it.

We were corralled and branded. The brands were salted and stung something fierce. Edgy and irritable, we paced and blustered, acutely aware of our confinement and anxious to excise ourselves.

We were totally stuck with each other. The cottage was less a dwelling on the shore, and more a prison on a rocky shoal.

But we were not completely without resources. For the short term, we managed to, more or less, work together. We devised some creative group activities as a distraction – creative in proportion to the challenge of the environment.

As the volume and frequency of Mom and Dad's fights increased, so did the freakishness of our entertainments: who could consume more strawberry-flavored sterilized milk than the other guy without belching; toast crunch contests even on Pop-Tarts; between rolls of thunder, how many times could you swim under the raft without coming up for air? There were demonstration sports: bubble blowing and gargling of juice without spilling or getting smacked; how long before you flinched from the sting of an Indian sunburn; could you take the hardest punch in the stomach your brother could wield and not crumple and die like Houdini? *No pain, no gain* was the motto of anything we tried.

I wanted no part of it. But the trajectory of refusal led straight to the black hole of Stupid Little Sisterhood. Elevation to Lonesome, Git-tar totin' Cowhand was not to be, though I retained wellsprings of hope. But clucking "good fellow" as we rode imaginary ponies or using the long end of the boat line to practice rope tricks was not about to happen. As my brothers grew in height and parental-infused frustration, they made good use of the unchecked testosterone that spurred them. The closest they would succumb to was a game in which three hardened cowboys (them) tied me, the reluctant squaw, up to the nearest tree (and I was never given time to put together the necessary accessories such as beaded headbands or a fringed purple-suede vest). This was the sort of thing that happened to Timmy, so I knew I wanted to avoid going that low on the totem pole. I smartly selected the lone choice on the barren buffet: Whatever my brothers dished out, I tucked in and chowed down, no matter how distasteful.

I didn't want to be a wimp homo just mo'ing my pillow named Brucie. I did not want to be called *jerk off* (a disease that caused muscle spasms and made you look like a ree-tard – or so I thought). And I was not going to succumb to tattling, no matter how great the temptation to seek relief and save my own skin. Nothing was worth that much, especially me, a stinkin' girl, neither nice, nor even *niiiiiiiiiiice*.

I held on hard and fast for a game-changer. How or when it could or would happen were questions I was willing to leave unanswered in exchange for the absolute, if moronic, certainty that it *would* happen. Cross my heart and hope to die, stick a finger in my eye. And if I was even *half* sure that would work, I'd be blind before my eighth birthday. And happy, because somewhere at the unraveling edges of understanding, it was dawning on me that I was not.

Eventually Dad went back to the city, and the level of tension dropped to its usual fever pitch, and everyone felt a little better.

Except.

Except once or twice.

Since Mahow's visit, when he slept in my room, I hadn't made the long trek back to my own bed. I still occupied the "daybed" in my brothers' bunk barracks. I had gotten used to the whine and creak of the springs and metal frames of the army surplus bunks they slept in. I had learned to sleep right through James's articulate and bizarre sleep-talking during which he demanded mushrooms or scrambled eggs or waxed eloquent on the subject of how to properly tape a hockey stick. But once or twice –

Once or twice Buck had been dispatched to assist my changing from the ever sand-filled wet bathing suit to day or night clothes. When my mother dealt with this task, she efficiently scoured my front and behind for trapped sand. The female body, even the immature form, is an origami arrangement of precise and multiple folds. For its various functions, it's a more than serviceable design. For trapping sand, it is excellent.

Of course I knew that boys and girls were *different*. Anybody knew that. But that was one of the natural boundaries of being a grown-up person; girls were female and men were male; being a sibling I did not have a working knowledge of how these different physiological features figured and fit into *each other* and the Adult Universal Plan.

And I knew before I "spread 'em," prisoner-examination style, I *knew*

that this was not

not

not the best thing to do,

not the *right* thing to do.

But I didn't quite know why.

"Spread 'em," said Buck.

So I did. Because that was the position demanded. I was lost for reasons *why not*, so *why* wasn't even a question. Weighing my feather-light argument against Buck's heavy fist, I just did it.

I knew this was a game-changer. Not the one I wanted. Not a game I might ever want to play. Not one I saw for what it was. Not one that meant the hygienic clearing of the sand from my body.

Then, as now, I detach myself.

I detach myself, arm's length, in another place, in another time, in another paragraph to recognize some collateral culpability I was ill-equipped to begin to comprehend. At the time.

At the time I detached myself. Ad hoc. Arm's length. My arms have grown since then, in strength and sureness.

Buck took a wash cloth, cold and wet and mildewy. Slowly he moved it up and down, up and down though the open valley of my flattened cheeks, pressing just slightly in my anus.

I pulled away. Reflex.

"Not clean yet. You're still full of sand." His voice was… not…right…

Not right. He wasn't doing it right.

"You're supposed to use a dry flannel," I told him. "Mom uses a dry flannel."

"Shut up," he growled and pushed me. "I'm NOT finished."

I did what I had to – what any little girl had to: I had to man-up, *put up and shut up*. I had heard *that* so often I thought it was our family motto. I was compliant.

But years later, I insist, I was not an accomplice.

I put myself to bed that night back in my own bed.

"I haven't changed the sheets yet," my mother said when she saw me there. I pretended to be asleep.

You hold what ground you can. Once you've seen the bear tracks in the mud and seen the mess the coyotes leave of a hare, then you'd best do what you can do, bury your goods deep, or hang them high and sleep with one eye open.

It's the best any cowboy can do alone in the wild.

TEN

Tribes, Trials, and Family Feuds

SOME WEEKS LATER, the Turners came for a brief sojourn at Uncle Don's cottage.

We knew the Turners from the city. How, I couldn't say. I suspect Ralph Turner and Dad were in the Lions Club together, or something. Ralph was serious service club material. He was heavily into ham radio.

It was the kind of arrangement where we called them Auntie Pat and Uncle Ralph, though we weren't actually related. They had three daughters: Monica, Kathy, and DeeDee. Monica was around Buck's age, Kathy was a year or so older than me, and DeeDee a little younger. I was personally overjoyed to see them come. It meant my choice of female companionship was no longer limited to Timmy.

They stayed only a week or so. A good portion of that

time my brothers devoted to attempting to catch a glimpse of the impressively developing Monica in the act of changing her clothes.

Auntie Pat and Mom played Scrabble a lot, and the Turners brought about a hiatus to Mom and Dad's screaming matches.

I think my mother didn't like Ralph. He was an expatriate Brit. To him, everything in this backwater colony of Canada was slightly inferior. There was a serious shortage of proper English staples such as Marks and Spencer tea, and underpants and petticoats for his girls. There was not a drop of treacle to be had, just that maple syrup stuff. If we were going to join in on "God Save the Queen" and mean it, we really ought to have a decent recipe for scones and forget that English muffin rubbish. In England such things were regarded as horseshit.

Pat had long brown hair. Otherwise she was another hazy grown-up female figure in a sleeveless "shell" and stretchy black pants moving through the background with cheese and crackers.

Like most men, Ralph had short hair – brown and wavy. Unlike most men, Ralph had the unique ability to produce vast quantities of thin, trickling sweat. It gave him a perpetually glossy appearance.

I believe now, and suspected even at the time, that Uncle Ralph and Auntie Pat hated my brothers and me. But not without good reason.

Dad came up for the whole week of the Turners' visit. We actually went on a couple of Family Style Outings. Three, if you count the dump.

We took a daytrip to Bonnechere and visited the underground caves. They were a deliciously cool place to be on a hot August afternoon. They were an absolute Mecca for those who are really keen on 400-million-year-old fossils or hundreds of young (from a few hours to a few years) bats. The caves were quite extensive, long, and winding and, at places, very narrow.

"Hey, fatso," Kieffer whispered to me confidentially, "better watch you don't get stuck in here." And then he laughed.

"Ha, ha," I said, "so funny I forgot to laugh." But I cautiously looked ahead to Uncle Ralph and Dad, who were farther along the cave. Ralph's Bermuda shorts formed a square over his flat backside, roughly the size and shape of the freezer door atop the average refrigerator. And he still had a good half inch or so on either side. I had to be smaller than that.

Didn't I?

I casually employed a ballet-style extension of my arms, until they reached the cave walls.

"Don't touch the walls, please!" the guide shouted. Immediately, I dropped my arms and looked around as if he was talking to some other dopey fossil groper, even though every narrowed eye and pursed expression pointed to me. I didn't care. I'd confirmed I had plenty of room to grow and then some. My bum was not nearly as large as Uncle Ralph's.

The narrowness and dampness caused Mom to shudder and complain about claustrophobia. I suggested she put on her glasses, but she said that was like putting tits on a bull. I pictured the distinctly human bosoms of those *niiiiiiiiiiice* girls from *Playboy's* middle page randomly attached to a

Holstein in a field: *so* totally impossible. Grown-ups were weird.

Another day we went horseback riding at the stables and stayed for the corn roast after. I felt very grown-up when DeeDee cried and had to be taken off her horse, while I, three-quarters cowboy even at this point, was a confident, experienced equestrian. I was pretty much certain no one noticed when I just about fell out of the saddle after my horse had the temerity to advance to a trot without consulting me.

After the corn roast and hotdogs, after the country singers and square dance demonstrations had cleared the ring, the braver or stupider of the farm boys rode the bucking broncos. It was an open invitation. We asked if we could try, but Mom said "No."

There were some riding skills contests – jump the fence and collect the brass rings. It seemed like there were more prizes than competitors. So everyone was a winner.

And the best part came at the end of the evening when all the under sixteens were put in the ring, and an agitated piglet rubbed down with cooking oil was let loose. He who caught the greased piggy won.

It was never me.

By the end of that summer there was a lot of talk (shouting, actually) about not coming up to the cottage next year. It's not that I was listening. It was just that any living soul at any place in or around Go Home Lake couldn't help but hear.

I was beheading roses on the pathway behind the cottage

when what must have been *Act 2* began. The establishing scenes were more often baleful tableaux punctuated by irascible growls.

Curtain Up, Mother: "I'm sick and tired of being maid, cook, and court jester to these kids all summer long!" Her voice was the first to make the jump to hyper-sound. "I'm completely isolated up here. No phone, no car. No one over twelve to talk to. While you're off gallivanting all over the city, doing exactly as you please."

Father: "Quit bitching. You're never happy unless you're miserable. All summer long you've got neighbors on both sides."

"Nettie Barker is an idiot, and Lil is a mealymouthed snot."

"And you are so perfect, I suppose? You can't even put a decent meal on the table half the time!" Dad complained loudly. She may not have reached his heart by way of his stomach, but it was an excellent venue through which to aggravate him.

"You just don't appreciate anything I do!" Mom accused.

"That's because you don't do a damned thing!"

"You should talk!" Mom was well beyond furious now. She was miffed, hopping mad, fit to be tied. "You stroll in here, sit on your fat duff all weekend, and expect to be waited on hand and foot. Well I won't do it. I won't be your nursemaid with fucking privileges. Now what do you think of that!"

Sharply punctuating the end of that prodigious testimonial was an acute and piercing *crack* like the sound of wet wood breaking.

Followed by silence.

Some reflexive understanding caused me to realize I might best assume a position at least half a mile away. I turned and ran as fast as I could, as far as I could, away from the yelling and anger.

The back door of the cottage was opening with a creak and slamming hard. Thundering footsteps beat a path away from the house, in my direction. I had no clue if it was Mom or Dad, and less than no interest in finding out. As fast as my sturdy legs could carry me, I headed for the ice house and took refuge there.

I ducked inside the door and rolled into the corner darkness and held still.

Whoever it was stormed past. I tried not to breathe, not to blink, not to think. Very quickly, the path was calm. The storming adult was gone.

Though the coast was clear, I remained alone and motionless. The ice house was a slap-dash construction when it was put together what seemed like a thousand years ago. And it was certainly worse for the wear and the weather of the roughly forty years it had been standing. But now, as I began my second clandestine visit, I found my heart returned to a placid pace, my breathing took to its normal rhythm. It felt strangely safe in the ice house.

Whispers of half-formed fears and the mewling hums of starving hopes filled the hushed silence. But I was a long way from knowing that most of that disquieting rumble came from within me. Distant echoes from an achingly empty place that housed something sorely lonely. Something too young to recognize itself from among bits of broken furniture, dunes of loose straw, and discarded hardware. Something truthful but invisible loomed in ghostly profile beyond the stinging slats of sunlight. I climbed on top of the block table and lay down. I folded over in the middle, my belly filled with nervous churning. I concentrated hard, wishing fervently for something in the past, for Mahow to return to undo these impossible knots in my stomach. For the water level to go down so I could sail away to the island. I lay down flat, fixating and meditating with all my might, hoping against hope that Suzanne's metaphysical teachings might take hold, that I might levitate and fly away.

That didn't happen.

I lost a number of hours. I believe I fell asleep.

Something fantastical took place.

When we were finally called in to dinner, the cottage was nearly floating on a cloud of delicious fragrances. Savory and thyme seeped from the oven where a roasted chicken was keeping warm. Mashed potatoes, moist and buttery, waited patiently in a pot on the back of the stove. Peas were on the boil. Pickled beets and gherkins stood ready on the table, each with one of my whittled pickle forks on the side for serving. Dad was reading a magazine (all right, so it was *Playboy*, but he really was *reading* the articles). And Mom...well, Mom was standing by the stove, wearing a fresh, clean apron, one with a ruffle on the hem, and a Mona Lisa smile, while she whipped up some gravy.

Pinch me.

What was more amazing still, was that we ate dinner, all together, everyone using these odd super polite, unmodulated voices, like we were being featured on some CBC/NFB documentary about The Perfect Family. Because *we were the perfect family*. It was only natural.

Obviously I had fallen down in the ice house earlier and had a bad dream. The same thing happened to Dorothy, and she went to Oz. Now here I was, back in Kansas, ruby slippers just a little dirty, my brain whirring quietly along. "There's no place like the cottage, there's no place like the cottage..."

But wait! It gets better!

For dessert we had not Jell-O, not ice cream, not Everyday Cake. There was pie. And just to prove it was Valhalla, there were actually two pies. Lemon meringue times two. Seconds were a given. Thirds were guaranteed if you could pace yourself and save a little space.

Yes, there was a God. He was kind and bountiful and so very wise to know our favorite kind of pie.

The temperature in the room went up about ten degrees when Mom marched those pies out to the table. It was a byproduct of the light energy emitted from our beaming smiles.

"Now I want you to know how hard I worked to make these pies," she said as she placed them before us.

Yeah, yeah, we knew. But we were children. Mostly we knew we wanted a really big piece. *Me first. Make mine bigger than his.*

"I want you to *appreciate* it."

Sure, sure. Don't even worry about getting me a clean fork. I'll just lick this one off. Did I mention I wanted a big piece to start?

"So to make sure you appreciate it," Mom smiled sweetly and placed a wind-up kitchen timer down between the pies, "to make absolutely sure, you're all going to *admire* them for fifteen minutes."

Before I could even form the thought, James piped up, "What's *admire* mean?"

Mom sat down calmly at her place. She folded her hands in her lap. *Admire*...so sayeth Mom the Dictionary, "to *admire* something is to look at it carefully, think about all the nice things about it, like all the time I took to make it and how hard I worked for you ungrateful wretches and how nice it looks and all that sort of thing. If you can do that, admire it for fifteen minutes, then you can have a piece. Ready? Set?" She put the timer on, "Go!"

Since that fateful day I have written innumerable exams, given birth to three babies without anesthetic, and waited in the emergency room to hear if my husband was living or dead after he was run down by a taxi. Stacking it up against all that, I would have to say that the fifteen minutes we admired those pies were the longest fifteen minutes of my life.

We all waited as patiently as we were capable. We sat with these wacky, tripped-out smiles on our faces. We waited while eternity crept by at a snail's pace, vaguely wondering if the universe might stop expanding and time stand still before fifteen minutes passed and we were able to eat those pies.

Of course the time passed. It had to. There are universal laws and theories of relativity and stuff of that nature. Write a letter to P.E.T. and you could probably get a parliamentary committee to initiate a Royal Commission on the subject. And for certain you would get your pie. It would just be a matter of time – which appeared to be more elastic than anyone ever imagined.

The timer went off, we resumed life in this dimension, and heaping plates of pie were passed around.

The only thing anyone was aware of was the melodic murmurings of enjoyment that hung thickly sweet in the air. The thrilling taste of Nirvana melting on our tongues was stupefying.

But Dad was not eating his pie.

He looked at it for a while. He didn't touch it, didn't lift his fork. In time he raised his head slightly, only slightly, and looked at Mom.

It took a long time, because there was a lot of activity around the table, but when he finally caught her eye, he picked up his plate. He balanced it on his fingertips. He raised the pie above his head like he was hoisting the Stanley Cup. It was Pie In The Sky.

I thought he might make a speech. I thought he might be admiring the pie.

In one swift and smooth motion he overturned the plate, pie and all, and slammed the whole thing on the table.

The plate shattered. Everything shattered. Time itself shattered. Shards flew everywhere, meringue and blobs of Shirriff Lemon Pie Filling plummeted through the room and plopped festively on the ceiling lamp. It was a kerosene lamp. A flaky fragment of pastry even landed squarely on the wick, neatly snuffing out the light.

Inert, in semi-shadow, we all felt the impact.

Some said it was a single pie plate slammed by a lone pie man. Some claimed they heard plates thrown from the grassy knoll. But I have long maintained a conspiracy theory, as the great volume of pie and crockery that rained down upon us could not possibly have come from a single slice acting alone.

Dad got up. Went out to the car. Drove away.

He didn't even take the time to wash his hands.

ELEVEN

Lines in the Sand and Snow

DAD MUST HAVE returned at some point to collect us at the end of the summer. We went back to the city and went to school and weekly lessons and visited friends. We did all those incidental things that constituted a reasonable facsimile of life between summers. The Perfect Suburban Life.

James played hockey, participating fully in all the practices, games, playoffs, and fights. Kieffer menaced everyone on the block with his uncanny impressions of the Three Stooges, never quite getting the point that slapstick didn't mean you actually slapped someone with a stick. Buck continued with various projects, delayed only by the most mild of challenges, which sent him spinning into a tight downward spiral of rage and fury, necessitating the frequent replacement of anything breakable within his reach.

Me, I continued to study meditation, wishing myself into distant imaginary lakes and cornfields, until I reached that transcendental state where I could effectively separate myself from everything around me. I could lie on the floor and stare at the ceiling indefinitely and not even blink.

At night I went to bed and lulled myself to sleep with fantasy stories. No longer did I prime my dreams with images of pink-saddled unicorn ponies and herds of mauve and sunny-yellow cows to round up with the aid of cotton-candy-colored collie dogs. I took to imagining my family in ways they never would or could be: going on picnics complete with red-checkered tablecloth and a mammoth willow basket. We rode on matching bicycles, and everyone had a Fudgsicle after lunch. We took turns skipping stones in a babbling brook, and mine skipped the most, and my brothers cheered for me. At night we rode home, and everyone was so tired. My dad had to lift me in his arms and carry me to bed, where my mom dressed me in a white nightie with eyelet lace trim. Together they carefully tucked me in under the patchwork quilt, the one with the pink ruffles on it. Then they drew back to smile at me and sigh and murmur, "So beautiful. So perfect. So slim. And such splendid blue eyes."

In my dreams, I was a nice girl.

In mid-winter I got a new coat of wool melton with coordinating scarf and fully lined snow pants of the same material that I could wear to and from school and not freeze my knees off. The household dress code demanded that I wear dresses and stockings to school, ankle socks in the warm weather. So these pants were the most gorgeous and wonderful thing. They were nothing like the misshapen double-knit polyester pull-ons I generally had to deal with, or, more repulsive still, James's scratchy-sounding brown castoffs. These were authentic pants, sophisticated in styling. They had an actual waistband, a fly, and a heavy-duty hook-and-eye fastener at the top.

For their first wearing, I selected a dress that was shorter than the coat in order to preserve the exciting illusion I was wearing pants to school. I put on the coat and tossed the scarf over my shoulder so it hung down stylishly long, front and back, like Rupert Bear. I put my feet in the pant legs and then into my boots and pulled the pants up *just barely* over my bum.

I felt for the hook and eye. The fly splayed wide open in a *V* over my belly. This was not good.

I tugged at the opposing ends of the waistband several times. I sucked in my stomach and threw out my chest. I opened my coat and pushed my dress aside to see if I could figure out why this fancy snow-pants thing wasn't coming together.

It was, as Mama said so daintily, because all of me became a little hefty above the knee.

I hiked up my leotards affecting a sort of mild girdling about my middle. Flapping my hand behind me frantically ensured that my petticoat, dress, and even anything so thick as a sash ribbon wasn't increasing my circumference. Pulling as hard as I could, I managed to join the two halves of the clasp together above the zipper. I then zipped the fly *almost* to the top.

Hefty-shmefty. I was triumphant.

I rearranged my dress and coat over top. It was a fine effect. There was no telling what was being held back underneath. I could still mostly breathe. Not deeply. But what did that matter?

I stroked my gorgeous long scarf. I was wearing an *ensemble.*

But it did not include a watch.

I did not have a brilliant sense of time.

"What on earth are you doing going to school at this hour?" my mom asked on her way to plug in the percolator. It was an *automatic* coffee percolator. You only had to measure the coffee and the water and put them in and turn it on and turn it off at the right time. It did everything else itself.

"I have to go in early," I lied. It was way better than admitting I was so super excited about my new coat-scarf-trouser combo that I couldn't contain my joy. And she didn't need to know my belly couldn't be contained either. I was uncomfortably aware of the strain on the waistband of my snazzy pants.

"What for?" Mom asked irritably. Once in a while my brothers had to go to school early, most often for sports practice or sometimes to work on a project. More than once it had been because the school system was crap (as my mother explained), and teachers didn't teach worth a damn, so we didn't learn anything. So kids would have to go over everything twice or three times just to get it. It was all the hippie school board's fault. It was like some kind of detention. But the teacher always tried to candy coat these sessions by calling them Extra Help. Then my mother would looked pained and say again "We never should have left Montreal."

"I have to work on a project," I offered brightly.

Project was a catchall descriptive term. In the primary grades it was applied to everything from making a mural of the undersea world to creating a replica of Buckingham Palace out of cereal boxes and paper-towel rolls.

Of course there was no *actual* project. I was only partway through grade one, and I could barely read. Just tying up my own shoes or learning to blow my nose myself could be considered a project. Thankfully my mother didn't ask me *what sort* of project.

But, "You're going to be early," my mother warned me. "Really early."

"I know," I insisted. Actually I gulped the words as I bent over to pick up my schoolbag and mitts, and any residual bits of air that were squeezed out of me with the sudden strangulation of my diaphragm.

My mom shrugged. "Suit yourself." There was coffee calling.

So off I went, trussed and bundled and as warm as toast. I walked by myself. In kindergarten I was supposed to walk with one or more of my brothers, but as the year wore on, I became evermore embarrassing to be seen with. And I didn't help my case by deploying my version of The Happy Family Little Sister as I imagined her. If I saw one of my brothers on the playground or in the hall, I would step up with a posed smile and practiced cheer and inquire, "How has your day been, dear brother?" Kieffer or James – Buck was in another school by then – would pretend they didn't know me. I might try, "Isn't the sunshine lovely today?" but that might just get me a shove or a punch in the arm in response. Occasionally

I would raise some helpful point like, "Don't forget! Mom says you shouldn't burp with your mouth open on purpose in assembly."

It was only about three-and-a-half blocks to school. Ten minutes if I really dragged my feet. And I really did, though it didn't help much in the way of speeding up that particular morning.

There was no one else on the sidewalk at that hour. It was *that* early. I would have liked to have bumped into a friend or foe in order to have them see my new outfit. For sure they would think I was wearing pants. "*Penny* is wearing *pants*" would be the buzz. "She's wearing really *nifty* pants that *match* her coat and scarf." But I wasn't too worried. I knew I looked good and felt fabulous, if a little light-headed due to my inability to breathe properly. The news would be out soon enough.

I rounded the corner to the side where the primary grades hung out until the bell rang. I stopped and stared. The playing field and paved areas were vast and expansive. They looked like they had grown overnight. They went on for miles. The senior wing of the school where the grade four to six-ers ruled was practically in another country.

I had never seen the place so absolutely empty before. Swiftly moving clusters of bodies, ages five to twelve years, in late-baby-boom numbers, usually blotted out most of the school's geography. I felt like an early explorer gazing upon uncharted territory for the first time.

After standing and gawking for a while, I simply got cold and stood in the doorway out of the wind. I tried sitting down, but that was too painful. It felt like I was about to be cut in two through the stomach. *And* it made me realize I should have considered going to the bathroom before I got all dolled up in my new duds.

But it was okay. Soon the rest of the kids would be filling up the grounds, and I could ask the teacher on duty to let me in to go to the bathroom.

I clip-clopped around a bit being a wild horse in a meadow. But the blacktop was patched with ice, and I almost fell more than once. I shot at the birds flying overhead with my imaginary pistol. But being a cowboy was not a suburban aspiration. I might be able to keep a pony in the backyard and wear the hat on weekends, but there was never going to be a greased piglet to catch or a chance to shoot a gun.

It was beginning to truly dawn on me that it was really, *really* early. Rather earlier than I'd first thought.

I speed-walked around a while to keep warm and distract myself from my bulging bladder. I am sure I looked a bit like a stiff-legged duckling. Hoping against hope, I rattled the doors at the primary and the senior entrances. Everything was locked up tight and the metal was cold and made me colder. And more anxious to pee. I weighed the possibility of making it around the back of the school, through the parking lot, and to the teachers' entrance, but nothing led me to believe there was any possibility in that. Probably no one would let me in anyway. Teachers were mean like that. They liked to see little kids suffer outside in the cold and the rain. They probably laughed about it while they smoked themselves silly in the teachers' lounge before class.

I was getting to a really serious point. I knew it was time to look around for a place where I could pee and not get caught.

Inside one of the brick surrounds of the main doors looked to be the best spot. There was plenty of shadow, and from the left or the right someone walking close to the school wall would not be able see into the opposite corner of the doorway.

I duck-strode back to the primary doors. Those doors were a poor choice. Far nearer the public sidewalk and main street than the senior doors. So they were nearer also to the risk of being seen.

But desperation has the tendency of narrowing one's notion of what safe and reasonable might be. A full bladder, especially, is all about the unbalanced *now*.

My scarf flew off in a cold gust as I made the last awkward steps across the blacktop. I was not so far gone that I didn't take care to avoid stepping on cracks in the pavement or lines painted for four-square and hop-scotch. That would only bring bad luck. Superstition was stupid, yes. But I needed every advantage, no matter how farfetched. Anything to help hold back the impending flood of pee.

I made it to the primary doorway. I hauled up my coat and dress and tugged and fumbled madly at my fly. I crossed my ankles, fell into the wall and lost my grip, and had to start again.

"Little doors stay shut, little doors stay shut, little doors stay shut," I chanted instruction to my defiant urethra. I counted "one, two, three" and tried repeatedly to release the clasp on my pants "one, two, three, one, two, three," over and over in hopes the sequence could at once distract my desperation and magically announce the opening of my fly.

Eventually it worked, after a small forever.

I scraped my pants and leotards and underwear down fast and furious and bunched them up below my knees. I squatted awkwardly, lost balance, but caught myself by thrusting my elbows out behind me. My bladder emptied immediately.

I am sure I sighed and crooned *Aahhhhhh* in delighted relief.

It was certain they saw and heard me even before I imagined their horrible existence possible.

Two senior students stopped to stare. They were stunned. They were amazed. But not at my coat-scarf-snazzy pants ensemble.

They looked to be in grade six and stylish with zippered boots that went up to their knees and long, combed, clean hair. Frozen in disgusted stillness, mid-recoil, their attention focused on the steamy tsunami parting the snows as it rolled toward them from my moon-like backside.

I sprang upright, yanking my layers with me. But the effort, while speedy, was hapless. My underpants remained stretched between my calves while my leotards and pants were caught at separate levels of exposure. My privates were on full public display, still avidly demonstrating one of their primary functions: waste management. Pee was still streaming out of me, now directly filling my drawers.

Jumping out of the river of pee as it came too close to their faux-leather knee boots (with gold rings on the zipper pulls), the girls regained consciousness and their capacity to speak.

They didn't screech in horror. They did not accuse me of having a dirty twat.

One girl turned to the other. They grabbed each other's

shoulders to steady themselves from the shock, and one said to the gap-mouthed other, "Did you just see what I saw?" She probably wished she was hallucinating. Better that than just having witnessed the naked nether regions of a chubby grade one kid, squatting and pissing on school property. That had to be a sin.

Naturally there was no getting over that. For them, or me.

The grade six girls in boots took the glorious high road and held nothing back in their report. News traveled quickly from their teacher to mine to the office to my mother, who refused to allow me to come home until lunch. It was her contention that sitting among a jury of my peers in a damply malodorous urine-scented fog all morning would result in the experiential education I was in need of. I think the teacher was not exactly thrilled to have this sub-lesson taking place under her offended nose, but she was too polite to say anything about it. My classmates, however, were not so inhibited.

"Penny smells," they complained openly. "Penny smells like pee."

Once lunchtime came I ran home and changed my clothes. The coat, pants, and scarf were scrunched up and tossed in the garbage bin in front of me. I said I felt sick and wanted to say home from school.

My mother said, "*I* am sick. I am sick and tired of cleaning up after you selfish little beasts. You're over two years of age. You haven't got a piano tied to your right arm. You are perfectly capable of using a toilet. If you feel sick to your stomach, it's your own darn fault."

This was all true.

I was *not* a *nice* girl. I was hopeless.

As if publicly wetting myself and the loss of my beautiful pantsuit were not enough, I continued on my path of total humiliation. Most days I just tried to pretend I wasn't there. And I was pretty good at convincing myself. I forgot vital things like brushing my teeth or washing my face and hands. When I put on clothes, I just picked them up off the floor and put them on – the same ones day after day. They didn't have to match. They didn't have to be clean. I went to school wearing my worn old pj's once. Didn't even care.

Penny has a pissy, dirty twat.

Anybody knew that.

Mom and Dad went about their business. Dinners came in the usual rotating schedule. Dessert was served without violence on the side. They had a couple of big blowups, but the daily dose of yelling was reduced to a consistent sarcastic growl.

But late at night, when the house was still, and the stars twinkled, and the moon shone brightly high above Dewmist Crescent, you could hear a scuffle on the floor, as though they tripped while they were dancing. Dad would slam the door and the car would squeal out of the driveway, and Mom would sing a weird, repetitive little song in monotone about silk buttons found in the dirty sheets on her bed....

TWELVE

Rawhide and Glue

THE WORLD TURNED. Spring then summer came again and took us off to the sanctity of the cottage.

Life was going to be different around these parts. Better. It was going to be better. I was sprung from my grade one prison and grade two was far enough in the future so as to be invisible to my myopic child's eye.

The country of Here and Now was wide open. And it was gorgeous.

The cottage was becoming posh, almost spa-like. We acquired a hot-water tank, and the kitchen was renovated. The old front porch was shored up and the kitchen expanded into it. The finished product had about five miles of counter space and a huge industrial grill like the one at the Gulf Gas Bar and Restaurant. *Step aside, Doris. I'm flippin' the bacon now.* Because you can never have enough fried food.

From the *Twilight Zone* section of Mack's Home Appliances we also got a wringer washer, a semi-automatic deal that agitated and emptied on your behalf, though the unmitigated pleasure of feeding all the clothes though the wringers remained yours to revel in.

Mom was petrified of the contraption. When it was in operation we had to stand ten full paces back. I'm not sure what she thought; that the diabolic automatic motor could, at a whim, exact some indomitable suction force, pulling our arms, legs, and heads between the evil, crushing rollers, dumping us, flattened, into the wash water laced with super caustic washing powder, tossing us about in the drum until we were finally pumped down the drain?

The greatest luxurious addition to cottage life, as far as Mom was concerned, was the arrival of the second car, a Golden Pinto Wagon.

Now Mom could have "wheels" at the cottage. She was no longer limited to as far as she could walk (or persuade Buck to walk). Being a modern feminist was really working for her, though I was pretty sure she was still wearing a bra. Only *not-nice* feminists "let it all hang out."

The Pinto Wagon meant Mom was not some brainless, breathless housewife who had to walk in the rain (uphill both ways) to the hairdresser twice a week. It meant she had a mind of her own. A will of her own! Anytime she felt like it – after rounding us up and locking us in the cottage for fear we'd eat a lead sandwich while playing catch with cinder blocks in the deepest part of the lake during a lightning storm – any old time she took a notion to it – if she forced us all to put on shoes and shirts and get in the car and do up our seat belts and stop fighting and go with her – she could just traipse out to that Golden Pinto, swinging the keys in her hand, hop in, and zoom off to Fitzgerald's General Store and spend her allowance on milk and bread and even hotdogs. But not too many. She had to keep some money for gas. Dad was supposed to come up every weekend and give her a little more money. But sometimes he didn't.

Mom told me he was working on some kind of surprise building project. Specifically what she said was, "He thinks I'm too stupid to figure it out. But he's about as subtle as a train wreck. I *know*. I'm telling you, he's screwing around."

I wasn't sure why she sounded so peeved about it. Dad's screwing really seemed like a *good* thing. The cottage kitchen was looking pretty darn good. The cabinets were screwed to the wall, the counter was raised four inches and screwed in place. Even the wringer washer was screwed to the floor, stopping it from traveling across the room as it agitated its load. I hoped with all my might and mane that Dad was building me a playhouse, or a corral to keep my pony in. But he was probably screwing around with some grown-up endeavor. Like maybe one of those cool padded leather bars in the rec room. Maybe even with a tiny fridge. And an ice bucket. Freshie on tap!

Whoa! My own private cowboy saloon. Sock it to me! That would be so groovy.

So, if Dad missed a weekend or two because he was screwing the fancy studs into the quilted upholstery of the rec room bar or setting up the shiny high-bar stools, it was okay by me. Don't know why Mom got all in a sweat over a little remodeling.

If we were really short on male muscle, we could always call on Suzanne's boyfriend, Brian. Wherever Suzanne was, Brian was sure to be close by. If we needed the raft tied up or the canoe dragged up on the beach or some jars opened, he was handy. The rest of the time he just slept in or hung out with Suzanne or could be found eating Auntie Lil out of house and home, as she put it. And he never wanted to hang out with us kids. We were pests and dunderheads. In many ways, Brian's visits were a lot like my father's. Except Brian never came with any cash. That kind of kept the Golden Pinto hitched up to the post more than Mom might have liked. So it wasn't a perfect system. But Mom could always dispatch Brian for milk and bread in Auntie Lil's Turd-on-wheels. I think it was an imported car. Domestic models all seemed to have names I recognized. Usually they were named after animals, like a Bobcat, an Impala, or a Cat au Lac (French for "cat in freshwater").

Brian had a friend named Pete, who arrived one fine afternoon in a red-hot, shiny new Mustang, thus making the afternoon even finer. Brian also had a brother named Gord, who drove a big baby-blue convertible, and he visited a few times. All that summer, we did not suffer for lack of vehicular style.

For long water-going voyages, we also acquired a small sailboat. The body of it was shaped like three of the four connected fingers of a KitKat bar, except that the middle finger, which was fitted for passengers (preferably the double-jointed variety), was not as deep as the others.

The vessel was supposed to be untippable. My brothers and I were not about to take that as read. With Herculean effort we managed to capsize it once or twice, but after we proved the point it was no fun anymore, so we couldn't be bothered. As a sailboat, it held little interest for us because sailing required a certain combination of patience and dexterity, neither of which we children possessed in any measurable amount.

But Brian's friend Pete was an able seaman, if ever there was one. The little sailboat caught his eye, and he went straight for it. He set up that sail in nothing flat and whizzed that little boat across the bay faster than any America's Cup contestant.

Success loves reinforcement, and Pete soon bounded up to the cottage to offer all interested speed demons passage on this meteoric craft.

"I want to go. Can I go?" I jumped up immediately.

There was not a chance of turning me down. Brian was off with Suzanne exploring nature; the boys had departed for the cave, or the swamp. Even Mom was gone at the time, tearing up the back roads in pursuit of milk and bread. No one was around to shove me out of the head of the line or tell me no.

This is the only possible explanation for my going fully clothed and without a life jacket.

"I'll go. I want to go. Can I go? Can you take me?"

There was no need to repeat the question, though I did several times out of habit. Pete affably led me down to the sailboat, affixed me to a KitKat finger, and shoved us off. *Bon voyage!*

It was fun, too. The light breeze I felt at shore could do impressive tricks when Pete encouraged it to try its strength against the sail on the open water. We glided easily across the surface of the sparkling lake, Pete swung the sail somehow, and we flew back again, soaring into the afternoon. It was grand.

Absurdly, I thought that Pete expected something of me, that I should make my appreciation clear, that I ought to *admire* his skill and his kindness. My thoughts raced around, searching for the exact right way to express my gratitude and happiness.

The way I was hanging my head and staring into the moving water must have concerned Pete. He wrinkled his forehead and regarded me with some concern.

"Are you all right?" he asked, a little edgy that I might be getting seasick.

Suddenly I raised my head to meet his eye. In my mind I saw images of happy children sourced from TV commercials and clips of the crowds at the Santa Claus parades: children who were *having fun,* children who were having *a barrel of laughs.*

By George, I think I got it! Inspiration thundered up from my diaphragm and I threw back my head and laughed for all I was worth. I laughed loud and long, because, by the limits of my plastic comprehension, that was what *happy children* did virtually all the time.

Thank God television was invented to tell me this, or I never would have known.

Pete looked at me strangely, took one more turn around the bay, and then steered the boat to shore. My throat was so sore from laughing, I was nearly inaudible when I croaked "Thank you," and ran off.

✳ ✳ ✳

The last of the spectacular modern conveniences to arrive at the cottage was a black-and-white television. Slyly described as a *portable* model. (Well, yes, if you were Charles Atlas.) This baby weighed in at a svelte eighty-five pounds.

It occupied an honorable position in the middle of the main room of the cottage. But we weren't allowed to watch it.

✳ ✳ ✳

Granny and Gramps set up in Don's cottage early in the summer. I know this to be true because I saw it with my own eyes. It was a week-long satire: "The King and Queen of Prim'n'Proper Go Camping."

It is difficult to grasp that they arrived in but a single car. For all the paraphernalia it took to sustain them, one might have reasonably expected a convoy of eighteen-wheelers. Granny's swimming get-up alone must have required a good-sized steamer trunk. She had to plan two days ahead if she was going to go swimming. Putting on the suit was an enormous production, because it was hardly a suit. It was a costume. A bathing costume, in the Edwardian style, with a cinched, quilted, boned bodice, trussed up in the back like a Christmas turkey, with stiff, puffy bloomers that you could have set a tea cup on. Later, in grade seven, I would see Sir Walter Raleigh wearing the same outfit in my history text.

Granny also wore a bathing cap, an accessory not entirely out of vogue at the time. My own little noggin was squeezed into one the odd time, at swimming lessons and at the public pool. But mine was plain white with my name emblazoned across the forehead. Granny's swim cap was obstreperous in design. It had attitude before anyone knew what attitude was. It made a statement. It said, "I am hideous!"

Crammed over her hair and fastened with the kind of strapping used to tie down loads of lumber on flatbeds, Granny's swim cap almost appeared to be in competition for our amazed attention with her bathing costume. So much so that it was easy to miss the shoes.

Little white, rubber party shoes with three dainty straps and three buttons.

Granny came down to the beach enveloped in a floor-length robe with a hood. *Wouldn't you?* Disrobing, she waded into the water and stood there, knee-deep – which was about ankle-deep for everyone else, for Granny was very small – and chatted with Mom.

We went in, we splashed about, we came out, sat on the sand, built sand castles, dug holes, held a diving contest, caught five crayfish, let them go, went back in, demonstrated underwater somersaults, found a garter snake, threw it in, watched it swim back to shore, fought viciously over the air mattress, blew a hole in it, swam and splashed until our lips turned blue, and we were ordered out.

Granny never made it past her knees.

I heard her remark casually to Mom as she slipped back into her robe, "Well, I don't think I'll ever swim in a lake again."

I thought I would cry. Poor Granny. Poor, poor Granny. She was going to die soon. Because your life had to be over when you no longer wanted to go to the cottage and swim in a lake.

Granny and Gramps spent a week at Go Home Lake, prudishly adhering to their unalterable schedule. Gramps read aloud from the Bible every morning at nine. On Sunday, they actually attended Church. They ate lunch at eleven-thirty, had dinner at five, and always used ironed linen napkins. I think they brought their own silverware.

Their visit, at least in part, was a luckless attempt for my brothers and I to bond with them a little. Had we not been from different planets, I am sure this would have worked out fine. But they were serene, staunch, and stoic, while we were manic, disturbed, and stressed. No amount of provoking and irritation could bring them round to our way. God knows we tried. When they left, I think they were glad to go.

Next to occupy Don's cottage were the Turners on their second visit. This was not much of a bonus. While James, Kieffer, and Kathy teamed up, Buck and Monica did their own thing, and I was trapped in a nightmarish threesome with Timmy and DeeDee. In one another they found their inner mirror images. They were kindred spirits. Here were two people who loved to be babied, stay pristinely clean, giggle over small dolls, and snivel till the cows came home. For the sake of being part of the action, I strained to get along with them. We played games that they favored, role-playing games modeled after well-known stories like *Chitty Chitty Bang Bang* or *Heidi*.

Timmy was Heidi. I was some ugly stepsister in a wheelchair or on stilts or something (don't ask me, I never read it) who, when meeting the doe-eyed Heidi, was obliged to articulate with a disgusted sniff, "You smell like cheese."

Had this made one iota of sense, I might have been able to deliver the line the two thousand times required of me. But there was no logic, no deeper meaning – there were no cowboys.

I insisted we play cowboys.

"Oh, yuck," was their weary response.

"Well, you have to," I informed them. On what grounds I took such authority, I couldn't tell you.

Timmy and DeeDee regarded each other with questioning looks. Being overly coddled youngsters, they were totally bewildered by the sight of another child belligerently telling them what to do.

They shrugged. "No we don't," they said innocently.

How could they say no? "You do so!" I sputtered. "You *have* to play cowboys with me!"

DeeDee looked at me, scowling a little. "No, we don't," she said with a patronizing chuckle.

Long before the moment of implosion came, I knew I was losing control. Rage is a palpable emotion. It bristles and burns, presents like a typical inflammatory reaction: fury, clenching, increased salivary flow, dilation of the blood vessels that feed the brain, ischemic strangulation of all normal sensibilities. Wheal and flare. It hurts.

I shook. I had a terrible awareness of my own dissolution. The muscles of facial expression cramped in contortion. With or without comprehending that my legs were moving, I propelled across the room, a shrill projectile of ferocious outrage.

"You do so have to! You have to!" I blared, pressing hard

against the constriction in my throat. I threw myself into them, flailing madly, the enormous energy of the tumultuous indignation that spurred me on hampered only slightly by the spastic nature of my ire.

I don't believe the words came to mind as an actual goal, but my master plan was to knock some sense into them by knocking their heads together.

There was much whimpering and crying, a few welts, a goose egg, a couple of bruises, and one bloody nose (mine) before Uncle Ralph came tearing in, peeled me off Timmy and DeeDee, and tossed me out the door – actually tossed me – like a "bag of rubbish," he said, and slammed and locked the door.

I stumbled to the ice house, punch drunk and dizzy with a bad anger-brain buzz. I flopped over on my back on the old table and willed myself to stop breathing. Not just breathing too hard. I wanted to stop breathing completely.

I must have looked like a cadaver in the middle of the room. The table had one short leg. I concentrated hard and focused on a slash of bright white sunlight between the planks on the roof. All remaining energy drained out of me. I felt it go. I let it go. And I stared at the ceiling and chanted in my mind:

"She sleeps…she's sick…she's dead…"

I wished I was.

Balancing the table on three legs, I levitated as best I could and floated far, far away.

In my dreams I was a cowboy, comfortable in the saddle, riding the range, white hat, blue sky, Indian luv beads….

My beloved horse and I trotted along the shoreline and

through the forest. In my whole life I have never been happier than I was then, in that carefully orchestrated dreamtime. It was...beautiful.

I awoke a very long time later. The sun had long since passed over the roof of the ice house, like the angel of death. The table leveled with a thump. I sat up instantly, my head throbbing, unable to breathe for the cohesive mass of blood and snot caked in my sinuses. My clothes were saturated with urine.

I crept out, got my swimsuit off the clothesline, and went down to the lake and washed. Mom found my pee-soaked clothes later and berated me for not getting to the bathroom on time. Nobody mentioned my fight with Timmy and DeeDee, so I figured everything was all right. But as I moved automatically through the liturgy and customs of the summer, it chafed at me constantly: nothing was all right.

THIRTEEN

Big Sky

PRESIDENT KENNEDY HAD pledged to the American people that they would put a man on the moon before 1970. He said this before he was shot and killed, we all know. But the wishes of the dead are considered paramount in Western society, so posthumously he fulfilled his promise in the summer of 1969.

This, I discovered, was how the television came to be taking up space at the cottage. During the course of a single viewing, Life As We Knew It would come to an abrupt end and the Space Age would begin.

Change was something I was hoping for. The current and intractable way of my corner of the "West" was wilder than this little nearly-a-cowboy could deal with. Different had to be better. It was some time later that I noticed the total absence of cattle in the star systems (save that lone, moon-jumping cow). The result being that my chosen profession was on the precipice of uselessness. It would be a very long time before I could comprehend it. By the dawn of that dark day I would recognize the dangerous redundancy of cowboys in general, not to mention the complete stupidity and inertia of the immovable social order. But that was tightly crumpled up, a story yet to unfold.

Buck and Kieffer took me out to a clearing between the road and the cottage and pointed out the moon to me. I was not astronomically inclined and had never thought to search for the moon in the broad day-lit sky. I believed to that point that the moon was either a winking green cheesy face or a yellow crescent against a blue-black picture-book backdrop. I saw a balled up cloud and thought *it* was the moon.

"I see it!" I exclaimed, looking in the wrong direction entirely. Buck and Kieffer tried a smack to my ear to improve my sense of direction. Thank goodness that worked like a charm: The remedial throttling that almost certainly would have followed might have left me unconscious for the Big Leap of history into modern times.

I looked squarely at the moon, pale and hazy in the early evening light. I blinked and twitched a little from the pain in my ear. The man in the moon did not wink back. That was faintly disappointing.

"If you look carefully," Kieffer told me, "you can see the lunar module."

"But you have to look really carefully," Buck said. "Look to the left of that big crater in the middle near the top."

I did not know what a crater was, and I was twelve before I could consistently identify my left from my right. But I knew what was good for me, and I saw the lunar module. I saw it. I remember it as clear as day, just like I remember watching the assassination of JFK, even though I wasn't even a year old at the time.

I ran inside the cottage and boastfully announced to the gathering crowd, "I saw the lunar module. I saw it on the moon. Outside. Just now. You can *really* see it."

Everyone began to laugh. Buck and Kieffer came in behind me and laughed too. I joined in wholeheartedly, laughing my guts out because I knew that's what happy families did. They were laughing at me. So I laughed as hard as I could with them.

As if the cottage was not crowded enough with the Turners, Auntie Lil and Uncle Marlow, Suzanne, Brian, Mom, and my three brothers, Dad and I went out in the motorboat on a proselytizing mission. Like Jesuit priests sent from NASA, we rounded up the ignorant, television-less locals in order to save their souls by exposing them to the miracle of Neil Armstrong frolicking on the moon in the glare of the big, blue marble that contained us.

We collected so many excited devotees of space travel that I feared the boat would sink.

But we made it back.

In our absence, Uncle Ralph had been on the ham radio connecting with people all over the planet, who waited and watched as we did. That really put the global village spin on things. Presently Ralph was trying to erect a makeshift television antenna.

No one had thought to test the television prior to this auspicious day. When it was turned on for the pre-walk commentary, it was discovered that reception was nonexistent.

To rectify this media disaster, Uncle Ralph was using a toy bow-and-arrow set to shoot a framework of copper wire into the trees.

A great cheer rang out when he managed to catch it on the highest branch of the tallest tree. To the best of my knowledge, it is there to this day. Houston, we had contact.

Glued to the set, we watched a man who looked like Walt Disney, but wasn't, describe the details of a space suit. Mom passed around crackers topped with Squeeze-a-Snack, just like the ones we saw in the Kraft Foods commercial, but gave us a look if we took more than four at a time. Ominously, it was announced that we were about to tap in to the direct link with the Apollo 11, and the entire world held its breath and watched.

At first there was just a grainy picture of what the world might look like from Rover's perspective: an expanse of dirt and gravel swiftly moving past our view. I think this was the module landing on the moon's surface. Perhaps it was earlier footage from NASA.

Possibly it was just film shot by some rocket-science intern swinging a movie camera with a macro lens over the pot-holed surface of the Burbank television studios parking lot. From the very beginning there were prominent conspiracy theories that insisted the whole moon landing was completely staged by the American government to one-up the Soviets, who had put a monkey or a duck or something into space more than a year earlier. Not a pony. But whatever it was never came back, or its eyes exploded, or both, which wouldn't play well in the living rooms of the nation, any nation.

It was claimed that the falsified event was conceived and broadcast from the television studios of Burbank, California, the same studio that (hint, hint) produced the rather wacky comedy program *Laugh-In*. The Americans had no shortage of odd and remote islands reserved for nuclear testing and the like that they could have made good use of. Why bother trying to maintain a wall of silence in the suburbs when they could have just as easily whipped up the whole thing, out of sight and out of mind, in the middle of the Pacific and staged a timely plane crash to keep the rumors down?

In the end, it was probably simpler still to stuff three bonafide astronauts into an actual space capsule and light a fire under them, cross about a billion fingers, and hope it all came out in the wash.

Up flew the Apollo 11. The eagle landed. The man in the moon, if he still existed, did not show any objection.

The moon walk was about to occur.

There was great rejoicing and calls for more Squeeze-a-Snack. Then, after a long and snowy-buzzy broadcast pause that lasted almost as long as we had to admire the ill-fated lemon meringue pies, ol' Neil literally got his star butt in gear and popped it out the hatch.

He walked the walk, talked the talk.

I would not bore you by repeating it. Oh, all right, since you begged me:

One small step for man, one giant leap for mankind.

My brothers encouraged me to vacate my primo seat, front and center just inches below the TV, run outside, and wave at Neil Armstrong because he was *sure* to wave back. I was tempted, and not just to relieve the cramp in my neck from keeping my head at a sharp enough angle to see the screen. I really thought ol' Neil might look down and see me, see a nice girl, and wave just to be friendly. But I didn't want to risk the almost inevitable disappointment. So I stayed put. James squished Squeeze-a-Snack into my hair.

FOURTEEN

Bad Penny Westerns

AS HAPPENED every summer, the rain moved in and stayed a while. Usually not more than a few days, but in an under-age-eye-view, even an afternoon was an eternity. All sorts of miserable things happened. The well ran dry of reading material (*Tales of the Crypt*, *Spiderman*, and *Richie Rich* comics). The appeal of board games waned, especially when it was difficult to round up all the pieces. They tended to be lost when the board was flung across the room – a move that was rarely described according to Hoyle. I was inclined to think outside the game box and use the old shoe of the Monopoly game as a glass slipper for a Barbie scene. The marbles from the Chinese Checkers might be used as buried treasure on the beach.

For that summer I am thinking of, those rainy days, the Turners were long gone; Brian, Pete, and Gord were back in the city; and not even *I* could stand the sight of Timmy any longer. History was left to repeat its awful self, and my brothers and I were left alone to amuse ourselves.

Amuse is probably not the right word.

For a while indoor cottage life was a fairly calm affair. Numerous times we re-enacted the moon walk, or the even more exciting re-entry of the space capsule to Earth. We fell into the ocean floor, and, with space-addled brains, we climbed into the rescue craft/couch even though we were riddled with yet-to-be-named ailments acquired from beyond our atmosphere. Our flesh crawled with moon beetles. Our brows burned with moon fever, but weakly, bravely, we made it back to NASA. There we told our frightening tales and had nice, refreshing glasses of Tang, *the juice the astronauts drink* and maybe a little freeze-dried ice cream. Of course, we didn't actually have any of the latter. We subbed in shredded bubble gum collected from hockey cards. It looked the same, even if it didn't go down as easily.

It was all fun and games, as they say, until somebody lost an eye. Or, in our case, our patience and our tempers. None of us ever succumbed to blindness, but blind rage was a mutual handicap.

A jab to the arm was the most frequent opener to the melee. It was followed by an ear smack, stomach punch, and if the recipient could still stand after that, a flailing, whirling series of strikes that sucked in anyone or anything near it, like a fling-you-off-to-Oz twister.

If Mom *was* around she would intervene in order to keep the breakage to a minimum – dishes, furniture, or, in the worst case, human limbs. Bodily harm would only set in motion an unbreakable chain of dire inconvenience. First, Mom would have to pick up the phone and persuade whoever was clogging up the party line that this was a true and terrible emergency and not just one of us mangy kids playing games. Then she'd have to call ahead and make sure there was someone with some sort of medical training at the hospital in town, lest we should be diagnosed and treated by a local geologist – the only warm body with a degree the county could offer. Because what could a doctor of aggregates do, other than tell us we were mineral-deficient and make us a feldspar cast?

Then Mom would have to hope she had enough gas to make it to the hospital and back and wrangle whoever wasn't a mess in the waiting area. No way could she be so lucky that we'd all be seriously wounded, and she'd be left alone for a bit while we were all sedated and mummified in bandages.

But if Mom was not around (the more common case), and a scuffle broke out, it soon developed in to a brouhaha. A lot of screaming and carrying on was probably heard up the way where Mom and Auntie Lil were playing Scrabble on the veranda. "For corn's sake," Mom would probably mutter, rolling her eyes just before she laid out all seven letters spelling "trapezoid" on a triple word square.

But the sound of battered heads and bruising muscle was less easily perceived by the maternal ear. James might be held at bay for a while by compressing his thumb to his palm. If you could catch him. More likely he'd grab Buck's arm and twist it behind him and push until it almost broke. Kieffer favored "Spock bites," eye jabs, and the classic boxing of the ears. Ever the youngest and shortest and most resistant to creative combat, I always wound up with someone's palm on my forehead, braced at arm's length while I punched at the air.

After I tired of that, I'd soon be found on my behind, crying. Exhaustion probably. The same culprit usually slowed the boys down to verbal spars and name-calling, such as "Homo!"

(I knew by then it had nothing to do with milk, but something to do with *mincing* and *sod*. Mincemeat was a kind of tart at Christmas. A tart in pastry was *nice*. A tart in go-go boots was *not nice*. Sod came in rolls from the nursery in the spring. You used it to, like, reupholster your lawn and make it all green and nice. Maybe because it was dirty on one side...)

"It takes one to know one."

Whatever revolting things it indicated, that *homo* was not a term of honor was totally clear. Then came "Stick a red hot ramrod up your rosy red rectum," which caused me to giggle nervously. I couldn't help but think of the blacksmith at Pioneer Village posing with a length of black iron, one end glowing from the fire.

To which the pat reply involved pointing to one's crotch and commanding "Suck this." Unbeknownst to me, this was something of a circular parry because it brought us back to *homo!* (implied), so the next droll brother-to-brother remark would be "Don't you *wish*?" or "Wouldn't you *love* that?"

Such a round should have been simple. Still, I struggled to keep up.

Really, there were a lot of things I didn't understand. So much could be put down to trends and fashions, growing in and out of things, the development of brain and body – such grand notions and mysteries that I would understand, so the parents and prognosticators of the day advised me, when I was older. Whenever that was.

The thing was, everyone else, my brothers included, would be older still than me. Forever. I would never catch up.

And somehow, more importantly, they would always be boys. The Boys. I would always be The Only Girl. Even when – and it was going to happen, any moment now – I was well and truly, really, really a cowboy – I would still be a girl.

But being a girl was far less of an impediment that I once feared it might be. I didn't even wear a bra to burn yet, but the feminist movement was working out for me. I could take on any challenge I wanted to. It said so on the news. So long as I wore a proper dress and didn't let my underwear show. That was how my parents fine-tuned the philosophy. And anything that required grunting (heavy lifting, rock-and-roll vocals, and emphatic farting) was best left to the male half of the population.

At the drive-in we had seen a monumental grown-up film called *Cat Baloo*. I took it to be a near documentary. It featured a cowgirl who graduated from finishing school. She had the best of both worlds. She could square dance, ride a horse, rob a train, and never dislodged the poof in the top of her hairdo. She wore blue jeans and leather chaps, a gun belt, and a fitted checkered blouse, tied snug at the waist. And on Sundays and special occasions, she filled out that white peasant dress, fresh as a daisy! She was a *nice* cowgirl. Even the boys thought she was nice. Even if she did sneak a peek at the occasional "penny western" by Kid Shaleen. She was so great they made a movie about her starring Jane Fonda.

That's the kind of cowgirl I was going to be in the future. The *near* future.

But in the here and now, I still had to manage to get along, toughen up, and hone my cowboy skills. The whittling was going great. And those rainy spells provided the perfect opportunity to work on my fist-fighting talents and ability to keep up with insults.

"Homo" proved all-successful in getting any given brother's ire up. Though I had to say it and move fast to avoid the cuff to the ear. But the witty repartee never followed the same steps as it did between my brothers. No one ever suggested "it takes one to know one." I figured I was given credit for that "woman's intuition" that let you know your cake was about to burn or your cousin would never be happy married to that milkman, what with the postman always ringing twice and all. And if I avoided the cuffing, I might duck in and say it again – "homo homo homo" – because it went so well the first time.

And I thought I really was on my game once when James spread his legs, advanced two steps in the conventional process, pointed to his fly, and told me, "I'll prove it. I'm no homo. Suck this."

Okay. I knew the next line! I knew how it went!

"Whip it out!" I squealed, so pleased with myself I could hardly contain it. I could be *just as funny as the next guy.*

Except I wasn't the next guy. I was still a girl.

James actually moved to undo his fly and reach inside his y-fronts for his penis. His "woo-ee," as I would have known it.

It was no picnic.

"You wish," I said more quietly, uncertainly. I backed up a bit. And I backed up the whole exchange in my mind trying to figure out what had gone wrong. I was so sure I'd said the right insults in the right order. But the results were all wrong.

James pushed his pelvis forward and extended his penis from his pants, seemingly without having to prop it in position like boys did when they peed, so they wouldn't spill on the floor or toilet seat. They did anyway. But they were supposed to clean up.

I avoided looking at it. His woo-ee. It was kind of ugly. And I could smell the dried up pee even from four feet away. He never cleaned up.

"Yeah. I do wish. C'mon. You said, 'Whip it out.' You gotta do it now."

"Do what?" I asked. What was the next thing in the series? I thought we'd said all the pieces.

"Suck," James wagged his index finger at his woo-ee, "it." Very unpleasantly, it waved back.

I was suddenly and uncomfortably aware of the hair on my head. It felt greasy and itchy. I burped. The burp tasted like pee. Unconsciously I wiped my lips.

"Why?"

Why did I ask? I could think of so many reasons *why not*. There had to be a reason. Something I missed. Some way to dislodge the (dis)taste and the smell and the ragged line burned in my brain as this idea raged through it.

James stroked his woo-ee the way a game-show hostess felt her way along the surfaces of the prizes she was showing off. Like it was something everyone wanted. "Because it feels good. Guys like it when girls suck their cocks."

"That's disgusting!" I said, rubbing my mouth again. The pee taste was growing in my dry mouth. Burning. My tongue felt sick and prickly.

"You said, 'Whip it out.' It was your idea," James complained. Like I took his favorite comic and stuffed it in the woodstove. He was going to make me pay him back.

"That's disgusting," I repeated, my mouth behind my hand, those words being my only, weak, defense.

I was saved – a stinging respite – by Buck coming up and punching me hard in the back. It knocked the wind and thankfully the pee smell out of me. I hit the floor like a bag of hammers, landing on my shins. I started to cry. Out of relief. It was a solid and familiar place. I was happy to be there. As low as I was, I knew which way was up.

Another movie we saw that summer left me with a lot more unpleasant questions about what disgusting things guys liked and *expected* from girls. Did girls have to do that sort of thing? Even Cat Baloo girl-cowboys?

A rare and wonderful Pink Panther cartoon was shown before the feature. That was good. The commercial with the dancing snack foods never got too old for me, though the speaker instructions were deadly dull. Once the actual movie began to roll, the wheels fell off for me. It was just a lot of fast talking, a lot of ladies in fancy costume dresses, and a lot of men in striped suits and curly mustaches. I got the idea it was supposed to be funny. But I couldn't tell you why anyone would think so.

"You're too young to understand," my mother answered my cockeyed expression as I watched actors swallow their cigars whole at the sight of the slightly raised hems exposing ankles and pantalet trimmings.

Never accurately calculating the discomfort of layers and layers and bustles and corsets, I longed to return to the belle époque of such well-trussed styles. Certainly a hoop skirt would hide anything "a bit hefty above the knees" as well as below them. And those nifty lace-up short boots! No need to worry about my rather cow-like calves not fitting into zip-up knee boots. I'd be the height of style and in high heels!

But in this film the object was to move out of, or beyond, these charming garments. There was something totally hysterical about even slightly naked bodies in this film's perplexing plot. Under normal circumstances, as far as I could tell, bodies looked nice when nicely clothed, like in a TV commercial, or at the grocery store, or when they were displayed fully *un*clothed, in which case they were *niiiiiiiiiiice*. I got that much.

Female skin got the biggest laughs. Men's collars popped, brows shot up, steam tooted from their ears – all for less leg than was usually exposed beneath the average high-school girl's kilt. (That was legislated, where Suzanne went to school, to be no more than five inches above the knee when the subject knelt on the floor. One might wonder if *he who measured* experienced a similar hot throbbing of the eyeballs upon discovering the gap from linoleum to hem was five and three quarter inches or more.)

This movie had a lot of music in it. The kind without words but lots of humming and a few "la-la's." There was nothing good, like The Fifth Dimension or Glen Campbell. The main girl in the movie was always taking part in some sort of dance show. She never wore a tutu or a flowing dress and never danced in a circle of pretty ladies, or with a man in a black suit, like in other movies I had seen. In fact, she hardly danced. She just kind of walked around the stage like she might slip at any moment. My mother said this style was called The Bump and Grind.

"Why is she wiggling like that?" I whispered as the lady wobbled her shoulders and hips in opposite directions while moving her hands up and down her sides.

"Her girdle is too tight," my mother told me. "She's trying to sort it out."

The only thing that looked to be "sorted out" was the lady's enormous bosom, which was in danger of escaping her very low-cut dress at any second.

There was some sport in this. Images of the audience, on the screen and in the car, included daft grins, bemused shock, and gobsmacked wonder. Almost the same as when Bobby Hull scored a goal on *Hockey Night in Canada*. Right down to the same sort of hoots and calls.

A dry "whoopee-do" was all I could muster. And though it was more contained and quiet than the "oh yeahs" and "woo-hoos" I was in the midst of, I got shushed anyway with an added "Just shut up. Just 'cause you don't get it doesn't mean the rest of us can't enjoy it."

No sooner was this said than something so astonishing occurred on-screen that nothing short of electric happiness erupted in the car. It was only a half-second flash of wide-screen naked boobies, but it brought about a full four solid minutes of cheers and gestures. I'd seen the breasts, but missed their impact. I was sure I'd missed something – whatever shot on goal that brought about the storm of ear-ringing adulation. Not wishing to admit I was lost, I joined in.

"Money see, monkey do," Mom always liked to say when anyone did anything on the stupid side. Like when you might race after someone who cannonballed off the rocky side of the dock, and you both cut your foot one after the other. Good little monkey that I was, I added my own jeers and slobbering whistles. Even though I couldn't whistle. I stuck two fingers between my lips, squeaked, and spewed saliva all over Buck's shoulder. Naturally he turned around and smacked my hand into my face. My lip was nicked by my tooth, but my mother was totally unsympathetic as I bled all over the place.

Mom rolled her eyes and found an only slightly messed up tissue in her purse and handed it to me. "Be quiet, and wipe your mouth. You have a spot of blood on it," she said, and she tapped on the corner of her own mouth to indicate the source of the flow. I must have been in a weakened state because I applied pressure at the opposite side.

"Buck hit me," I whined, as if she hadn't seen so herself, since she was sitting right there beside me all along.

"Well, if you would behave yourself and not imitate your brothers like a nasty little monkey, then you wouldn't have spit all over him, and he wouldn't have reacted like that." How I could be so obtuse on so many levels was beyond her comprehension. She sighed and grabbed the tissue back. She wet it with a little ball of spit from her tongue and "cleaned" my face by smearing cigarette-flavored saliva all over it.

After the car ran out of enough oxygen to keep up the cheering, there was a short pause, then James said with airy satisfaction, "Wow, that was a woo-ee tickler."

I didn't even think about saying anything. And I tried not to think about anything either, especially anybody's woo-ee.

✶ ✶ ✶

Within the week, while Dad was still around, a Grown-ups Only night took place at Uncle Don's Cottage. Uncle Don was there, with a different girlfriend this time, a considerably more domestic model, who was keen on putting on a supper party. Cocktails at six. R.S.V.P. She wrote invitations on pretty paper and handed them out on the beach one afternoon.

"What on earth am I supposed to do with this lot for an evening?" our mother complained to Don's girlfriend – Mimi? Loulou? Something you said twice – as if she had a lot of nerve asking Mom to come up with a solution on her own. She'd left us alone before, but not past sundown (when the bears came out, she thought).

"Well…" said Double-Name Dame, "your oldest son looks very responsible." Mom and Double both paused and looked at Buck, who was studiously picking his toenails. "And you'd just be a few steps away," she added. "It's not like they could get into any trouble."

"You'd be surprised," Mom said. But the thought of dressing, eating, and speaking like an adult was just too great a temptation not to risk whatever disaster we, or the bears, could invent.

So under Buck's authority, Kieffer, James, and I were

left alone in the cottage under strict instructions not to step foot outside for any reason. Such a directive was probably to ensure we didn't go anywhere near the lake and drown ourselves and ruin the dinner party. But for emphasis, Mom provided modified urban legends of things that ate young people who ventured out after dusk. Something worse than bears: limbo-locked, un-dead hunters who roamed the dark shadows and filled anything that moved with poisoned shot.

I was not happy to be in Buck's charge, but I was sure as anything I was not going to go outside for any reason.

We ate dinner at five o'clock from paper plates, so there were no dishes to wash. The rules were reviewed, Buck's authority reaffirmed, and bedtimes declared. I felt a little woozy because it seemed like a very long time before Mom and Dad were coming back. It felt a little like they were never coming back.

My lip quivered a bit when they walked out the door. I fought back tears. I didn't want to hear how I was over dramatizing and faking to get attention. Pleased with her purse and perfume and strappy sandals, Mom assured me, "Your day will come." Only it wasn't going out and smelling nice I was jealous of. I was simply scared about staying in with the pee smell, burps, and farts so dear to the boys' hearts, and how they might impose their thrills on me.

I kept to myself, drawing and coloring pictures. The boys read comic books and thankfully ignored me. After a while, Buck told me to brush my teeth and go get ready for bed. I wasn't sure he was honestly telling me the right time, but I was a bit bored and out of sorts. An uncommon longing to be with my parents was making me feel a little insecure, though

I didn't really want to be with a bunch of boring, smoking grown-ups who just talked and talked and told me to be seen and not heard. I just didn't want to be where I was. Alone. With my brothers.

After I brushed my teeth and washed my face with a slightly mildewy cloth, I went to my room to put on my pj's. Buck was sitting on my bed holding them. "You have to get ready for bed," he told me. I reached for my pj's, but Buck smacked my hand away. Hard.

"Hey that hurt!" I shouted.

"You *have* to get ready for bed!" Buck shouted back, louder.

Intimidated, I stepped back and tried to figure out what was wrong with this picture. I was doing what I was told. I was inside and behaving myself, and I had really, actually brushed my teeth, not just wet the toothbrush and *said* I did. But something was off. The smell of the mildew was sour on my face. I just wanted my mom and my pj's.

"Now!" Buck barked so loud I jumped.

That brought Kieffer and James running in, grinning, wondering what trouble I was in and how much fun could be had with it.

"I need my pj's," I said contritely, venturing a weakly pointed finger in their direction.

"What are you going to do, put them on over your clothes, stupid?"

My stomach turned and I felt like *yes* was the right answer. But I wasn't stupid. I knew the *expected* answer was no. So that's what I said, "No."

"So take your bloody clothes off, dunderhead." Buck

groaned, tormented by the heavy responsibility of having to tell his brainless little sister every little obvious thing.

Whether I knew I was or wasn't an idiot didn't matter. What mattered was that I wanted to look smart, to look like I was getting along. Because otherwise, there would be hell to pay. Even if I didn't understand the metaphor, I understood the inescapable unpleasantness of Buck reporting that I had been nothing but a pain: It would mean the unrestrained application of pain to my backside.

I thought of the frogs I'd set free and envied them their freedom.

I turned my back to my gawking brotherly audience and slowly, awkwardly started to pull off my clothes.

But another very strange thing happened. Buck, Kieffer, and James encouraged me. They cheered me on. They took turns imitating some line or phrase of bellowing horn music, badly, of course. I could not help but find their attention kind of funny, kind of a game. Their musical efforts were very funny, and I improvised moving my arms and legs to the rolling, cacophonous notes. It didn't take much for me to become slap-happy with their jeers and cheers. I was soon waving my shirt above my head and throwing it in the air. My skirt and underpants came off in one piece, and I gave my impression of the Bump and Grind like that lady had done in the movie. I pretty much brought the house down with (what I thought were) my extraordinary interpretive dance and imitation skills. Surely now my condescending, easily annoyed brothers could see my brilliance and sophistication. I was a dancer, and a talented one, and they hooted their amazement.

So enthralled was I, that I failed to notice the simultaneous game of "pocket pool" that accompanied my artistic display. Perhaps it was this preoccupation of hands that delayed the thunderous applause I was anticipating. Or perhaps they just wanted more.

Buck tossed my pj's on the floor at my feet and rose to leave. Kieffer and James moved to follow.

But it didn't have to be over. "That was the getting undressed show. Now I'll do the *getting dressed* show!" I announced, truly believing it would be equally joyously received.

Of course it was not.

"Who gives a shit about that?"

I sat down on the floor, made myself as small as possible, and pulled on my pj's.

In the next room the boys laughed themselves silly over my dance. They crashed around and stomped their feet mimicking my ungainly motions. My performance was reviewed using such anatomical terms as *asshole* and *cunt*. I was declared tit-less and useless and lard-laden. I was incredibly funny.

So funny I forgot to laugh.

Holding my breath against the sobs that cut it short, I slipped into bed and pulled the blankets in tight around me and over my head. And I put the pillow over my head. It smelled stale and damp and the sheets were worn and sandy, but it was better than whatever was outside that was so horrible I couldn't understand it. Not outside the cottage, where I was told it would be, but outside the bedclothes where I ended, and everything else in the whole world began.

FIFTEEN

Inside Out

MEANWHILE, BACK in the suburbs, our split-level home was sliding slowly, insidiously off balance from the inside out.

"Were you born on a raft?" you were asked if you left the door open.

(Presumably the lonely mariner whose lot in life confined him to the single plane of a raft, his view unmarred by doors or other upright structures, would be ignorant of the fact that doors were meant to be closed, unless one was passing through them.)

We may as well have been born and entirely reared on the wide-open sea for the way we learned to weave and lean with the swell and tow. We tumbled through openings. We slid offside through the front door on the way to school in the morning, skidded through again for lunch, and then later, finally landed on deck at supper hour.

There was always a storm brewing on the horizon. Our hatches, unhinged and unlocked, flew open and shut, this way and that, and all the contents and reason spilled up and over. Up and over the side. Heave-ho, and over he goes. Man, woman, and child overboard. Out of the frying pan, into the fire.

What will we do with a drunken sailor?
What will we do with a drunken sailor?
What will we do with a drunken sailor
Ur-lye in the morning?
Put him in the brig until he's sober,
Put him in the brig until he's sober,
Put him in the brig until he's sober,
Ur-lye in the morning.

The house on Dewmist Crescent was without a brig. I think I would have loved solitary confinement. In the General Population we just hobbled about on sea legs, punch-drunk and seasick. We might have considered a mutiny had we the bounty of intelligence required to feed the fire to burn the captain. But there was no captain. It was every soul for himself, and, like scurvy dogs, we bled and oozed. Our thinly stretched skin ruptured. We hungered and thirsted and yearned for stable land and fair weather, a little relief from the gale forces.

"You're not sugar. You won't melt," our mother insisted if any of us had the temerity to ask for a drive to school in bad weather.

I tried to argue that her statement was, at least for my Little Girl self, not entirely true. Modern poetic science had revealed that sugar was not on the list of *Little Boy* ingredients. That was limited to "snakes and snails and puppy dog tails," whereas "sugar and spice and everything nice" was what *Little Girls* were made of. Mother's response to this brilliant argument was: "Well, I never got a drive to school when I was growing up. I walked, no matter what the weather…." And then she went on and on about the long and wearisome Quebec City winters that lasted fourteen out of twelve months a year and were too rough for Scott of the Antarctic to endure, and it was a wonder they weren't all eaten by polar bears.

That was the end of that. My brothers and I put on our raincoats, rubbers, boots, or snow pants. I put up my clear bubble umbrella until I broke it (probably in a fencing match), and off we went into monsoon, mudslide, or avalanche, our mother closing the door behind us. One could say slamming it.

We knew precious little of what happened behind other front doors. Front doors lined the streets and neighborhood, green or gray or black or white, with mail slots and boxes. Sometimes for holidays there were wreathes with bows and baskets with bows to collect parcels. Doors were dressed for seasons and swung back and forth flashing bright, sparkling glimpses of the life stoppered by them.

It stood to basic reason that there were families and dogs and furniture and roasts of beef on Sundays and cereal in the morning, running water, soap, and laundry in the basement, and junk in the garage. Everybody had a hockey net. And a car. Usually two. Everybody had children – three or four, though five was not uncommon. Six was the cutoff of respectability: any more and my mother shook her head and said, "Well they're either Catholic or careless."

Catholic was what the kids were who went to St. Clements Separate School. It was so separate, it was in a totally different building on a totally different street than the normal, regular school, where I and the other normal, regular kids went. I understood that to be Catholic was to be *ir*regular. But with my Good Anglican Sunday school understanding, I knew I was obliged to feel sorry for them. Probably they were a few bricks short of a load and disinclined to paddle their own canoes. And if my mother was right, they were a tad on the disorganized side and couldn't keep track of their children. Superfluous offspring just sort of spontaneously infiltrated their homes, and they were powerless to stem the flow. Perhaps their front doors were faulty.

Other than that, they had fish on Friday and Christmas lights, just like the rest of the normal people. And the only actual, real-live Catholic kid I knew had a swimming pool in her backyard. Given that circumstance, I was committed to being the best Samaritan ever. I considered her my Best Friend Ever – in hot weather.

The rest of the time I had other Best Friends Ever – when I could persuade one to ask me over to her place after school. Generally this worked only once per child. So overbearing and overwhelming was my little personality that I plowed through best friends like a hot knife through butter. My vision blurred by an implacable silver lining, I mistook this process as my being so popular that I was perpetually adding Best Friends Ever to my roster. It was years before one harshly honest child informed me that any child who took the time to know me encountered no difficulty whatsoever in disliking me. Actually, it was more along the lines of "Everybody hates you." And *she* was the fat kid that everybody picked on, who smelled like dirty feet and garlic.

Obviously, she hadn't a clue what she was talking about.

I renewed my vow to fill my stable with Best Friends Ever, blinders on and furiously ignorant of how being my buddy was merely a turnstile through which I stuffed and dragged every unsuspecting, malleable girl my age in order to enhance my self-esteem.

I wasn't a single-purpose mercenary. Even if I couldn't fit myself into a friendship, I was determined to wedge my way into other kids' houses. I was fascinated by their un-mangled toys, by the way their mothers brought juice and cookies on a tray for a snack, by the quiet, middle-of-the-road music on the radio, by their console television sets. It was a strange and trippy sort of obscured reality, something like what I imagined being high on drugs might be like.

These children were living in a dream world. Their rooms were tidy, their beds were made, and their siblings had no interest in us. They peacefully ignored us! They had unscented, sedate dogs. They had bright, white teeth and resplendently combed hair, neatly styled with ribbons that matched their outfits. Their socks matched! Not just one another but also the stripes or spots in their blouses! They wore pants! Proper ones with belts and pockets. They took music lessons, or dance lessons and had costumes we could put on. If not, they had a trunk of dress-up, discarded adult party clothes with hats and gloves and sequins.

And perhaps they had their own motivations, but at the end of the playtime (after I had asked for extra sugar for the tea and spilled it on the carpet, split the seams of the tutu I insisted was not too small for me, and annoyed the dog until it peed), one parent or another always drove me home. Even when there wasn't a drop of rain.

Once it was Andrea's dad who drove a blue two-seater sports car. He also had a beard. I got a spanking because my mother reckoned only secret agents and child molesters drove such automobiles, and Andrea's dad had to be the latter because no self-respecting international spy ever wore a beard unless he was *posing* as a child molester.

She pulled me though the front door before she gave me a hard shake and a volley of wallops to the behind. There was no need to alert the neighbors to the fact I deserved a good spanking. That's what closed doors were for.

These were rough times. Squalls between our parents tore up our days and nights and pelted us with toxic spray. We spent much time below ground, in the rec room, in the safe harbor of the television. We escaped, when we could, to other kids' houses, the school grounds, and the park. We returned just as the streetlights came on, as slowly as possible. And when we did, we habitually left doors open, maybe to let a little light in, maybe to let the smoke and dust clear a little. A last ditch rescue. We left doors open in vain hopes of pumping oxygen into our stifled home. Trying to spark more life, less fire. Out with the bad air, in with the good.

The forces that brought this about, while natural, were out of any sort of order. Not serendipitous, like snow in June, or finding money on the sidewalk. These forces were occult, unnerving, like a total eclipse of the noonday sun, or a flash flood.

* * *

Proof was in the pudding, as they say, or more literally, in the cold soup: Vichyssoise.

Our mother had surely gone mad. "It's an appetizer," she explained. "Your father and I enjoyed it at The Club."

The Club was what passed for a golf and country club in our little pre-planned community. It was sort of a TV dinner version of a country club. There were elements of the real deal, but they were sort of over-processed and starchy. There was a golf course and probably a locker room. And a dining room that served mostly the same things everyone made at home, but with way fancier names. Everything was served on a white tablecloth you didn't have to iron yourself.

Father didn't play golf. Mother wouldn't be caught dead doing so. But from time to time Auntie Lil had them as guests for some "occasion," the nature of which was immaterial. The drinks were free. For that they could cheerfully ignore any feted event or individual.

This was the first time, since The Lemon Meringue Incident, that Mother had taken an active interest in anything to do with cooking. This was totally from another planet. For sure she had some brain disease brought back from the moon by the Apollo 11.

"It's cold," one of us complained, while the rest of us regarded the chopped green things floating on top. "It's *chilled*," mother corrected, "and those are chives." She slapped the back of my hand to get me to stop trying to drown them with my spoon. Not that I was the only one, but I was easiest to reach, being stuck in the most undesirable seat at the table.

For all of the past that I could remember, probably since time began, my brothers and I rotated weekly through the side chairs of the table while our parents remained stationary at either end. Like all good satellites, we had purpose as we circled. Chair One put out the cutlery, Chair Two got serviettes, Chair Three was "on vacation," and Chair Four, the most burdened chair, was the server-clearer. But for shouldering the weighty yolk of that horrendous seat, Chair Four got seconds on dessert. Always. Even if you picked at your Vichyssoise.

Then came The New Deal: a more complex division of labor based on gender-assessed talents and fixed future potential. Seating was assigned on social-historical tradition as informed by current philosophical and political climates. Buck, the First Born, was seated to our Father's right, Man Junior of the house. Kieffer, the Spare Heir, was seated to Buck's right. James, needing a heavy hand to keep him seated and eating his vegetables, was placed to Father's left. I, at my mother's right, having two X chromosomes and presumably all the joy in the world for "woman's work," was loaded and locked on the server-clearer's thankless spot. I was Little Mother, the dedicated helper. I could like it or lump it, but I was strongly advised to like it, because it was my lot in life. Even a Career Girl was genetically determined to minister to the cleanliness, godliness, and feeding of the manly men of her life.

The boys, so as not to become weak, oily Mama's boys, would assume the masculine tasks of the house: shoveling the driveway, mowing the lawn, and re-staining the raft (the one at the cottage, not the one we were supposedly born on).

Trouble was, these *boy jobs* were reduced by season and divided by three, while the one of me was stuck day in and day out with the endless grind of servile drudgery.

Such calculations were not addressed in The New Math, or recognized by The New Deal.

The Second Dessert Rule was abolished. There was no getting away from the Vichyssoise. Or the stewed tomatoes.

The boys were all "on vacation" all the time.

Split. Level. Oxy…

…moron.

That was me….

SIXTEEN

Pony Express

MY CUP RUNNETH OVER with joy! As Cottage Time loomed large on my horizon, it was with great rapture I learned that the riding stables near Go Home Lake had burnt to the ground.

This was to be the Summer of Dreams Come True.

With the barn reduced to a smoldering heap of charcoal, the horses were left out in the cold, so to speak. The proprietors and hired hands had enough to worry about, trying to clear the mess and raise a new barn without attempting to contain a bunch of skittish horses too. Most were distributed to local farms. The Clydesdales were kept under big army surplus tents on the grounds to help with the work. Only a limited amount of pestering persuaded Dad to volunteer to take a pony for a few weeks.

My heart nearly burst.

There was no dealing with me. I walked on air. I laughed spontaneously. I dug out that old white hat, jammed it on my head, and refused to take it off.

"Mom, how come we have to take off our hats at dinner and she doesn't?" one of the boys asked resentfully. It was bad enough I was getting a pony. Did I have to get everything I wanted?

Why, now that you mention it, yes...

"Because a lady need never remove her hat, unless asked, very politely, to do so in the theater."

This made no sense to anyone. Not to me, because I was a cowboy. Not to the boys, because I was no lady. I was not really human to them. I was a snot-nosed sister.

When the pony arrived, I was radiant with happiness. The pony was white. Her name was Flash. I wanted to ride her immediately.

Uhhh, hold on a minute there, pardner. "Where's the saddle?"

"A saddle costs a lot of money," the hand from the stables said, "I ain't leaving one with you. If you want to ride her, you can ride her bareback."

There was, however, a bridle. I knew how to steer. But the problem of how to mount her remained. I was too big for Mom to lift. The boys tried to give me a boost, but gave up quickly when Flash kept moving and I kept falling flat on my face and crying with frustration, thereby proving once and for all that I was a snot-nosed moron sister and no lady. I tried leading the horse into the water next to the dock so I could climb down on her rather than climb up her side, but she wouldn't have any part of that. She could be persuaded to stand by a tree stump that was a bit too short, which almost worked, until I pulled on her mane one too many times and she lost patience and galloped away. Not far. But far enough that I was forced to concede.

Flash won the battle that day, but not the war.

I was nothing if not determined. For days on end I employed every tactic and enterprise that I could come up with, showing inventiveness and creativity well beyond my years. I used positive reinforcement, apples and carrots, and negative reinforcement, yanking her mane or slapping her neck so that she whinnied and reared her head in annoyance. I thought pony-like thoughts, begged and cajoled her, all to no avail.

Over the course of the summer that followed, with patience, hard work, and understanding, I learned to hate that pony.

At least I was not alone. Flash managed to get everyone's knickers in a knot.

Mom hated her in principle and in theory. The pony was one more animal for her to pick up after, the same as me and my brothers. Auntie Lil hated the pony due to the alarming propensity with which she discovered, invariably by stepping in them, "horse dumps" all over the place. The boys hated the pony because I was so unbearable about it, and Timmy hated it because even when *I* hated it, I still liked the pony better than I liked him.

Not feeling the warm tide of unconditional love flowing her way, Flash took to hightailing it out of there every opportunity she got.

Brian, Suzanne's boyfriend, went to get her once or twice, attaching her by rope to the back bumper of whatever he was driving at the time and towing her back at about two miles an hour, while Suzanne rode up on the hood for fun. The boys were sent for her when she went astray at Rover's place, though I guess it was safe to go there if you didn't have wheels. And any number of times Flash made her way quite far down the road to make time with a lonely Appaloosa kept by a widowed farmer.

"The damned thing must be in heat!" Mom exclaimed in exasperation after the third or fourth time we fetched her from there.

I'd never heard the term. Fearing it meant she was sick, I asked, "What is it? Can it be cured?"

"It's an itch between the two big toes," Mom said coyly. "It can only be fixed by another horse."

Clearly Mom knew nothing about horses. They didn't have toes of any size.

The sense of urgency with which someone was dispatched to retrieve Flash diminished quickly. It was difficult to catch a hot-to-trot pony.

Now that my brothers and I were perfectly capable of fending for ourselves, according to our mother's standards – we were all over three years of age; there was no one sitting on our chest; no one on the bay had a piano so we couldn't possibly have one tied to our right arm; and none of us believed in the Jolly Green Giant, so there was no chance of him chasing us down the street – we were left alone to do so more and more often.

Mother and Auntie Lil were on better terms than in the past. All of Lil's kids were pretty much grown, including our beloved Suzanne. She was around the cottage a lot, still often with Brian on her arm. And he sometimes brought one friend or another along. I yearned to spend time in their company.

I would have given my right arm to be *their* little sister. And I put a lot of time and energy into imagining fantastic scenarios that could have made that happen. Like maybe an angry bear would break into the cottage and do in my entire immediate family. Less angry with a nearly full belly now, but still itching for a little taste of "afters," the bear would then consume anyone over twenty at Auntie Lil's. I would manage to escape somehow, riding away on Flash, who would have magically sprouted a saddle and bridle for the event. And even if she didn't, she would be my Only Hope, and she would not let me down. It was against her nature.

Fact: every horse, no matter how distracted by itches, can always make its way back home. I needed only to tie myself to Flash's back in order not to drop off from exhaustion and hunger by the time I reached Suzanne's. Not Auntie Lil's cottage across the way. That was filled with gnawed-on cousins, aunts and uncles, and a belching bear. The pony would take me home to *Toronto*, to Suzanne's doorstep, about a half-mile from my own urban abode. I would find the pony in the fray and mount her. Flash would do the rest.

Thank goodness, because I had less than no clue. Turn left or right at the top of the hill on the bumpy road? I couldn't tell you any more than it would be a harrowing journey.

I would arrive eventually, all wrung out, looking and feeling quite Catherine-esque in a Victorian lace nightgown, my flowing chestnut tresses brushed out in waves over my lace-trimmed collar, my pale complexion whipped into rose-milk perfection from riding Flash across the moors (because they couldn't let a pony on highway 401), Brian looking as anxious as the tortured Heathcliff and Suzanne bursting into tears of joy to see I was alive…praise be to God! ALIVE!

Even at the time I knew that would never work. But not because Flash, if she actually could find her way home, would go to *her* home, the riding stables. And not because there was a dearth of moors in the provincial geography. And certainly not because Suzanne might be too preoccupied with finding herself an orphan at the whim of an angry bear to worry about lowly, and generally annoying, little ol' me.

No, it was a disquieting, amorphous feeling. Something to do with my pissy twat that was so unspeakably grotesque and my naked form, which, if I bent over backwards and extended myself in some way that was the right way whatever that right way was…I could crack the code and bridge the gap from nice to *niiiiiiiiiiiice.*

And the world would beat a path to the door.

It was clear to me, somehow, that was not the kind of beating that would inform my future.

I knew that Brian and Suzanne would have been just as happy to see me dry up and blow away. My only consolation was that they regarded me as only one insignificant pest, equal to all the other pests in a large hive of pests. Hallelujah!

✳ ✳ ✳

When Flash was off seeking therapy for that mysterious itch, I found myself, as usual, testing various ways to stave off boredom. Once I took out the canoe by myself thinking that singing "dip-dip, and swing my paddle, flashing with silver" several times over was a reasonable substitute for actually learning how to pilot such a vessel.

It was not.

It was a windy day and I was short and wide and the canoe was long and narrow. The wind and I were equally stubborn. I jabbed the paddle into the water and tried to push, but all I did was form an effective keel, an axis upon which the wind could spin the canoe in circles. I rose and jabbed again on the other side, giving myself a nice wet smack on the side of my head in the process, and spinning in the opposite direction. Had I not been so aggravated, I probably would have had a lot of fun. But frustration caused me to scream and yell any number of words I knew I wasn't supposed to say. I couldn't figure it out! Did I have a left-handed paddle or something? Was I caught in the tide or the undertow or a whirlpool or something? Did the Bernoulli Principle have me in its evil clutches? It couldn't have been that I was hapless, feckless, and foolish.

But it was.

I was very clearly informed of this fact once pulled back to shore by Brian. He'd been dispatched with a boat with a fifteen-horsepower motor when somebody heard me "screaming." *They* thought I'd been calling for help. *I* thought I'd been swearing like a mule skinner (a close, if vulgar, cousin to the cowboy).

I was confined to my cell for the rest of the week and

forbidden to go out in any boat again, ever, by myself for the rest of my life.

Fine with me.

Landlubbers – that's what cowboys were. And durned proud of it.

SEVENTEEN

Borders and Horizons

"D'Y WANNA PLAY a game?" Buck had a checkerboard under his arm and a bag of pieces. But not checkers – little pointy-knobby black-and-white pieces. Two of them looked like horse heads.

I considered the offer from behind the same *Richie Rich* I had read about a hundred times already. Mom maybe told him to come.

Kieffer and James were off somewhere with pellet guns. I could hear the shot flying and the birds squawking warnings to one another. Little did they know that Kieffer and James were more likely to blind one another by accident than they were to hit something they were shooting at on purpose. Mom was in the main room, knitting – probably eye patches for Kieffer and James. I guessed she was getting tired of

Buck "reading" the *Playboy* magazines piled up on the coffee table. I could hear him unfolding the pages and mumbling "Niiiiiiiiiiice…." It was getting on my nerves too.

"What game?" I glanced at the pieces in the bag. Those horse ones looked pretty good. Maybe it was cowboy checkers.

"Chess," Buck said.

"I don't know how to play that," I said. I went back to *Richie Rich* and waited for Buck to tell me how stupid I was for not knowing how to play chess. But –

"It's easy. I'll teach you," Buck offered.

Now, this was a whole different kettle of fish – a rotten one.

The last time I took instruction from Buck it was on the subject of reading. He was chuckling over the comics from the weekend newspaper, and I wanted him to read them to me.

"Read them yourself," he sneered, because he knew I couldn't.

"*Pleeeeeeease*," I whined. That brought Mom into the conversation.

"*Teach* her how," Mom told Buck. A brilliant move on her part, effectively shutting us both down and keeping us occupied, while she carried on with her rum and Coke and book.

Buck sighed and spread the comics out on the floor. Jethro came over and sniffed at them a bit, thinking they might be good to eat or pee on, but Buck pushed him away. Not before he deposited a giant gob of dog drool on "Family Circus." Too bad. I would have liked to start with that one. It was all about a large-hipped woman and her husband and their several knee-high children. They were cute and round-headed. Buck turned the page and smoothed over the lump of drool. He pointed to "The Wizard of Id." The drawings were simple, and, more to the point, so were the words and lettering.

"What's this letter?" Buck pointed to an *I*.

I told him. Then he pointed to a *T*. "What's that one?"

I correctly identified that one too.

"Now put them together," he said.

"Eye-tee," I named the letters out loud.

"Wrong!" Buck said, like he was the host of a game show and clapped his hands together. "You have to sound them out."

They just don't teach phonics properly in Ontario. I remember being a child in Quebec and standing up reciting the alphabet in class: "*A – ah. B – buh...*" – with irritation our mother recounted the entire alphabet and its various sounds. That our school system was totally lacking was one of her favorite subjects and a handy excuse for our failure to thrive in class. Except Buck, who went as far as grade two in the hallowed halls of the only English primary school of the pre-Quiet Revolution 'hood where we lived. She only ever got as far as *G* when we stopped listening.

But Buck took the hint; "*I* makes an *ih* sound and *T* makes *tuh*. Ih-tuh – it."

"Ih-tuh – it," I repeated after him. He pointed at the letters in the word bubble, and I said it again.

"Right," commended Buck.

I was reading! I was winning! What a thrill!

Buck turned the page to a new selection of comics.

"*Hmmmmm.*" He sounded like a drumroll. He pointed his finger, twirled it in the air, and dropped it with a flourish in another word bubble. "Now read this," he commanded.

I stared at the page at a similar short word. Just sticks again. There were no curly letters. "*Ahhhhhhhh,*" I mumbled, unsure where to start.

"Wrong!" Buck declared instantly and punched me *hard* in the shoulder.

"Hey!" I complained. Mom was only about as far as *P* on the Good ol' Montreal Phonetic Stand-Up Alphabet. She didn't even miss a beat.

"I don't know!" I told Buck and sat up straighter, hopefully out of swinging range. He flipped the page back to the "Wizard of Id" and pointed again at *it*.

"What's this word?"

"Ih-tuh – it," I said again correctly.

"Right." Over went the page again. Buck pointed to the same second word. "Now read this word."

I knew it looked a lot like Ih-tuh-it, but the letters were not exactly the same. The comics were hand drawn, hand lettered. It was a little harder to sort them out because of this.

"One…tuh," I drawled uncertainly.

Punch. A sharp shoulder pain told me I was wrong. "Ouch!" I turned to Mom – who had gone back to her book – and whined, "Buck hit me!"

"Did not!" he countered quickly, looking believably affronted.

"Well if you wouldn't torment him…" she began, confident in the fact that she'd given me the same advice so many times before I could fill in the end myself. I swallowed and turned back to the place where Buck was pointing. I tried squinting. That didn't make it any clearer.

"What's the first letter?" Buck prompted.

It really looked more like a number to me. "One?"

"No!" Buck punched me again. I just scowled. So much for the initial thrill. I wasn't reading at all. I was an –

"Idiot!" Buck shook his head in disgust. "You are an idiot of the first rank." And he punched me one more time to punctuate the fact.

I learned to read at school, never venturing to read for the teacher unless I was forced to, even though the punch-the-shoulder method of reinforcement was not widely used among the primary teachers of our local school board.

By the time grade three rolled around, I had established myself as the most hopeless speller of all time, in any space or time or universe, ever. Bar none. *There is a spelling gene, I swear, and I don't have it.*

I was good at phonics as it was taught in class: a series of neatly packaged vowel and consonant regulations. I committed every one to memory and drew them swiftly out like swords to slice the gurgling heads off the evil Spelling Hydra. And every time I thought I had it beat, out grew another exception to the dithering and flaccid rules of phonics.

Nice girls, with white knee socks and tidy hair, could spell and use a ballpoint pen and write in cursive. I could not be so trusted. I was the only kid in class to leave grade three without the coveted "pen drivers license," a blue construction-paper pseudo-permit taped to the corner of each successful student's desk. Because I couldn't spell.

"If you can *read* you can most certainly *spell*," a school teacher once told me. "You are just not paying attention. You need to pay attention and try harder."

I was mesmerized by the splendid festooning quality of cursive writing, but I was barred from using it because I was doomed to erasure after erasure by my phonetically sound but dictionary unacceptable spelling.

Sometimes I wondered if I really could read. And then my arm hurt just thinking about it.

Remembering Buck's first pedagogical enterprise made me leery.

"No. I don't want to play chest," I decided.

"Oh, c'mon. And it's chess, anyway. Not chest. Nobody wants to play with *your* chest."

Fine with me. The more of my person left out of any game the better, including my tender, punchable arms. I felt a strong attraction to the horse-shaped pieces. What could go wrong with horses in the game?

"Maybe I will. Maybe I won't," I said, then added, "Not if you're going to hit me."

"I'm not going to hit you…" Buck sighed. Like I was a total dunderhead for even thinking such a thing. "In fact," he offered, "I'll teach you how to play, and if you win, I'll do whatever you want."

"Like take me skating?" I asked excitedly.

"Sure. Right. If the lake freezes over all of a sudden. It's summer. Get a grip."

So, if I couldn't exert my will on an actual, living, stubborn equine creature that seemed to deeply comprehend my cowboy dreams and do everything in its power to thwart them, I had to be able to direct those little black-and-white horse-head figures.

"Those are called knights," Buck explained. The king and queen, pawns, rooks, and bishops were each identified as were their limited movements on the board. He showed me how to line them up, queen on her color, king beside her, with all the others flanking and protecting their monarchs.

I was a bit shy on historical knowledge. Buck had to employ an eclectic mix of references – Richie Rich to Jason and the Argonauts – to get it in my head that this was a game of yore and war and planning and victory.

Sweet victory, which if obtained, would bring about the more-precious-than-gold prize of power. Power over Buck. Nothing could be finer.

I paid the closest attention possible.

I was keen and paired the pieces with their move patterns almost immediately.

I played my cards as close as possible to my chest. I held back, allowing no twitch or "tell" to betray me. Buck might have thought he was going to play me for a fool, but I would have the last, and most hearty laugh.

Fingers crossed.

I could do this.

By a sunny window in the boys' room we sat at a wobbly card table. An example game was enacted so I could see checks, set-ups, and checkmates, and how the pawns, being idiots of the *first* rank, I surmised, were the first to topple. The queen could go anywhere and topple anyone, but just as in real life, one had to be cautious. To put one's queen in jeopardy was akin to having one's mother fight one's battles for one. Mother Dear may well have been able to box the ears of the local bully, but her success would ensure crushing defeat to any small bit of respect (hers or one's own) that might remain. Die standing, or live on your knees. Any cowboy knew the right choice. Puffed up with bravado, I felt sure I'd never have to make it.

"So you got it, right?" Buck asked me after a careful half hour of instruction.

"Got it," I replied. I was a quick study.

Ready...

"You're sure?"

"I'm sure." I'd be a quick draw.

aim...

"All right," said Buck.

"Okeydokey," I confirmed.

...GO!

Placing one black and one white pawn in a paper bag, Buck shook them up and let me choose. White. A good sign. Didn't good always triumph over evil? I wore a white cowboy hat. I would carry victory away with ease on the erstwhile backs of those horse heads. Those *knights*, I meant. I would have to remember to call them knights so Buck would remember not to hit me.

Game on.

I was sort of perplexed at first. I confused the bishop with the rook and the king and queen with each other. But so long as I kept *fingers on it*, Buck would groan and grunt and shift his eyes and make funny faces to let me know which way I ought to move my piece. More than once I collapsed in giggles and a break in the battle had to be called. Until...

"Check...?" My hands were over the "face" of the bishop so I had to ask on his behalf if his imposing position was correct. Amazing! It was! But what the bishop and I were both blind to, was that it was not just check, but check*mate.*

Well, I'll be durned...just smear my ears with jam and tie me to an anthill. NO, don't really. It's just a cowboy's way of expressing surprise of a pleasant nature.

"Lemmesee now..." Buck pulled in his chin and assessed his king's sorry, cornered bottom. "Yup. You did it. I'm lost. It's checkmate. You are the winner."

I jumped up and did a war whoop and a dance of joy. "I won! I won! IwonIwonIwonIwonIwon!"

"Keep it down to a dull roar in there!" Mother shouted from the main room. I recognized the I've-had-it-up-to-here tone in her voice right away, so I immediately dropped my schtick to a shuffling chant: "You loser. You loser. You loser. You lose. Ha ha ha ha ha. You loser, you lose," which was just as satisfying.

Buck held up his hands in lazy defeat. "Sure. I lost. You won. So I guess you get to pick your prize."

"Really!" I squeaked. I had never even imagined such a fantastical possibility. The notion of choosing from a broader array than a sharp stick in the eye on the one hand to a slap in the face with a wet fish on the other was overwhelming enough. Here I won all the choice in the world. I didn't know how to cope. "I don't know what. I can't think. What do I pick?" I asked breathlessly.

Buck hummed in serious consideration. "Well...the weather's all wrong for skating..." By the way Buck turned his eyes to his own one raised eyebrow, I knew he had a really good choice. "We could go out for a boat ride."

I teetered on the edge of unbridled joy. "I'm not allowed," I reminded him.

"You're not allowed *alone*. But it's okay if somebody takes you."

Ever closer to falling into heaven, I ventured cautiously, prepared to be blown back to cold common dismay. "Will you take me?"

Buck raised both palms upwards. "You won. You get what you want."

Pfizzt. Just for a fraction of a fraction of a second. Electrified. Just enough to cauterize the moment.

One final reserve stilled me. "Really?"

Wide-eyed with wonder, Buck said, "Sure, of course," as if this happened every day and twice on Sundays. "Really."

I whooped like I'd won the whole rodeo and ran down to the water.

EIGHTEEN

Something Wrong with the Water

PINK SKY AT NIGHT: sailor's delight. Pink sky in the morning: sailors take warning. This is what I learned from my father.

Just before a tornado, the sky turns sickly green. This is what I learned from my mother.

* * *

It was a perfect day. A perfect, perfect day. Blue sky all around the world. Not a cloud to be seen, not even one of the fluffy candy-floss ones that most resembled bunnies or unicorns or baby lambs. And there was golden, shining sun: the lemon drop kind. The honey kind. The kind with power and glory in every splendid ray.

Did I run to the dock where the fleet was moored (the

canoe and the plywood rowboat and the KitKat sailboat), or did I glide swiftly and gleefully over a ribbon of sun-shining sunny sun? I don't recall. Did I grab my life jacket and doff my flip-flops as I sped, or did I grow gossamer wings and discard every dank, moldy, and leaden sorrow in my heart to become weightless? Who could say?

But somehow I found myself pressed joyfully against the stern of the sailboat by Buck's push off from the dock, strong and smooth. He adjusted the keel, and we were away.

Oh, I loved the water, loved the lake, loved the bay. I loved how the surface sparkled and dappled and slapped against the sides of the boat sounding a jolly "ha ha ha." The lake spoke in laughter. It looked up at the sky and reflected it back like a giant blue eye, twinkling, sharing the giddy understanding of how I adored it.

The blinding brightness of the afternoon blurred my vision and mottled the scenery with rosy purple spots. I blinked against the light and lightness of the moment. I took deep, cooling breaths of the oxygen rising from fragrant water lilies, the waving green lily pads, from the frogs and the fish and the turtles and from living water itself.

But.

Very soon we slowed. Then more or less stopped.

Buck tugged the sail into place. He tied it off in two places. Scowling officiously, he regarded the mast and the boom with sideways looks.

"Well," he announced. "Looks like there's not enough wind to take the boat around the bay this afternoon."

Big hairy deal. "So use the oar to paddle back and we'll get in the canoe, instead."

Buck's usual bored, stink-eye glare seemed to have returned to his face when I wasn't looking. "You use an *oar* to *row*, stupid. You use a *paddle* to paddle." His tone was just as stinky.

"Oh. Yeah. Right. I knew that," I said with utter confidence. Though I really didn't. It was a wide-ended stick you pushed through the water. Same difference. It wasn't a hockey stick. I knew *that*.

"So if you knew that, then you must also know, Einstein, that there isn't one in the boat. That's a safety law. The provincial pigs could arrest us if they saw we were out here without a paddle. You're supposed to put one in before you go out on the water."

As my brain clambered to discover my way on Buck's implied map of doom, I scanned the sailboat bottom and KitKat floats for anything even faintly oar-shaped. I would have made myself happy with a hockey stick.

Buck shook his head, revolted by the fact his one and only sister was as dumb as a dishrag. "Nice going, forgetting the paddle. We are now up the proverbial creek without a paddle."

I was tempted to challenge him. We were on a bay on Go Home Lake. We were nowhere near a creek. The nearest one was Bird's Creek. And that was only a name – a place where there was only a gas station and a feed co-op. Maybe there wasn't even a creek there. I'd never seen one. Birds for sure, if you counted crows, but never a real-life creek. I knew I was in serious trouble. I didn't dare suggest to Buck he might be mistaken on this one little thing.

Ominously, I looked around at the still lake, the now darkened water. "What are we going to do?"

"Nothing," Buck said. As if nothing was something.

Nothing was pretty serious to me. It was easy for him to say. *He* didn't forget the paddle. He could and would put the blame on me.

I could hear my mother's voice clearly through the throbbing fear in my head. "Well, if you hadn't just run out there without the slightest consideration for anyone but yourself, Buck wouldn't have nearly starved to death, and Brian wouldn't have had to leave his job building hospitals for The Poor People and rescuing kittens from trees to make his way through the whitecaps and ice shards…"

Oh. No. Ohno. Ohnoooooooooo…

"What do you mean nothing? We can't do nothing."

"Double negative!" Buck buzzed in to correct my distressed grammar.

"Wha – pardon?" I was getting seriously worried. And Buck was just talking nonsense.

"Because we *cannot* do *nothing*, then we *must* do *something*."

I didn't get it, but I was willing to agree. "Yes. That's what I say – we have to do something."

"For sure," Buck said. "What do you want to do?"

Since when did anyone ask the little sister of the family what she wanted to do? Since *never*, that's when. The whole uneasy scenario was making me woozy. I felt distinctly green about the gills. "How should I know!" I demanded incredulously.

Calmly, quietly, Buck suggested, "Do you wanna play a game?"

I looked at him blankly.

"To pass the time. Until the breeze comes up again. And we can get back to the dock." He looked about the sky, stuck his finger in his mouth, and held it up to test the prevailing air currents. "Shouldn't take long," he assured me.

"Yeah. Sure. I'll play." I answered, quickly, eager for distraction.

"Let's play *Trivia!*" Buck proposed, right off the top of his head.

Of course, *Trivia*. Why didn't I think of that? Oh yeah... because I had no clue what that was.

So for the second time in a day, I found myself in a parallel dimension in which my eldest brother, Buck, was patiently and quietly explaining how to do something. And absolutely no part of it involved causing me pain when I messed up.

Had Buck been spending some quality time reading up on B. F. Skinner's principles of behavioral therapy? Had Buck been blessed with the understanding that random, positive reinforcement was not only humane but largely effective on Rotten Little Sisters? Mahow expressed distress at the way Buck shoved my head underwater for asking why he didn't swim. Maybe Buck felt bad about that. But was it even possible that Mahow was right and Buck was wrong?

Probably not.

But here I was with Buck up *The Convertible...no The Prevertable...no The Proverbial...*some make-believe creek I couldn't pronounce without a stupid paddle, and it was all my fault.

Mother always said "Take what you get, and be grateful."

Trivia was what I got. So grateful I had to be for the distraction.

It was pretty simple, really, as Buck explained it. One of us was supposed to ask the other one a question about anything at all. Something that we knew, and they didn't. If you got the answer right, you won. If you got it wrong, you lost.

"Easy, right?" Buck asked.

I thought for a second – too much time.

"Easy, right!" Buck demanded again, almost immediately.

"Right," I said.

So at least I got the first question right. Everything else I got wrong. Wrong, wrong, and wrong again. It was all wrong. All that was asked, all that was said, all that was unsaid and understood and unreasonable and unwanted and un un un no no no I don't want to I didn't want to.

No.

Buck went first: "If a plane crashes on the border of France and Germany, where should the survivors be buried?"

Going down in flames. I had nothing. Less than nothing.

"What's the answer?"

"I'm thinking."

"No thinking. Just say the answer."

"Ummmmm…"

"Say it!"

"I think – "

"Don't think. Just answer. Now."

"Well, where was the plane from?"

"Doesn't matter."

"But it all depends, doesn't it?"

"No it doesn't. Don't be stupid. You are just so stupid."

"But – "

"Butts are in cigarettes! Time's up! What's the answer!"

"I don't know."

I didn't know. To the nth degree. No. I felt no. So much no and so much not know, my brain felt turned inside out. And all the bulk and weight and gobs and bricks and shards and slings and arrows and sleet and fire of all I did not know hailed down upon me.

Nature abhors a vacuum. I was literally struck with the knowledge I was one. Struck dumb. Paralyzed. Blood rushed to my head. My eyeballs throbbed. Everything in my vision misted in pink.

Gravity, of course, won. Buck, of course, won.

I didn't know. I did not no.

But Buck won.

Ours is not to wonder why. Ours is but to do or die.

I didn't want to die. So I did.

I did without putting any thought into it. Buck had made it strikingly clear during the question-answer half of the trivia process that thinking was not preferred.

What was preferred was for me to lift my dress and remove my underpants. Had I done any thinking, I for sure would have thought *no*. I don't think I would have wanted to do that. But, no, I know I wouldn't have done it. No. Know. No, I can't forget.

My underpants were soiled and stained and malodorous. They contained a streak of feces, a smear of urine, and the threadbare proclamation "Tuesday" across the front. I don't know what day it was. Probably not Tuesday…

No I did not know what day it was no.

I felt sick and green.

I know I didn't want to.

But, "You have to. I won," Buck reminded me sternly, even though I did not protest.

I could not say "I know," I could not say "I – no!" I could not say not say not say not say

no.

✳ ✳ ✳

I could smell my own dirty twat. But the scent in passing was insufficient for Buck to extract his fairly won prize. I spread my knees and exposed my filthy sty of a body part as directed by the Rules of the Game. Hoyle was never party to this. There was nothing familiar about these procedures. No rules. But I would never look it up. I would never want to remember. I would never want to know. I would regret forever not being able to…NO. I would regret forever being petrified like craggy fossilized driftwood stinking of ancient decay and unfathomable rudeness, the crux of the matter that I could neither see nor comprehend from Buck's pornographically fueled adolescent brain stem. Just spread and comply. Imitating the crux of the tree. The foul, rotting remains of an extinct life.

Buck's hangnail-festered fingers, one or two at a time, were dragged and scratched, over the hairless pink skin of my flattened vulva. The unresponsive clitoris was clipped by his raggedy, black fingernails. The rise of the smell of my unwashed nether regions.

It's not like it hurt. It was like something else. Something I didn't know. Something…no.

Buck hit me in the face. That hurt. James smacked my head with a hockey stick. My ear bled. That hurt. Kieffer gave me an Indian sunburn because he got mad when I ate the last caramel in the jar, and that hurt that hurt that hurt so much.

Not the insipid weight of Buck's dehydrated calloused finger pads skidding across unnamed anatomy, piquing tissues that were ignorant of their purpose. Drawing nothing painful, but the antithesis of pleasure. The vocabulary would not for many weeks and months and years spike upon the word *rebarbative.*

I just knew no. No. NO.

"Whee!" Buck exclaimed, intoning the voice of a fairy tale gnome, one gone violently insane. "Whee!" every time he slid his despoiled digits back to front over the friable reluctant skin interrupted by orifices yet to be fathomed by the girl child that I was. I knew poo came out of a bum hole, and pee came out the front. Anybody knew that. You didn't talk about that. I didn't know what that other hole was for. Nobody talked about what that might be. Its purpose had to be repellant, disgusting. Incomprehensible.

"Whee!"

Why did he smile so sideways?

"Whee!"

"Your face is so screwed up," Buck felt compelled to remark. "If the wind changes, your ugly face will stay that way."

if the wind changes, I am released
I know but

"Whee!" Just – I – no. Just no. I don't know what it all is supposed to mean but no. NO. I know it's NO.

*My face remained unchanged, fixed permanently in defeated
disgust. Had I been beautiful once it was fleeting and fled, hur-
ried and harried by*
"Whee!"
now textured by gore and revulsion
"Whee!"
I would be ugly forever
"Whee!"
At some point there was a game that was played and
won and lost. At some point there was lost a game that was
not understood. At some point the point was dulled beyond
comprehension, and at some point before it all unfolded, I
had the chance to redeem myself with just an oar, a paddle….
dip-dip, and swing my paddle, flashing with silver
"Whee!"
"no"
I found a fragment of my voice. I know, late for no.
"Wh – "
"Nnn"
"eee"
"NO"

The wind changed.
Buck put up the sail. I pulled up my underpants. The
boat returned to the dock. I was in it. I was gone. Something
was missing. I didn't know what. But the NO lingered, effer-
vescent and endlessly looping like the undersea earthquake
followed by the tsunami followed by the cholera followed by

drought followed by famine, internal squabbling, and a complete breakdown of all known order....

No, I know that's too much.

But, at the time, it was so much.

NINETEEN

Trouble on the Horizon

FLASH.

Marcy, one of Auntie Lil's daughters, brought her boyfriend to the cottage. We were invited to address him as Uncle Mo-Mo.

It crossed my mind to ask if this was because he mo'd his pillow – and what was that all about anyway? But I'd learned the hard way to repress such curiosities. Questions asked and answered tended toward the vile and the humiliating.

I wanted neither. There was already an overabundance.

Flash.

I renewed my devotion to my pony. The riding-tall-in-the-saddle I'd dreamed of was yet to take form, but I could still brush her and stroke her nose and talk to her.

Flash. She was a good listener. She listened to me say all the nothing I had stored up.

Flash. Not only the name of my pony but also an apt description of how my brain was operating. A carousel of images, dark and bright, pungent and acid, were thrown up behind my retina. Where no one else could see. Where I could not help but see.

I grimaced involuntarily.

I was constantly being told, "If the wind changes – "

I KNOW!

Flash. If I could get on the pony and ride her, I would ride into the wind and change everything.

Marcy was quite smitten by the pony. She was a part-time model and had legs "clear up to her armpits" the adults liked to say. So with little effort she straddled Flash and, with no effort at all, attracted every soul with a camera within a three-mile radius. Even my mother, who had long ago declared her hatred of "that everlastingly shitting beast," came into the sun and the radiance of Marcy's smile to snap a photo on her Instamatic.

Uncle Mo-Mo charmed Flash into taking her bit and bridle. And, romantically enough, he held it as he led pony and princess-like Marcy about the shore and through the meadows near the cottages.

Flash. I tried to memorize that pretty image to play among the hideous ones.

When Uncle Mo-Mo returned Flash to me, he helped Marcy down, then lifted me high in the air and set me on the pony's back. He slid the reins into my limp hands and said cheerfully, "Your turn now."

I sat tall in the *prevertable* saddle. Just sat there.

"Are you afraid of the little horsie?" Uncle Mo-Mo asked.

"Wha – pardon?"

"You want me to help you down?"

I checked my face. I was sure I looked happy. "No," I said. *Flash.* I think I flinched. My legs were spread. But I checked; they were over the pony's back. I smoothed my dress and made sure my underwear didn't show.

Waiting a moment more in case anyone wanted to take my picture (no one did), I made that clucking noise cowboys make before saying "giddy-up" and pulled the reins taut. Flash began an easy walk.

Away on a pony…not fast, not laughing. But away on a pony.

The summer Flash came, Dad seemed to stay away more. For all the commotion concerning pony retrieval operations, being banned from watercrafts, the flash tics I could not quite hold steady, I hardly noticed. Weekends came and went, unmarked by his visits. The goods and chattels once bound to his presence were sourced by other methods. Mother had her own car.

We still had enough sterilized milk, margarine, and canned and frozen goods to support a small, hungry nation for years on end. And it's not like we'd eat a fresh vegetable without a gun held to our heads. But the occasional trip to the general store was required to replenish the supply of hot-dog buns, hamburger buns, and white bread. Seems we didn't need Dad for necessities – just the car. And a little cash.

Until that summer, I had not put a lot of thought into money. It was something that was offered up to buy things: gas and coffee and licorice whips, if you were lucky. As far as I knew, it just magically sloughed off the linings of men's pants pockets. Once, Les Sutherland gave me five cents and a wink "just because." Les was about two hundred years old and wore false teeth that rattled. He may as well have given away all his nickels. All you could buy for five cents was a pile of black balls. Les's rattly plates could never cope with that.

So, without Dad's pockets being mined on regular weekend rotation, we had to find another source of cash. That was the bank in town.

A small-town tour was planned. The itinerary was simple. Hit the bank, get some cash, prowl around Stedmans, get a few groceries at the IGA, and wind it all up with milkshakes and floats at the Kawartha Dairy.

We all piled into Mom's car and didn't even fight that much. Buck sat up front in the auxiliary adult role, gaseous with self-importance. I sat in the back between Kieffer and James, who were just the normal kind of gaseous and overwhelmed by the hilarious sounds and smells their bums could make.

But it was better than being pressed up next to Buck — even when we closed the windows to avoid choking on the dust we stirred up as we drove over the old gravel road that led to the highway. Mom was humming at the wheel. We sang "Up and Down the Bumpy Road," a brilliant ditty of our own creation sung to the tune of "London Bridge." Rover made an appearance. He snarled and snapped at us as we passed. I twitched a little, but not as much as in the past. God was in the bright church on the hill, and all was right with the world. We slowed a little when we passed the burnt-out riding stables. We *admired* the progress they were making on the new buildings. It made me think that the summer and Flash would come to an end pretty soon. But I wasn't sad. The summer hadn't turned out the way I had hoped. And I hoped the flash-tic problem might just be choked out in the winter freeze.

In town, the joint was jumpin'. Everybody and their pet pig and the quaintly dressed Mennonites were there.

It was a challenge to find a parking spot, but Mom managed to get something not far from the front doors of the dairy. Mecca. Knowing that was the end of the road, we willingly walked the four blocks to the bank.

Past the giant, heavy front doors, the inside of the bank was cool and dark green. Like an arboreal forest but with long, high counters. James and I fiddled with the pens on chains at the counter. Kieffer pretended to be absorbed in the contents of pamphlets on mortgage rates and how to apply for a car loan. Buck availed himself of one of the comfy chairs that banks always seem to have for no definable reason. Mom filled out her little withdrawal slip and trotted off to the teller.

"Lemme see that – " James grabbed the pen I was playing with and tried to knot up it up by the chain with the other one he already had in his hand.

"You look with your eyes, not your fingers," I reminded him sourly. He ignored me, of course. I didn't care. I ambled around the island of counter on which the pens were tethered and considered whether a root beer float or a strawberry shake was more appealing. Root beer was more cowboy-like.

But strawberry ice cream was just –

Mom was yelling at the teller. She yelled all the time at kids, extra at her own, and sometimes at Dad. She didn't generally yell at other grown-ups. The teller was kind of young-looking, kind of kid-like, so maybe it was just a reflex.

Still, something was wrong. Bad, maybe. Buck and Kieffer had stopped and were watching her ream out the young man in his little wicket. Even James paused, broken pen chains waving in his hands, and listened. She was so shrill, it was not easy to make out what she was saying. By the time I turned my full attention her way, Mom dropped her voice about eighty tones to the point where every syllable caused the building to vibrate. Now everyone in the bank was still. We all heard her say distinctly and furiously, "Just go get me the manager."

Mother glared at us, snapped her fingers, and pointed. James, Kieffer, and I scurried to join Buck in the comfy chairs.

Including Mom, there were five of us, but only four chairs. Mom came over and stood next to us, locked in position, arms crossed, one foot tapping....

"Good morning, madam." The manager, a sort of shiny man in a shinier suit, extended his hand politely.

My mother looked at him and sneered. "Maybe *you* think so." She offered a nasty look in place of her half of the handshake.

Manager Shiny dropped his hand and clasped it damply with his other one. "Yes.... I understand we have a bit of a problem, yes?"

"No," Mother snapped. "*We* don't have a problem. *You* and that mealy-mouthed twit over there have a problem."

"Oh, my. Well, my, my…." The manager blustered and then smiled and became even more shiny and reflective as sweat began to form sequined droplets on his face. "Perhaps we could just speak very quietly, madam," he urged Mother.

It was a bit like tossing a log on her fire. *Vhoof!* She burst into flame and fury. "I'll speak as damn well loud as I need, until you hear me! I came in to make a simple withdrawal and *his nibs* over there can't figure out how to give me my money."

His Nibs closed the little gate to his wicket and slunk out from the behind the counter to near where we were all stationed. Not too near. Probably he was a little afraid of my mother. Probably with good reason. Somebody was going to get a smack here. Like my brothers and me, His Nibs couldn't be sure it wasn't him.

Shiny and H. Nibs shuffled together and mumbled for a minute. Patting Nibs limply on the shoulder, Shiny urged him back to the safe haven of the tellers' stalls. He then turned to my mother and said with a constipated smile, "Just give me a few moments, madam, and I'll see what I can do."

The manager nodded curtly and scuttled off. Mom just did her best to stare holes into his flesh. She never once blinked. I thought I could smell singed polyester. Now that the first act of the floor show was over, the other patrons and staff in the bank settled back in to their business. A mercantile hum rose up, softly covering the sudden anxiety we had been exposed to.

Manager Shiny took a seat in his office. One wall was glass so we could see what he was doing. But it wasn't much. He twirled a rolling index card file, selected a card, and flipped it open. Another employee came in and handed him some papers. He made one or two phone calls. On the line he didn't say much, mostly just nodded, shuffled through the papers, and nodded again. Then he hung up, stuck his fingers under his necktie, and straightened it. He rose and walked purposefully out to my mother. He paused to take a breath and said plainly, "I'm sorry, madam, but your bank account is in overdraft. Cheques and withdrawals will not be honored. This institution is not prepared to advance any funds in support of an overdrawn account."

Wha – pardon? And what did that mean? The bank manager phrased it three different ways and I still didn't understand.

Translation was not immediately forthcoming.

Act two began: The Fight Scene. *Clang!* The manager and Mom came at each other from their opposing corners. The verbal punches flew fast and hard. She had no intention of going anywhere without her money. He had no intention of giving her any of his, not with Dad's infamous credit rating; she wanted her money; he said she didn't have any; she said just transfer it from the Toronto account; he said it was dead empty....

Nothing. Nada. Zilch. Zippo-canorie. L'oeuf. Absolute zero.

One of these terms finally got through to her. Mom stopped short and gawped at the bank manager. TKO. Her mouth hung open.

Mother. Was. Flabbergasted.

There was a collective cautionary "*Oooooooooo*" from the, once again, still and staring crowd. Like my brothers and me, they all worried and wondered what our smoldering mother might do next.

For onlookers, it was probably anticlimactic. Mother just snapped her mouth shut and turned on her heel and left. We bolted from the green, comfy chairs reluctantly, automatically, and sped after her.

Mom had no choice but to leave. She was called out, pulled up lame, short shrifted. And even if, on the off chance there had been money available to her in some bank somewhere, the bank manager, with his sweaty face and jiggly jowls, had all the power. He jangled the keys in his pockets, and Mom could not get a cent if her life depended on it. That's the way it was.

Well past the bank and along the sidewalk, Mother found her voice. "We are leaving!" she declared.

Leaving the bank, right? We're leaving only the bank.

This was not to be so. The front door of Stedmans, with its mosaic tile entryway, came and went. It was history behind us. Breaking the minute mile, Mom bypassed the IGA. Approaching the theoretical speed at which time slows down, she blazed directly to the car, the keys already in her hand.

"Aren't we going to the dairy?" one of us asked her.

"No. We are not," she said. Too calmly.

"How come?"

"Because," she turned and looked at us. She spoke as if it were the most obvious thing in the world. Like *we are putting on our rubbers and our raincoats because it is raining, and we are made of sugar. We will melt if we get wet.* "Your father has cleaned out the bank account. I don't have any money. Not one red cent. Get in the car."

We drove back to the cottage deflated, uncertain.

I wondered if we were poor people now. Would the church give us a cow? If we got a cow, then for sure we'd need a horse. And a proper dog that could herd it.

When we got back, our brainless dog was barking madly for joy to see us. He had crapped in the kitchen in protest of our going to town without him. My mother dragged him to his smelly pile of feces and stuck his nose in it. She hit him.

In her frustration she hit the dog much harder than she should have. Much harder than she meant to. The dog yelped and bolted. He hurtled himself at the back door and tore a huge hole in the already ripped screen and disappeared into the woods.

At the same time something tore a hole in my Mother's retaining walls. She fell to the floor and flowed out in all directions all over it. She cried and wailed and wept and bellowed. It was like watching the moon walk, without the heady air of excitement and the Squeeze-a-Snack.

But it was just as ominous and incredible.

Buck stepped back. He tried to separate himself from the scene. He slid noiselessly onto the couch, melding into its lumpy form, drawing up one knee, one arm, one magazine in blurry slow motion. Anyone coming upon the view might have thought he was part of the furniture, a boy-shaped throw pillow with a *Playboy*. Everything was so alien that it could have been normal.

The cottage wobbled with Mother's percussive sobs.

Everything was wrong. I had no clue what to do. My default *What would a cowboy do?* was lowered to well below that solid standard to the murky, bizarre depths of *What would Heidi do?* I could only revert back to the kind of person who put the dreaded Heidi seed in my brain. I could only do *what Timmy would do*: I threw myself, blubbering, on top of my mother.

Though of no comfort to her, my emotive tackle did serve to shock her back to the moment. She pulled us both upright, gave me a good shake and shouted, "Stop crying, or I'll give you something to cry about!" which should have been funny because neither one of us stopped crying. But at least all parties could breathe again. Mom was back to so-called normal.

I took a seat at the table and dribbled and mewled. Mom collected herself and blew her nose on a dish towel. You could see the way she was looking around the room that she was counting heads. Finding none but the dog missing, she carved out a little space and time for herself by delegating jobs to us all.

"James, go on up to Auntie Lil's cottage and ask her if she has an extra loaf of bread. Kieffer, take the liver treats and see if you can find the dog. Buck, put down that rag, and go bring in some wood. Penny, pick up the dog dirt in a serviette, and wipe up the mess. Then clear the table, and put the dishes in the sink."

Dishes? Why did I have to get the gross job? I was barely tall enough to reach the stupid sink. "*Awwwwwww,*" I moaned, my crying spirit refreshed. "Do I hafta?"

Mother launched herself at me and slapped me. As hard as she'd slapped the dog! The shock of it stunned me.

"I ask you to do one thing for me, and all you can do is complain!" She laid into me with all she had. "Your precious daddy can get you a pony, but he can't give me enough money to feed you damned kids!"

"He's not my precious – " I protested faintly.

"SHUT UP!" Mother screamed and jerked like she was going to slap me again. I completely shut up. I shut down. I sat down on the floor, halfway under the table. "SHUT UP AND DO AS YOU ARE TOLD. WHY CAN'T ANY OF YOU DO AS YOU ARE TOLD?"

Maybe because we were glued in place by the force of her anger. The boys quickly found their feet. Kieffer and James were out the door and on-task in a half second. Buck was close to it when Mom had a sudden change of heart and stopped him.

"Penny, I'm sorry I rose my voice." *And the slap. Were you going to mention that?* "Buck, why don't you take Penny out for a little boat ride?"

My stomach turned. My eyes teared up again. I swallowed hard and tried to find my most appealing, loving child voice. It just came out whiny. "Please, can I stay with you?" Mother hated whining.

"For crying out loud, would you just go with your brother on a damned boat ride, and leave me alone!"

Buck looked at me with that sideways smile. "C'mon Penny. We're going for a boat ride. Wheeeee!"

TWENTY

Well's Dry and River's Dirty

SOMETIMES FLASH would pace around in her little field. In those last days of summer I would pace with her, holding her softly by the mane. I let her lead. There was nowhere I wanted to be. And it was better to do what she wanted. She never really wanted anything. Though I am sure she was happier to see me with a sugar cube in my hand. If I could get hold of one of those, I brought two: one for each of us.

Sometimes my mind would flash unwanted pictures. The internal screen upon which they were shown distended with my efforts to repress them. The images were distorted, more so in repetition. The omnipresent threat that a change of wind would freeze my face in a flash-induced grimace caused me to grit my teeth. Two molars, weakened by decay I wasn't aware of, fractured. It didn't really hurt. But the sharp edges and biting my tongue did. I bit my tongue a lot. Not that I noticed. Until there was too much blood to swallow and I just sort of let if all out of my mouth. I didn't spit. That wasn't allowed. I wiped it with the back of my hand and constantly picked at the dry red crust accumulating at the corners of my lips. It looked like I was rusting. Maybe I was. But that didn't hurt either.

Just days before Flash was due to be returned to the now fully rebuilt riding stables, I decided to give riding her one last try. Uncle Mo-Mo was long gone, so I had to make do on my own. I walked with Flash a long time around in circles. We came to an understanding. I no longer tried to fling myself to her back in frustration. Not elegantly, but effectively, I managed to brace my grip on her mane and throw one leg over her. The other one followed. But in my single-mindedness to make the mount I neglected to bridle her up first. All I could do was sit there, prostrate and ineffectual, the most useless cowboy in history.

The boys liked to start each day arguing over crazy boy issues, like whose cereal crackled more loudly or whose fart was worse. But they gave up more easily and parted ways sooner than before. Fighting took so much out of you. Now and then you had to take a rest from it.

One day, late in the afternoon, Kieffer, still wearing his shoes and everything, came careening out of the woods, thundered over the dock, and tossed himself headlong into the water. He had stepped in a wasps' nest. When he was pulled out and stripped down, and the tally was taken for the sake of public interest, he had seventy-two bites in all. He was as sick as a dog. Mom hovered over him while he wailed and sweated and puked. The whole place stank to high heaven, and we had to manage for ourselves as far as meals were concerned. It wasn't so bad. At least it provided a distraction.

Flash ran away. No one ran after her. There wasn't much point in chasing a dream that was dead.

My father came one weekend and packed his car and Mom's car. He shut the cats and the dog in crates. Buck got to sit up front in Dad's car. I was glad.

I didn't say good-bye to the cottage. It didn't deserve it.

During the fall, in the city, Suzanne's boyfriend, Brian, moved in with us. He'd been "kicked out" of his own home and was persona non grata in Auntie Lil's. There were whispers and hisses but few actual words to explain this transfer. One phrase that was consistently clear, *Brian got Suzanne in trouble*, filled me with a jealous rage. My brothers were ceaselessly getting *me* in trouble, but were *they* unceremoniously turfed from their digs and set adrift on the open seas to paddle their own canoe, or fish or cut bait? Hell no! They remained well-situated in those purely ceremonial positions at the dinner table while I shuffled plates to and fro, staring down the bloody stewed tomatoes with not the faintest hope of an extra bite of cake.

I would have been quietly overjoyed to see any or all of

my brothers "shown the door and given the gears without so much as a pot to pee in," as Mother said of Brian's situation.

Though having a pot to pee in didn't ensure a standard of aim or neatness. I avoided the bathroom on the back level where the boys' rooms were. It was speckled with dried pools and splashes of urine. The over-ripe aroma of a territory too well marked by threatened animals. The toilet bowl was less a target and more a point in the landscape to decorate with piss. Seat up/seat down? The question did not compute. Just enter emptying the bladder. Let nature take its own wobbly course. To direct the urethra with the hand was to surrender freedom. The only loose rule was to keep one's back to the door.

If absolutely desperate, I would cover the seat in paper, public bathroom style, back in, and keep my front to the door, only because to close myself in with the stench was to be intimately acquainted with suffocation, the thickness of urine odor being as oppressive as what it was.

It had to be that the well-traveled cowboy found himself answering the call of nature more than once during the long cattle drive. Yet despite the steady diet of *beans, beans, the musical fruit, the more you eat, the more you toot,* I refused to accept that the bodily waste of any given cowboy could possibly be anything stronger than neutral. No cowboy on the planet ever suffered from a pissy, dirty twat. When a cowboy said ever so decorously that he had to *make water,* that was about all he made. There had to be a way to rise to this level of digestive metabolic balance. I had to find it, or die (from inhaling caustic urine) trying.

Then came the season of Anal Expulsion.

Based on a set of complex mathematical equations and formulas that stump a Nobel prize-winning economist, our Mother concluded that toilet paper was an unspeakably overused commodity in The Boys' Bathroom. Perhaps she felt that limiting this luxury would lead to an improved outcome in the aim-and-flush department. It only worsened the urine spray. No surprises there. As far as Number Two went, if one wanted to *take a crap*, as was said by the hip, one first must present oneself to the Maven of Toilet Tissue and put in a request. Sadly, anyone that happened to be female and tended to use toilet paper for sanitary upholstery and for every elimination event, namely me, had to ask for toilet paper, too. Even though physiology demanded a sit-down position, which made missing the bowl considerably harder.

When I put forth this argument to Mother, doing a little jig of bladder urgency as I did, she was unimpressed. "Suit yourself; then you can't use the upstairs bathroom anymore. Maybe that way you'll learn to keep your gummy paws off things that are none of your beeswax."

I feigned blank innocence but I knew darn well she was referring back to my snooping in the linen closet and publicly making a fool of myself (she said). Other than the ubiquitous spare rolls of toilet paper, a sack of Epsom salts, calamine lotion, some cleaning products, and the Good Towels that we were forbidden to touch, the closet housed two mysterious and gorgeous boxes. Powder blue and embossed with a single white rose, each box had a perforated hatch open on top, which I could just barely reach. So in plowed my dirty, nail-bitten hand. I groped about blindly for treasures hidden and drew out two forms of the same object. I was utterly nonplussed. One box contained what looked a lot like pocket-sized tissue packets all neatly wrapped and folded. The other contained the same packets rumpled and wadded up and loosely wound in toilet paper. The *now-rationed* toilet paper.

Well, that was just *wrong*. Totally wrong. Such beautiful boxes should be used for a far more elegant purpose. I could make Barbie boudoirs, princess castle walls, wardrobes for Wendy Walker's outfits – such beautifully printed containers were infinitely too lovely to store stacked paper hankies and gobbed up snot rags! Somebody probably wasted some of those fancy tissues on a nosebleed too, because there looked to be a good sized blob of blood on the one I fished out.

Growling, indignant with rage, I stomped down the stairs and thrust the samples under my mother's nose. She was in the kitchen making percolated coffee for Mary Wrangler who was hanged over the kitchen chair. Mostly she was sitting on it, but she was slouching and holding her head with both hands, and my mother always called that *hung over* in the past tense, after Mary Wrangler left. *Hanged over* must be what it was when it was happening now, and the person was slouching right before your eyes. *Hang up the phone now, please. The phone was hung up.* See?

"Mom, when you empty the pretty tissue box in the linen closet can you NOT put the dirty ones in it so I can have it for make-and-do?" I said, a trifle impatient with her obvious disregard for such beautiful boxes.

"What the...?" Mother scrutinized the evidence before her, then clucked in disgust, "Oh for Pete's sake. Put those back where you got them and stay out of the linen closet." She snapped her arm like a switch blade, pointing up the stairs.

"But can't I have the boxes when you're not using them?"

It was clear Mom was peeved, but I didn't get why. "Go! Now!" she shouted.

"But…" Of course, I started to cry.

"Right now this minute, or I'll really give you something to cry about!" Mother said, turning me by the shoulders and giving me a shove.

I wailed ebulliently with every step, feeling stung all over by the gross injustice of such beauty being squandered on wastepaper and filth. It was all the more vexing as I was chased up the stairs by my Mother's and Mary Wrangler's appalled laughter.

I figured it out eventually. The boxes were my mother's stash of sanitary pads: a box of new and a box of used. With this knowledge, I felt even more humiliated, even though years, *and Mary Wrangler*, had passed.

So my brothers and I were on strict toilet-paper rations.

This was in no way a passively accepted rule.

Underpants were streaked brown. People smelled a little worse walking away. Sphincters were clenched shut until reaching a well-equipped school cubicle. Or, in the case of James, more creative efforts were made.

James took a liking to the Picasso-esquire appearance of his shit smeared on the gray-blue bathroom tile of The Boys Bathroom. In artistic protest, he inscribed BITCH*BITCH*BITCH in liqui-shit as high and as low as he could reach on all four walls. Nowadays such a thing would be called an "art installation."

I don't know art, but I know what I like.

It was unlikable.

The limit was six squares to a bowel movement, four for a female urination. Numbers were stringently enforced.

One might bank unused sheets. Hide them under pillows or between the pages of an under-read classic. But when the digestive reflex worked its magic, and the urge came, you had to be sure to leave enough time to approach She Who Held the Loo Roll to request the requisite ration of sheets.

Mother kept a roll next to her chair in the living room, among the *Good Housekeeping* and the *Redbook*.

Once I asked Mother why I was subject to this frustration when it was not I who had soiled The Boys' Bathroom in so many evil ways.

"Waste not, want not," was her patently obscure answer.

I never understood that phrase.

I still don't.

If you don't waste the toilet paper then you won't want for vegetables? If you eat all your Brussels sprouts, then you'll have reams of super-soft, quilted three-ply to clean your bum?

Then just as abruptly as the ration law was enacted, it was repealed. The Boys Bathroom was cleaned and the paper replaced on the roll holder.

This occurred the *morning* of the *evening* that Brian arrived. That was the only hint that a change in household organization was about to take place.

Some time after dinner, but before dessert, a chair was pulled up to the table, an extra cake fork was laid out, and Brian was welcomed to our little unsafe harbor, in hopes he'd find a better place.

Even at the time I was baffled by the notion that our place could be considered in any way a *better* place. Better than a slap in the face with a wet fish, maybe.

Or maybe getting Brian was like getting the dog. If you squinted one eye and held your head just right, it looked good on her: Good ole Mom! The headlines would read: Hard-Working Mother of Four Takes Up Lazy Neighbor Mom's Slack by Putting a Roof Over Misunderstood Teen's Head. Maybe it was just that Brian was tall and could reach stuff off the high shelves. The *why* of the thing was lost in the rush to deal with the *who, when,* and *how.*

There was a lively shuffling of places in the house. A new room was hastily knocked together with two-by-fours and paneling, and Buck was stuffed into it, while Brian took up residence in Buck's former room and painted it entirely flat black: ceiling, walls, *and* windows. Multiple cans of spray paint were used. Once it was all dry, Brian used a compass and a razor blade to create circular windows in the square frames. The parquet floor escaped with merely a haze and dapple of drips. He hung a series of black-light tube fixtures down the center of the room and put up some psychedelic posters. I loved going in there wearing white. If I could find anything white. It glowed bright pale violet. It was so cool. So marvy. So mod. I wanted to do the same in my room.

"Don't be stupid," was my parents' response. "No nice little girl would ever have a black room." I might have been touched that they still saw potential in me, that I might one day become nice. But persistent doubt was seeping under the veneer of trust in which I had clad my mother and father.

In his basement bedroom, Buck papered the walls with *Playboy* centerfolds. When he was not at home, I would stand in the doorway and examine them. My reading skills had improved to the point where I could read the captions fairly well. "I think before I ball" was the footer of a picture of a damp soapy girl in a shower whose fulsome figure protruded through the bubbles. "Her father's a preacher and her mother's a nurse. Sunny is a nice girl." Sunny had a splendid hourglass figure, yards of blonde hair, high heels, and a lacy blouse with no buttons. Yes, she looked nice. Regarding my own squared-off trunk, speed-skater thighs, and dark hair pulled into tight braids, I knew I would never be nice.

I still held out some hope that I might be a cowboy. But not much.

Thinking my thick-trunked prepubescent figure was more barn than beauty, Brian took to calling me Piggy rather than Penny. Mother thought this was apt enough due to my size, but better yet, due to the continually untidy state of my room.

As they say, *Mother's trash is a child's treasure.* Or something like that.

I hoarded anything with a shine or a sparkle: foil tart tins, bottle caps, pop-can pull tabs, broken bits of costume jewelry, a bit of trim from an outgrown nightgown, bent keys, a few pieces of a plate with gold leaf. Whatever I could palm, I hid away and fashioned into elaborate creations. I pasted wads of Christmas-tree tinsel, retrieved from the trash, onto my dresser mirror and looked at it as the Star of David, or Bethlehem, or the Northern Star depending on the season, or the phase of the moon. I stared unblinking at it as I meditated on sleep, sickness, and death, in which I would levitate to freedom. I was an exile from Jerusalem, a stranger in a strange land, on the rivers of Babylon; or I was a noble emissary from afar; or an enslaved soul in flight. The uniform was different. The cause was the same. I soldiered on, bent under my burden. I toiled to cast off the inglorious stench of the pissy, dirty twat, to escape the pursuing hounds, overseers, governors, parents, and brothers, natural and imposed.

Brian called me Piggy or Piglet all the time. I asked him to stop, and he laughed. I asked my Mother to ask him to stop, but she insisted it was a term of affection, and I should be charmed by it. I wasn't.

"He calls you that because he misses his own little sister." And she insisted I go find him and ask for a cuddle.

"No way," I said, disturbed by various repulsive affections that Buck too often heaped upon me. I was baited and acerbated by them. Insinuating myself into some older boy's grasp for no useful reason was above and beyond what I planned to do. Ever.

Grabbing me by the wrist, Mother pulled me downstairs where Brian was building something at the basement workbench. She shoved me stumbling into Brian's arm, and he knocked over his work and swore.

"Shit! Waddya want, for crissake?"

I glowered.

Mom realized in a minute I was perfectly happy to stand there and say and do nothing for as long as it took for nothing to happen.

Putting her hands gently and atypically – *who are you, lady, and what have you done with my real mother?* – on my shoulders and speaking in a soft, loving voice, my mother, or someone who looked and smelled a lot like her, said, "I have a little girl here who needs a HUG."

Maybe Snoopy needed a hug. Bloody well not me. But a hug I got, as quick and as perfunctory as Brian could manage it and for longer than I could stand it, even if it only took a second.

I dashed off as fast as I could, feeling humiliated and furious.

I didn't want brothers or others to touch me. No matter the frank reason, there was always something unseemly underneath. Maybe my mother had learned to bear and forebear. She was an adult. I was not ready. She had to know that. Why didn't she know that? I didn't want any part of what boys liked and where they wanted to put their dirty hands. Lucky Brian's little sister, far from the extent of his reach. Lord knows what he did to her. I thought, then, all brothers treated their sisters the same way.

Brian probably did nothing to his sister. She was what, way back then, we used to call Mongoloid. Somewhere around when the metric system came in, she was measured up as having Down's syndrome, and we weren't allowed to say *Mongoloid* anymore or mention that the little girl was at least sixty pounds overweight. If you couldn't divide by 2.2 in your head and say it in kilograms, the most you could say was she was a *big* little girl. But she was nice. Even if she wasn't, you had to say she was nice because she was retarded and couldn't help herself and would never grow up to be a *niiiiiiiice* girl.

She would never be fat enough to be called Piggy.

My mother pasted a cartoon strip to my bedroom door. A child stick figure is regarding her untidy room. Out of frame, her parent's question is, "Lolly! Look at this mess! Are you a nice little girl or a piggy?"

Stick-thin Lolly considers a moment, then offers, "How about a nice little piggy?"

My Mother capitalized P and crossed out *nice*.

It was plain where I stood.

My mother got a new gold charm for her bracelet with Brian's birth date and the date he arrived engraved on it. It was bigger than the one she had for me.

TWENTY-ONE

The TKO Corral

IN A MARRIAGE-RESCUE maneuver, Mom and Dad went on a trip together. It was a good plan, in theory. But our guardian for that time was Brian. To say he was not happy in his work didn't begin to tell that tale. He managed to wake us up in the morning. Then he went back to bed.

Every day I got up, got dressed, usually in my customary haute couture mix of whatever I picked up off the floor, mixed myself a Carnation Instant Breakfast, and went to school. I came home at lunch and ate bread and butter and brown sugar. I went back to school and tried, almost always unsuccessfully, every afternoon to obtain an invitation to someone else's house. Anyone else's house. Had I a classmate that smelled of brimstone whose name was Beelzebub, I would have been happy to follow him home and through the flaming front door.

Twice Brian held house parties. There were no hats, games, or loot bags, as I still thought parties should have.

I was directed to go to bed and stay there. So I did. One night I sat in the closet eating saltines that I had absconded with earlier. Kieffer caught me and told on me, but Brian could not be stirred to care. No one could. The music was loud, but the party guests were draped about in a haze of sour-sweet "cigarette" smoke. Even my brothers. Even James, who slept only a few hours nightly on average and was constantly in motion, was oddly sedate. He lounged and dozed with a natural expertise I found very strange.

Bruce Humphries, whom I had thought was going to be a pony surprise summers ago at the cottage, joined in the festivities. He stumbled up the stairs and into my room, mistaking it for the bathroom. Then he laughed himself silly at the joke. Between peals of giggles he managed to make it to the toilet and relieve himself, door open, his poor aim left on display for anyone to see. Brian, similarly tittering, collected him and ushered him back down the stairs.

"Is he drunk?" I asked Brian, wide-eyed with wonder. The greatest wonder being that I actually believed I was witnessing the first drunk person of my life.

Brian grinned wide and replied, "Does the Pope make big potty in the woods?"

The second party night I was dispatched to bed again. I was happy to go. I changed into my nightie and arranged my toys and got into bed. But as I lay there, tuning the party noises and loud music into a background buzz, I noticed my closet door was moving slightly. I looked at the window. It was open a bit. But there was no wind, really, and the curtains weren't moving. Curious, I slid out of bed and moved closer to the closet door. Even as I stood right next to it, it opened and closed, just a bit, just slowly. I took the handle and pulled the door all the way open.

Buck was standing in the closet. His shirt was unbuttoned. His pants were unzipped. One hand was inside them. The other hand dropped from where he had rested it on the door handle.

I tried to focus, tried to assign some sense to the moment. Then the flash in my brain and the spike of dirty crotch smell went straight up my nostrils – but no tic.

I just screamed.

That brought a few dulled but concerned guests staggering up the stairs, Brian and Suzanne included. Before they arrived Buck was out front of the closet and his pants were zipped, and before I knew anything else, everyone was sharing a good laugh at how Buck "scared the living shit out of me." I was a baby and a chicken. I went to bed and did not sleep again until my parents came home.

Mission Marriage Mend was a complete bust.

Mom and Dad fought, louder and harder than ever. While they used to stick to an incendiary repetition of pop hits such as money and jobs and household upkeep, now they escalated to putting on fights of operatic proportions. One could scarcely determine what language they bellowed in, though I could still make out some of their signature catch-phrases, such as "nursemaid with fucking privileges" (Mother) or "now the shit is *really* caked to the bowl!" (Dad).

I don't know where my brothers were. I didn't want to know. I knew where I was, cornered with the sting of a burning prod always on my side. I sat by and watched the progression of my parents' misery like an oncoming stampede. There was no high ground, rocky or moral, to take to. I covered my head and prayed.

she sleeps…she's sick…she's dead…

One Friday after school, Auntie Lil and Uncle Marlow came and collected Mom. It took both of them to help her up and out, hobbling, weeping, caved in over a box of tissues she held close to her chest. I stood halfway up the stairs and watched them waltz her past me, toward the front door.

"Mother is going to be all right soon, dear," Auntie Lil said to me, smiling weakly. "She's going to be fine."

Really? She doesn't look it.

I wish I could honestly say I was concerned. But I was not. I was just relieved that some small intermission had been called between the Acts of Intensity.

I returned to my room and lay down on the floor, stared at the ceiling.

she sleeps…she's sick…she wishes she were dead

I floated away.

It wasn't the same night, it was another night when the police came and dragged Dad off. Could have happened more than once. I'm not certain. Hearing the buzz and static and broken voices on the police-car radio, I got out of bed and tiptoed down the stairs. The front hall was flooded with the rhythmic red glow of the flashing light on the patrol car. In the cast of the blood-colored strobe my parents momentarily ceased to argue with each other. Instead, they sparred and spat abuses on the young officers, who stood in the door. One of them noticed me.

Looking up, he squinted to focus on the slowly descending body in the shadows. "Here comes a little more trouble," he interjected between my parents' hurtling epithets, nodding my way. Perhaps he thought Mom and Dad would tone it down a bit, say things in a little more family-friendly way.

Not sure where he got that silly idea.

My parents instantly redirected all blazing fury onto me. The one officer, the one who spoke, I think he sort of sighed and looked pained. The other one looked very tired. Mom and Dad snapped to united attention and glared fireballs at me, the misbehaving child. It was something they could agree on.

"Get back to bed and stay there!" Mom shrieked at me.

"Now!" barked Dad. "Before I rock you to sleep with the biggest rock I can find!"

Well, a change is as good as a rest, right?

The whiff of fresh, meaty anger gave my parents more (unreasonable) reason to snarl and tear up the once-still suburban night, and each other.

I didn't stick around to see the next part of the show. I

scurried back to bed and under the covers, through a black rabbit hole and under another flag and star and nowhere anywhere.

While I was away, time happened and things passed. They were none of my beeswax, and that was fine with me.

* * *

Dad was gone for two days before I asked why.

"He's in lockup," my mother said sharply. "He drank himself stupid and sick, and they took him away."

What shall we do with a drunken sailor, ear-lie in the morning?

I broke out in a raw, abrasive sadness upon his return.

Thinking he was on some level sorry for me, or trying to show some sort of apposite brotherly love, I let Buck pull me into his lap one day in our parents' bedroom. He had been watching TV (and reading Dad's magazines), and he called me in as I passed. It was early evening, and Mom was well into making a meal, or a rum and Coke, probably both. Dad was not yet home from work, but he was out of jail. Who knew if he had to present one of those cards from the Monopoly game.

Buck had hardly looked my way in a long time, and I thought it was safe to toss him a bone. Or a rope. I gave him enough to tie me up, hold me down, and pull up my shirt. He ripped the blue and green pattern of buggy eyed owls as I pulled back. I tried in vain to keep myself covered. Once he'd exposed my skin, he rooted out the un-grown nipples and slopped his white coated sticky tongue across each one.

I grabbed his hair with both hands and screamed as I pulled with all my might and his greasy hair slipped through my grasp and my chewed fingernails pinched into my palms and I screamed and screamed into that vacuum that nature abhors and I screamed and nobody came.

It was a long, cold winter.

TWENTY-TWO

The Iron Road

1971. IT WAS A NEW AGE. A Modern Age. The Future. There was even a TV show, *Here Come the Seventies!* geared to introducing all the modernness that we would soon be riding the bright shiny wave of.

I looked for signs of a new era.

Darlene-Dirtybutter had given up the practice of napping and could be viewed perpendicular to the ground most of the time. Her nose still ran like a tap.

Expo '67 was four years ago, ancient history by the standards of a child, so Francine had nothing on me. Sure, she had actually gone to Expo. She had seen the three-hundred-and-sixty degree movie and the home of the future. But now it was way, way in the past. I still had a cottage, and last summer I had my own pony. It was not quite fibbing to extrapolate and plant the seed of a suggestion that I was going have it again this year.

I convened a meeting of the girls of Dewmist Crescent at the junction of the willow tree and driveway at the front of my house. Darlene, Francine, and me. The Nixon girls, Nancy and Nina, were cordially *not* invited. They had recently hosted a kids' party in their backyard next door. I knew this because I climbed to the top of our monkey bars and stared at them through narrowed eyes until Mrs. Nixon banged on our front door and told my mother she had to come and make me get down. My mother did this by staring at me through narrowed eyes from the garage door, so I knew it to be an effective way to inflict misery on others. My current plan was to punish Nancy and Nina by hanging out with my real friends where they could clearly see us from their front window.

It took a bit of doing, but I managed to put my evil plan into action. Lucky for me, I only had to give two red licorice strings (each) to get Darlene and Francine to come. Still one left over for me. I stuck it in the side of my mouth like a switch of grass. I'd seen cowboys do this in the movies. It fit well with my presentation. Swiping the licorice from Kieffer's not-so-secret stash was worth the risk. They were a bit hard and stale, but that bought me time to draw the story out as the girls gnawed their way through the bribe.

"A pony?" Darlene gasped in amazement. "Wow!"

"Yep. It's pretty great." There was no denying it.

"A real pony?" Francine qualified. "Like a *real* one?" She wagged a licorice at me, dubious about it and my pony tale.

I looked at her like she was an idiot. She was. "Yes." I

spelled it out for her. "Y-E-S. Duh. A white pony. A pony named Flash."

This was great: bragging without lying. It felt pretty good.

I was sympathetic, naturally. Francine had to resent my real white pony. She had nothing to counter with. And I knew she loved red licorice. She would have had to give it back if she wanted to call me a liar. Rules Of The Jungle.

"Oh, you just think you're sooo big," was all Francine could come up with. She concentrated on the combined tasks of chewing and looking doubtful.

But Darlene was still with me. "Did you ride it all by yourself?" she asked all dreamy and breathless.

"Sure did," I said, deftly avoiding admitting that I only did it once. "If you ever come up to my cottage, you can ride her too." I issued this promise with the complete confidence that it would never happen.

"Yeah, well, before you go this summer, your dad better clean up that crappy-looking lawn you got there," Francine said, jerking her head in the direction of the big, blank front windows of the house. I never really stopped to look at it before. The sod did look kind of ravaged. Crabgrass city. And Jethro, the dog, forever bolting out the front door before any-one could chain him, had de-sodded and shat over a wide swath through the whole middle of the front yard. The still-immature willow tree did nothing to hide the mess. A wet spring had worsened Jethro's efforts and added to the stink of the place. There was no repeat of the crocus disaster of our first year in the house. Nothing sprang up in our lawn except sour smells and shit heaps in various shades of sopping brown.

"My mom says your house is bringing the property values down," Francine reported with a tart little simper.

With difficulty, I ignored this. "We'll probably get off school early to go up to the cottage. Maybe a month early." To regain the upper hand I reverted back to lies. It didn't feel as good, but I craved control. I needed control. The red licorice was swiftly disappearing.

"Wow, for real?" Darlene displayed a wide licorice-studded grin below equally wide eyes, and I thought I was gaining that control – then, "D'you want me to ask my dad to help your dad fix your lawn?" Darlene asked earnestly, by way of thanking me for my generosity.

Francine sniggered.

Pfffft.

That was that.

I knew it was over. A white pony no longer counted as currency. The future had, unwanted and unkind, arrived.

Dad was on a business trip when school closed. Neither my brothers nor I wanted to wait for him to come home to drive us to the cottage. We could not get there fast enough. We tormented Mom to lay in the provisions, unhitch the Pinto, and take the wheel.

Mom did not like to drive. Especially not on the highway. She said that having learned to drive in Montreal, she was a better driver than people in Ontario. Her fellow motorists were so dreadful at this task that she feared being on the road with them.

Be it the strength of our arguments or the inability of our mother to resist our implacable and acrimonious begging, the mission was taken on. The car was jammed to the gills with groceries and clean clothes and the dog and my brothers and me. Buck sat up front with an unfolded map. Unable to see out the back window because of all that was piled high inside, Mom closed her eyes and backed out to a muttered prayer, "Jesus, Mary, and Joseph on a flying broomstick, I can't see a fucking thing!"

We didn't leave until nearly noon and didn't stop at Doris's grill. We just drove the whole day in the sunshine drinking warm pop straight from the can and peeing on the side of the road when we had to.

It was glorious.

We drove the whole way, never exceeding the breakneck speed of forty-eight miles per hour, making easily fifty-five stops along the way. Not that we cared. We were on our way to the cottage. Nothing else mattered. It was not the same as being on our way to happiness or even hope. But the cottage was the closest thing we had to hope.

That was the last sunny day of 1971.

Owing to a natural aberration of the weather cycle, rain and cloud set in and did not let up for weeks.

The general effects of that much precipitation were predictable. Overcast and gloom were incessant. The lake was cold. It was too cold to swim, even for us, and too choppy to row, canoe, or sail. Mildew threatened to take over the world.

It did stop raining periodically. We went outside when we could. In the mud. There was mud everywhere. It caked shoes, knees, elbows, stuck in hair, dried in chunks in our beds. It was an especially loathsome substance when the pump blew and we had to hike up the mud path to the despised outhouse. As you sat on the splintered bench, reasonably worried that you might fall in, it seemed a genuine possibility that the whole soggy structure might implode with you in it, sinking deep into the mud and molasses-thick mélange of feces and urine that fairly bubbled beneath you.

The surrounding cottages remained empty. Reasonably afraid of the predictions of long-range forecasters, the other summer inhabitants stayed well away. Auntie Lil and Uncle Marlow came once to see that theirs and Don's cottages had not been washed away in the deluge. Marlow fixed the pump, and they left the next day. Suzanne never came.

The blackflies and mosquitoes took over.

Mom talked about just making a break for it and leaving "this goddamn mess for your father to clean up," but it never happened. Time without breaking, ever, felt like it had stopped.

It was like living in a Hitchcock movie. It was dark enough all the time that you could believe the world was black-and-white. The rain poured down constantly in big sloppy drops that could only be produced by special effects artists. The blackflies did not know the end of their predetermined season. They lived long and hearty in league with the squadrons of famished, vehement mosquitoes that sprang in ever growing numbers from the pools of stagnant water that had us surrounded.

We went through aerosol cans of Off! like a hot knife through butter. We were probably personally responsible for ripping open the original hole in the ozone because of the number of aerosol cans we emptied. For all that, the Off! scarcely made a dent in untold legions of pernicious insects who smacked their little bug lips in glee each time one of us cracked open the cottage door.

Bugs are fewer on the water, so on a less windy day we tried to go out to the island. Most of a morning was given over to bailing out the rowboat and hunting down the oars. By the time we finally reached the island, we found it had sunk completely. The one brave tree it supported was dying by degrees – drowning and rotting simultaneously.

At the cave there was a small lake covering the floor. It wasn't deep, but we knew not to venture too close. We knew what still water meant. Even from a distance you could hear the grim, insanity-inspiring buzz of the mosquitoes.

We didn't dream of going to the swamp. It had already come to us.

Dad arrived out of nowhere one day. It was not a good day. There were no good days in a charnel house, particularly one in which the inhabitants suffered greatly from acute vexatious cabin fever. No one so much as stood or said hello when he entered the room.

We were playing Monopoly. I was out because my empire-building strategy was based strictly on purchasing properties in coordinating colors. I remained at the table leafing through a magazine that featured articles on the Partridge Family. Free Parking was piled high with luminous pink, yellow, and green faux cash. The pressure was on to see who would get it. Buck, Kieffer, and James, the shoe, car, and flat-iron respectively, were all rounding the corner, in double-dice distance of winning the pot.

First to roll got a "chance," Get-out-of-jail-free card. That could come in handy. *Save that one for Dad.*

Second up: snake eyes. Low rental property. Decided not to buy.

Third roll: the dice hit the floor and one rolled under my chair. Kieffer retrieved the other one and presented it as a four. I picked up the one beneath me and held it out to show them, "I got it."

"What was it?"

I looked at the die, now sideways in my hand. I knew it was a high number, lots of dots. I considered the patterns. "It was this one," I showed the six, "Or this one," I showed the five.

One of them, the high roller, would fetch the dough in Free Parking. The other one gave him bupkus. Six eyes burned holes in my flesh as my brothers willed me to get it right, or not. I didn't even know whose turn it was.

"Uhhhmm," panic was rising. I was going to get it in a big way, no matter what. All of the day's frustrations – hell, all of a life's frustrations – were going to land on me hard. And it didn't matter if I was right or not. I was a train wreck in the making, on a ninety-degree slope gaining momentum, and the breaks were out. "I don't know." I started to cry. "Roll again. Roll this one again."

That was that. Blow to the head, and I was on the floor, dizzy and distant without a clue. The Monopoly board went flying. Little houses and hotels rained like lemon meringue pie and plastic shrapnel all over the room. Mad money fluttered in a maelstrom of sound and fury. The walls quaked with the reverberation. All who could stand, which was everyone but me, joined in a kinky dance of combat, an interpretive melee, absurd and unappealing, where the participants grappled and swung at each other, changed sides, and began the steps anew.

I tried *she sleeps, she's sick, she's dead*, but the cacophony of shouting battered my senses. I could not concentrate. Nausea came in thick, sour waves, pinning me in place.

The boys tried to kill each other, oblivious to the impotent commands of our parents to stop.

"Stop. Shut up. Why can't you damned kids just shut up?" Mom's voice was higher, so it could be identified in the wall of screaming, directing Dad into the oncoming traffic. "For corn's sake, make them stop. Make them shut up. They're your children too. You make them shut up!"

She meant for him to halt this head-on collision with his bare hands. Lashing out in pure anger, he knocked down my brothers like pins in a game. They popped up just as fast and struck blindly at whatever, or whoever, was within range.

The scene moved steadily from bad to worse, from worse to unimaginable. Mom was in the middle of it all, trying to stop it, getting hit, hitting back. In the eye of the storm. In the path of destruction.

From my mole's-eye view I watched curiously as my brothers retreated, their three pairs of filthy feet clamoring to get through the doorframe as fast as they possibly could. I craned my neck to see what they ran from so fearfully. And there was Dad. And Mom. She was sprawled on the floor, bent like a piece of rusted metal, with Dad hunched over her, beating the living shit out of her.

Don't look.

I looked anyway. I couldn't help it. There was nowhere to go and no way to get there. It was like I was glued to the floor. Mom tried to cover her head with her arm. Did a lousy job of it. Got clobbered all over.

I stared at the ceiling, tried to find a bright spot to focus on. There was none. I wanted to float away. To ride my horse over the beautiful land, stop at a stream, and eat a picnic, one that wasn't squashed, one that stayed right-side up on the plate, one that I did not have to admire.

Glancing back over my shoulder, I could see Dad was running out of steam. But every now and again something new must have occurred to him and he stepped up the pace, found his second wind. Mom might have been unconscious, maybe only stunned. I couldn't tell. Either way, she looked like death warmed over.

It was then I had a vision. Perhaps it was a premonition. It was the 70s. Extrasensory perception was the next big thing.

I knew we would get out of here.

From way down there on the floor I could see a tranquil horizon, a big open sky, and a sun setting golden and shining in the west. These dreams, these days, and this place would be dust in my wake. Mad Mag was dead. Kicked in the head by a dead horse that was beaten once too often.

We would live.

But we would never return.

TWENTY-THREE

Ghost Town

MOM AND DAD were officially divorced in 1974. That same year, the Watergate scandal played havoc with regularly scheduled programming, prompting me to hate all Americans without mercy. That probably wasn't fair. Even in his home country, how could anyone prefer Richard Nixon's sweaty face constantly filling the TV screen? He said "I am not a crook," but he stole Tony Orlando and Dawn from us all.

In the late autumn, for reasons known only to himself, Uncle Don drove his car into the Rideau Canal. Where he left the road and entered the water the canal was hardly deep. His car was barely submerged. His seat belt was still on. He made no effort to escape. He fully intended to be (or not be) where he was found. I suppose that's called suicide in the vernacular.

I might have been sad or shocked or horrified. But I drew nothing from within when I found out, not even a blank. The end of Don was inevitable, similar to the end of any season, any day. On balance, my feelings remained the same. Dawn to dusk. Don to death. Spring forward and fall back. I would remember certain days, the bat in the jar and the colors of a caftan, days of cold rain and days when the rain was relief, now here, now gone. Like the cottage. I wasn't tied to it, or tied down by it anymore.

Now was something different than it used to be.

Now and then I wondered if Don wasn't on the right track, figuratively and literally. The road less traveled, for sure, but hardly baptism by fire. Baptized under the fresh, clean, cold water, he was immersed, never to rise again.

There's no such thing as a phoenix, anyway.

But I wanted to believe there was room for me, eternally asleep in silt sheets, at the bottom of a broad lake of sweet water.

In 1974, as well, the cottage was sold. Due to the inability of our parents to forge anything like a jointly parented family in a single region, that was the last time my brothers and I were in the same room at the same time. We became forced Bedouins, following not the sun, but our father across the country. We set up camp with our father's mother, our own mother, our father. Then, fractioned, one set out on his own, one remained with our father, and two of us went with our mother, back from whence we came.

We took a bus through the Rocky Mountains. I stayed awake the whole time, looking out the window at the yellow line and the miniscule verge of the road and yawning abyss, thinking, *I am far too close to the edge.* I don't think I have ever moved from it.

Since then we have, as I so brilliantly predicted, lived. We have rarely been happy. That is the stuff of fiction, for cowboys, and devotees of nostalgia.

✱ ✱ ✱

Once upon a time there was a beautiful princess who dreamed of being a cowboy. She lived her life under the Big Blue Sky of Go Home Lake. One day she was driven away and set adrift by an Evil Prince. She was stripped of her heart and innocence. The King and Queen, who failed to notice the gaping hole, declared her Not Nice for having provoked her brothers, until they were powerless to control themselves. Whatever she got she richly deserved. She was banished from Sweet Dreams, banished from Goodness, eventually banished from Go Home Lake. She became as ugly as her past, and throughout the world she was known as Piggy of The Pissy Twat.

Don't tell.

My mother cannot abide a tattletale.

"Oh Gloomy Gus! The past is past. It's over and done with. Why cling to it? Let bygones be bygones."

Such advice drives me to the edge. A short drive. I look out the weather-worn window of my own mind, searching for some mental boundary, an effective yellow line that would show me where I stop. Stop burning, being afraid, being angry, falling down…yearning for the abyss.

"Oh, Sarah Heartburn. You just like to prove you can cry on cue. Why dredge up all those dramatics? You're never happy unless you are miserable. It's all behind you now. It's long past."

But it isn't. It's on me now. It hurts like I'm burning alive.

"You are imagining things. You were too little then to remember anything."

No, I remember. I'd like to forget.

"That could not have happened."

It most surely did.

"Show me the proof. Show me the scar."

It's on the inside. I can't. I'd cut it off and bottle it if I could, and throw it in Mariana's Trench.

"You must have misinterpreted."

I didn't.

"Not that I believe it, but even if it happened, what does it matter now?"

It matters. I still carry it, hunchbacked and aching. It slows my step and halts my progress.

"Don't say such nonsense. I can't stand your shrill whining. Are you about to get your period? Just excuse yourself, go to your room, and stay there until you're civil."

Do not pass Go. Do not collect $200.00. Do not pray for relief. It is not yours to enjoy. Go to Hell. Go directly to Hell. If you wouldn't provoke your brothers…you got exactly what you deserved.

I'll give you something to cry about.

★ ★ ★

She sleeps.

I was old enough to know that dreams were unreliable

when I began dreaming of the house we used to live in. I knew it was sold and gone, and I'd never darken the doorstep again. Same for the cottage. But the cottage, whether it stood or fell, was eaten by worms, or destroyed by the elements, was far beyond my reach. Literally. Even if I could commandeer a car and make it as far as the last paved road, I was sure to be stymied by the unmarked dirt roads or pass out, choked by the dust, before I discovered the route to our spot on the lake.

I could scope out the house on my own steam. I never told anyone. I'd turn onto the old street as though it was just a bridge of convenience from where I was to where I was headed. I'd walk slowly past the old house, and, pretending not to, I looked.

There stood the house and I. We faced each other blankly. Then I walked away.

She's sick.

Recalling and forgetting demanded expenditures of energy I never had. Memories piled like old photographs and dried papers, randomly mixed and layered, failing to decompose, *dust to dust*, like other formerly living things.

My head ached with the weight of all it hoarded. But I was powerless to discard anything. I just kept churning the mess of the *now* that once was and isn't and can't be again, over and over. I remained close to the edge, hoping that some of the past would just slip over, wafting downward indefinitely, until it was out of sight, out of mind.

It's much advised against – to burn bridges.

Such advice drove me to it.

Incandescent with rage, eyes blazing, aflame with fury.

All bridges went up like a tinderbox and burned down faster than you can say "Wheeeee!"

She's dead.

I saved no Penny for a rainy day.

To say we drifted apart, Penny and I, would not be untrue. No adult is forever the child they once were. The tides of time draw the past and present wide apart, in keeping with the laws of nature.

But Penny's departure was less soft drift and more hard driven. I found her on the ground. I picked her up, held her close, and told her she was loved properly, that she was nice and good and none of any of this was her fault. I made a wish and threw my Penny over the edge. Into the abyss, for kindness. Fierce kindness. It had to be done. I couldn't carry her anymore.

Acknowledgments

Many thanks to Hunny, The Girls and the Boy Sister, my fellow Quads who consistently picked up the pieces and glued me back together when I needed it, which was ALWAYS.

I am unceasingly grateful to the good folks at Second Story Press, especially Kathryn Cole and Kathryn White who ran my work up the flag pole and ensured it was properly edited so it can fly gloriously (fingers crossed) and the charming Melissa Kaita who has graciously addressed all my anxiety fuelled e-mails with patience and sorted me out.

Finally, thanks to Brent Bambury and the fine makers of CBC One's former show GO, who put my efforts on the radio, stuffed me full of confidence, and told me I was an actual writer – who knew?!

About the Author

MEGS BEACH wanted to be Jane Eyre when she grew up and practiced writing with long-winded penpal letters. She was a dental hygienist for over twenty years and now divides her time between her three daughters, various creatures, writing, and refurbishing furniture. In 2009 she was runner-up in CBC Radio One's Canada Writes Contest. She and her husband, Scott, live in Toronto, Ontario.